RAVE REVIEWS FOR LOIS WINSTON AND
LOVE, LIES AND A DOUBLE SHOT OF DECEPTION

"Lois Winston ratchets up the suspense and heats up the romance in her captivating second novel, *Love, Lies and a Double Shot of Deception*. Fans of *Talk Gertie to Me* should be very pleased!"
—Lauren Baratz-Logsted, author of *How Nancy Drew Saved my Life* and *Vertigo*

"Readers will fall in love with the handsome Logan Crawford. They'll learn of the lies and deception Emma Wadsworth must face after tripping over a dead body. A *dead* body! But most of all, they'll be unable to put down *Love, Lies and a Double Shot of Deception* since Lois Winston has woven this romantic, suspenseful and page-turning novel like the pro that she is."
—Lori Avocato, bestselling author of the Pauline Sokol Romantic Mystery Series

STEAMY SECRETS

Logan came up behind her and slid his arms around her waist. "Regrets?"

"Funny. That was going to be my question to you."

He spun her around and stared into her eyes with an intensity that made her knees go weak and sent her pulse racing. Slowly, he slid his gaze down her body, taking his time, inch by inch. "A million. But none where you're concerned."

"You might. Things could get ugly."

"I can deal with ugly. You did what you had to. If the story comes out, the public will sympathize with you, not castigate you."

Will they? she wondered, when her entire life was served up for all to devour. *Will you, Logan? Or will you turn your back in revulsion? If you're even still here.*

Logan studied the worry lines furrowing Emma's brow. There was more. He sensed it. Another secret she kept hidden away. Something far worse.

Love, Lies and a Double Shot of Deception

Lois Winston

LOVE SPELL NEW YORK CITY

In loving memory of Ben and Rae Schaffer.

LOVE SPELL®

June 2007

Published by

Dorchester Publishing Co., Inc.
200 Madison Avenue
New York, NY 10016

ISBN-10: 0-505-52719-7
ISBN-13: 978-0-505-52719-6

The name "Love Spell" and its logo are trademarks of Dorchester Publishing Co., Inc.

Printed in the United States of America.

Visit us on the web at www.dorchesterpub.com.

ACKNOWLEDGMENTS

To my editor Leah Hultenschmidt for her enthusiasm and support and to the rest of the Dorchester staff for taking such good care of my babies.

To my agent Carolyn Grayson who continues to put up with me, even though I haven't bought her a new car yet.

To authors extraordinaire Christina Skye, Kasey Michaels, Lori Avocato and Lauren Baratz-Logsted who found time in their busy writing schedules to read *Love, Lies and a Double Shot of Deception* and supply me with such fantastic quotes.

To Judy Spagnola of Book Trends Promotions for her unwavering support as well as her friendship.

To P. J. Mellor for helping out a fellow author in search of a title.

To retired Philadelphia lieutenant Margaret "Mags" Allen for making sure I got my facts right.

To Janice Boot, long-time friend and the best cheerleader an author could have.

And finally, to my dear friends and fellow authors Karen Davenport, C. J. Lyons, Irene Peterson and Caridad Pineiro for always being there for me.

Love, Lies and a
Double Shot of
Deception

Prologue

*The journalists have constructed for themselves
a little wooden chapel, which they also call the
Temple of Fame, in which they put up and take
down portraits all day long and make such a
hammering you can't hear yourself speak.*
> Georg Lichtenberg,
> 18th-century critic and scientist

"Home sweet hell," Emma muttered as she turned off
the main road and guided the Mercedes down the tree-
lined drive toward the house. Her estate. Not that she
had any desire to return, but what choice did she have?
Drive around Philadelphia into the wee hours of the
morning? No, exhaustion precluded that option. She'd
thought about checking into a hotel for the night, but
she doubted the small Chestnut Hill hotel would have
any available rooms this late, and she had no energy
left to drive into Center City. Better to slip upstairs and
hope Phillip had forgotten their earlier confrontation.
Better yet, if she were lucky, he was still passed

out where she'd left him and wouldn't wake until morning.

Right.

She laughed bitterly. When had luck ever paid her a visit? Unless it was rotten luck. She had that in spades. And every decision she'd made in her adult life only compounded her problems. Phillip headed the list. First and foremost.

"Emma the masochist, that's me." She coasted to a stop on the cobblestone drive, set the parking brake, and turned her attention to the house she both loved and hated.

Only something wasn't right in Satanville.

Darkness enveloped the stately colonial, and only the repetitive clicking and chirping of the cicadas and crickets broke the stillness of the late August night. Less than two hours earlier, when she'd first pulled into the driveway and slipped inside, the house had been ablaze with lights, the air filled with raucous partying. Phillip's rowdy friends never called it a night this early.

Emma pushed open the unlocked front door and flipped on lights as she made her way down the central hallway toward the kitchen. Catering platters, still piled high with deli sandwiches, lined the kitchen counters. The back door stood ajar. Outside, half-empty beer bottles and bowls of guacamole and salsa dotted the pool deck. Nacho chips and beer nuts littered the patio furniture and crunched beneath her feet. Still-smoldering cigarette butts filled ashtrays. The sickeningly sweet aroma of pot hung in the air.

Where is everyone?

She stepped over a wet bikini bottom and noticed the suit's bra dangling from the diving board. Several other garments floated in the calm water. Something had disrupted the alfresco festivities mid-debauch.

But what? Who? Why? She'd like to think one of her civic-minded neighbors had ratted out her husband. Maybe at this very moment Phillip was cooling his Bruno Maglis in an eight-by-ten cell.

Wishful thinking. Phillip wielded too much power.

She headed back to the house and climbed the stairs to the second floor. Damp towels and an occasional swimsuit littered her path. A strip relay race? Nothing would surprise her.

As she entered the bedroom, she nearly tripped over a figure sprawled across the carpet. Phillip. Right where she'd left his sorry, passed-out-drunk ass. She cast a wary glance toward the bed. Empty. Maybe her luck was looking up for a change.

But she didn't dare leave Phillip on the floor. Reluctantly, she bent to rouse him; he refused to budge. Then she noticed his face. Halfway buried in the thick pile, his features were contorted into a grotesque waxy mask, his lips pale, his one exposed eye staring blankly up at her.

If she didn't feel guilty as hell, she'd celebrate.

Chapter 1

Five and a half months later

Winter wonderland, my ass.

The stinging wind whipped at Emma's exposed cheeks and brought tears to her eyes. Lowering her head, she trudged around the enormous mounds of black snow piled along the curb, searching for a semisafe path to the sidewalk. Finding none, she grabbed a parking meter and hauled herself over the smallest of the soot-encrusted icebergs. Some people would go to any lengths for their morning cup of java, and she was one of them.

As she yanked open the door to Chapters and Verse, the "Spring Movement" of Vivaldi's *Four Seasons* greeted her. Someone had a really warped sense of humor. Or hoped the power of positive thinking could affect weather patterns. Still, the music held a reminder that the harsh realities of early February in Philadelphia would eventually give way to sunshine and flowers come late March. Maybe. Last year they'd suffered through one of their worst blizzards ever the first week in April.

Emma shivered, thoughts of daffodils and crocuses quickly replaced by the chill rippling through her damp body. Shaking the moisture from her hair, she deposited her coat on a chair in the café, then headed for the coffee bar.

"Morning," said the barista. "The usual?"

"Please."

With her morning shot of caffeine and sugar in hand, Emma trolled the stacks of books, occasionally pulling a volume from the shelves and sliding it under her arm. She needed the predictability of this daily routine. It helped her get through the rest of the day. Every day.

Why the hell do I stay?

If she had any courage, she'd leave. Sell the house. Move away. Start over. But she couldn't leave, and her reasons had little to do with a lack of courage. Life in Emmaville was just too damn complex. One part guilt, one part masochism. But how could she leave the only tangible reminder she had of life before everything had turned to shit?

So she stayed, losing herself in work that at least gave her the satisfaction of knowing her efforts helped others. She pushed herself each day until exhaustion overcame her and she fell into nightmare-riddled sleep. Tomorrow morning the cycle would repeat itself. *I'm a twenty-first-century Sisyphus, eternally damned to live out an unending punishment for my sins*. Not that she had a clue as to whatever sin first condemned her years before, but she'd certainly committed a whopper since then. Whether a sin of omission or commission, it hardly mattered. The result was the same.

Still, what would be the harm in a short escape?

She deserved that much, didn't she? Emma closed her eyes and conjured up a distant memory of a sun-kissed Adriatic coastline. Hell, why not? She opened her eyes and headed for the travel section.

Logan Crawford's mind kept drifting back to the events of last night, an evening definitely not worth remembering. Even her name escaped him. Normally it wouldn't have mattered, but this time he was saddled with Candi-Randi-Bambi-whatever-the-hell-her-name-was for the length of his stay in Philadelphia. As head of the city's redevelopment office, she was his official escort-slash-liaison, the person assigned to make certain he chose the City of Brotherly Love as the East Coast site for his corporate headquarters. And last night Candi-Randi-Bambi, a woman who wore her ambition emblazoned across her surgically augmented chest, made it abundantly clear just how far she'd go to get him to sign on the dotted line. And it was far from brotherly. Or sisterly.

Logan doubted he was the first billionaire businessman she'd bedded in her quest up the corporate ladder, but he'd wager a good portion of his sizeable fortune that he was the biggest—the *wunderkind* West Coast urban developer who was giving The Donald a run for his money. Only Logan had better hair—as the media was quick to point out.

With a snap of his fingers, he could provide Candi-Randi-Bambi with an express elevator straight through the glass ceiling, and she knew it.

No way in hell.

Last night when he stared down into Candi-Randi-Bambi's come-hither eyes, he saw the reflection of a disillusioned, unhappy man. And damn, up to that moment he hadn't even realized he'd been disillusioned or unhappy. He had wealth; he had power. So what was up with the sudden emptiness and dissatisfaction?

Beryl would say it was because he led a shallow life devoid of emotional commitment. As much as he protested to the contrary, he knew she was right. Maybe it was time to leave the bimbos to Trump.

Struck by the epiphany, he'd bolted from Candi-Randi-Bambi's bed. They'd used each other. She'd spread her legs hoping to advance her career; he'd taken advantage of the offer. Sex without emotional entanglements, the pattern of his adult life. He got the release he needed, and the woman got a notch on her bedpost. Only this time it hadn't worked. After thirty-eight years, Logan Crawford realized it was time to grow up. Only damn it, he didn't have a clue how.

Still reeling from the self-revelation, he'd canceled his morning appointments and headed his rental car north, needing some time alone to think. After driving for half an hour, he found himself in a quiet, upscale section of Philadelphia. A bookstore on top of a hill beckoned like a siren.

For the rest of his stay in Philadelphia, he vowed to spend his nights curled up with a good thriller rather than a cheap thrill. Now all he had to do was find one. At the moment he couldn't even find the damn fiction section in the boundless maze of shelves that wound around the first level of the two-story megastore. Lost in the travel section, he spun on his heels and—

THUD!

Chapter 2

Books flew left and right. A woman bounced off Logan's chest and toppled backward. Logan lurched for her, grabbing her arm as her knees buckled. Somehow he managed to keep her upright, but her coffee didn't fare as well. The plastic lid popped off the cup; the beverage erupted, spewing across the front of her ivory sweater.

"Shit!"

"Certainly looks like it," she said with a slight chuckle to her voice. Without looking up, she added, "Sorry. Did I get you, too?"

Logan glanced down at his own sweater and khakis. "Looks like you took the full assault, but it's not your fault. It's mine." He bent to retrieve her books, several travel guides to the Greek Isles and Italy. "Ever been?"

"Once, a lifetime ago."

As he handed her the books, he took note of the petite woman with nearly purple eyes and an unruly mass of almost ebony waves that fell across her shoulders. He reached into his back pocket for his wallet and pulled out a twenty. "For your cleaning bill."

She clutched the books to her chest and backed away from him. "That's not necessary."

"I insist."

"No. I'm just as much to blame. I thought I was alone and wasn't paying attention."

"Neither was I." He moved a step closer and took hold of her upper arm. "But contrary to how I behave at times, my mother did raise me to be a gentleman. If you won't take my money, I'm at least buying you another cup of coffee."

She glanced at his hand encircling her arm. "You're not leaving me much choice, are you?"

"Not unless you care to make a scene."

She glanced once more at her coffee-soaked sweater. "I think I've already made one." With that, she allowed him to lead her to the café.

Logan had the distinct impression she didn't recognize him, and he wasn't certain whether that pleased him or not. Only weeks before, a *People* magazine poll had voted him one of the ten sexiest men in the world, his photo emblazoned on the cover of that week's issue. Everyone recognized Logan Crawford—whether he liked it or not. Everyone, it seemed, except the woman at his side.

"What were you drinking?" he asked as they arrived at the counter.

She reached for a handful of napkins and began dabbing at the stain. "A mocha latte."

Logan turned to the barista. She leaned on the counter and ogled him, her mouth hanging open. Yesterday he'd sucked up that kind of adulation as hungrily as his companion's sweater sucked up the spilled coffee. His once insatiable need for attention now struck him as shallow. Like him. The great Logan Crawford. All smoke and mirrors. No substance.

After a lifetime of meaningless one-night stands, why last night's encounter was the catalyst to an emotional tectonic shift escaped him. All he knew was that something had snapped inside him, and today the attention he once craved hung like a six hundred-pound albatross around his neck.

His mother's words echoed in his head. *Be careful what you wish for, Logan.* He hadn't listened. He should have. Aggie Crawford was always right.

He cleared his throat and glared at the woman behind the counter, startling her out of whatever Logan Crawford-starring fantasy she'd drifted into. "One large mocha latte and a double shot espresso."

His companion continued to blot the stain on her sweater while the waitress filled the order. Damn it! She had to know him!

Get a grip, Crawford. When have you ever let a woman dent your ego? Throughout his adult life, he'd never allowed any woman close enough to attempt it. Other than Aggie and Beryl, of course, and they just tried their damnedest to keep him grounded. And here was the million-dollar question: If he no longer wanted all that attention he used to crave, why did it bug the hell out of him that the woman standing beside him didn't recognize him? Maybe he still had more growing up to do.

The barista placed two cups on the counter in front of him. "Six seventy-one."

Logan glanced at the cups and frowned. *Twit.* If she'd paid more attention to her job and less to him, she wouldn't have screwed up the order. "You forgot the whipped cream." He pointed to the larger of the two cups, then to the sign behind her listing the ingredients of the various drinks.

"Mrs. Wadsworth never takes whipped cream, sir."

He glanced over at the woman in the coffee-stained sweater. She nodded.

Logan reached for his wallet. After paying for the beverages, he grabbed both cups and followed as she led the way to a table where a coat was draped over a chair.

"So that's two things I know about you." He placed the steaming cups in front of them.

"Two?"

"Your name is Mrs. Wadsworth, and you don't like whipped cream." He grinned. "And now that I've given you a coffee bath, I think we should at least be on a first-name basis, don't you, Mrs. Wadsworth? I'm Logan."

She offered him a shy smile with the slightest hint of a blush creeping into her cheeks. Logan was used to women with calculating smiles that promised rewards for favors granted. He doubted she fit that mold. But maybe he was only projecting his newly discovered self-revelations onto her. Aside from his own family, he'd never met a woman who didn't want something from him.

"Emma," she said.

Her voice matched her appearance—graceful and serene, yet somehow haunted. Emma Wadsworth looked more like an angel than a flesh-and-blood person. Or maybe she was a witch. He certainly felt like he was falling under a spell. Logan was intrigued, and no woman had ever intrigued him before. But then again, before today, he'd never allowed any woman within intriguing distance. At least emotionally.

"Well, Emma Wadsworth, I wish you'd reconsider and let me pay to have your sweater cleaned."

"The stain will wash out."

"And if it doesn't?"

"I suppose I'll have a very unique souvenir of an interesting encounter." She glanced over the rim of her coffee cup. Her eyes sparkled with amusement. "What's Sotheby's going rate for anything touched by Logan Crawford these days?"

So she did recognize him. He took a sip of his espresso and studied her further. He wanted to know more about this woman who was eliciting such unusual emotions from him. Was it him or her?

But the barista had referred to her as "Mrs." Wadsworth. Even *he* had his scruples. Besides, Aggie would tan his hide if he ever took an interest in a married woman. No matter that his mother weighed all of a hundred pounds dripping wet and was pushing eighty. She'd find a way.

He noted the bare ring finger of her left hand and the sadness lurking behind her eyes. Had Mr. Wadsworth recently walked out on his Mrs.? Or had he died? "I didn't think you recognized me."

"Right. Putting aside all those national magazines with your face on the covers, you've been front-page news here all week."

"All week? I only arrived yesterday."

"But the city's PR contingent has been hard at work in preparation."

Most likely Candi-Randi-Bambi's handiwork. Once upon a time he'd have eaten up all that free publicity. After last night it chafed. *BusinessWeek* and *Fortune* were one thing. He'd take all the good PR he could get for his business, but the tabloid crap was getting old. And annoying.

"Philadelphia suffers from being sandwiched between Washington and New York," she continued. "We usually get bypassed by celebrities, so the media always makes a big deal over any who pay us a visit."

"I'm no celebrity. Just an ordinary businessman."

"A businessman with the power to create quite a few jobs here. That makes you a celebrity as far as the news media in this town is concerned."

"Then Philadelphia is unique. Everywhere else the news hounds are far more interested in my private affairs than my business ventures." He paused for effect. "Not to mention my newly anointed status as one of the world's sexiest men."

Her cheeks flushed.

He chuckled. "Did that embarrass you?"

"Hardly." But she avoided eye contact with him.

"Now I know three things about you, Emma Wadsworth."

"Three?"

"One." He held up his index finger. "Your name. Two." He raised his middle finger. "You don't like whipped cream." He paused.

"And three?"

"You're a lousy liar."

No, she thought. *I'm a very good liar. I've been lying to myself for years.* And to the world. For sixteen years, in fact. The citizens of Philadelphia liked and respected her; some even envied her. If they only knew the truth behind her false façade . . .

But of course, she didn't mention any of that to Logan Crawford. "What makes you think I'm lying?"

"Your eyes."

"My eyes?"

"And your hands."

"My hands?" Emma stared at her hands. They were wrapped tightly around her coffee cup—so tightly that her knuckles had turned white. She released the cup and shoved her hands into her lap. His comment *had* embarrassed her, but what did it matter? After all, it wasn't like she'd ever see the man again. She returned her hands to her cup. "Your reputation does precede you, Mr. Crawford."

"Logan. And don't believe all you read. Besides, we're only having coffee, Emma. Your husband has nothing to worry about."

Phillip worry? About her? Emma nearly laughed out loud. The bastard had cared only for her money. "There is no Mr. Wadsworth. Not anymore. He died a while ago."

"I'm sorry."

Don't be. I'm not. Just guilty as hell. The words almost slipped out. *Jeez, Emma, get a grip!* No one knew. No one could ever know. What was it about Logan Crawford that nearly caused her to reveal her darkest secret? Granted, the man was drop-dead gorgeous with his thick auburn hair, his too-handsome-for-his-own-good face, and his six-pack-abs bod, but pretty packages often disguised ugly secrets. She of all people should remember that lesson.

Besides, she'd read enough about the Lothario sitting across from her. There had to be some truth to all those stories. She wasn't the naïve fool she'd been sixteen years ago. Phillip had seen to that.

She fidgeted with a cable on her sweater.

"Is it uncomfortable?"

"No, actually, it's drying rather quickly, considering the amount of coffee—" She swallowed back the remainder of the sentence.

"Not to worry. It was my fault, whether you want to believe it or not." When her expression disagreed with him, he changed the subject. "When are you leaving for Italy and Greece?"

"What makes you think I'm going to Italy and Greece?"

He pointed to the stack of books on the table.

"Oh. Right. The idea only hit me a few minutes

ago. I was having one of those I-hate-winter moments and suddenly found myself wondering why I
put up with all the ice and snow."

"Cabin fever?"

For the briefest of moments panic crossed her face,
but she quickly masked the emotion. Or maybe his
imagination was playing tricks on him. After all, he
hadn't gotten much sleep the night before.

"More like an allergy to drab and dreary," she said.

"The Adriatic and Mediterranean are certainly
cures for drab and dreary. There's this little island—"

"Why, you're Logan Crawford, aren't you?" A
woman in her early twenties, pushing a baby stroller
and dragging a toddler in tow, parked herself in front
of their table. She nodded toward Emma. "Hey,
Emma, you know Logan Crawford? Cool! You don't
mind if we join you, right? I've never met a real live
celebrity before." She whipped out a notebook and
pen from her knapsack and thrust them at Logan. "I
have got to have an autograph. No one is going to believe I met Logan Crawford unless I have proof, you
know?" She jabbed at the paper. "Make it out to 'My
good friend Jana-Lynne,' okay? Capital J, A, N, A, hy-
phen, capital L, Y, double N, E. Got it?"

Emma raised her eyebrows. "Good friend?"

Jana-Lynne giggled. "Who's going to know as long
as you don't tell?"

The toddler at Jana-Lynne's side stamped her foot.
"I wants hot chocolate."

"In a minute, sugar. I'm busy."

"Now! You pwomised." The child started screaming. "I wants hot chocolate! Now! Now! Now!" The
baby in the stroller chimed in with a chorus of howling.

"Now see what you've done, Madison?" Jana-
Lynne scolded. "You woke Parker."

"Did not!" Madison threw herself down on the floor. "Hot chocolate! Hot chocolate! Hot chocolate!"

"Get off the floor," yelled Jana-Lynne. "Naughty girls don't get hot chocolate. Behave yourself."

After quickly scrawling something, Logan slipped the notebook and pen into Jana-Lynne's knapsack and whispered to Emma, "Want to make a run for it?"

While Jana-Lynne wrestled with a child deep in the throes of Terrible-Twos Rage, Emma and Logan slipped out of the bookstore.

"So that's what celebritydom is like," said Emma once they were on the sidewalk.

"Your friend was rude and obnoxious, but I've dealt with far worse, especially since that damn *People* article hit the newsstands."

Emma held her hand up. "Stop. I need to clear something up right now. Jana-Lynne is definitely not a friend. She's my neighbor's nanny."

"That's a relief."

"Oh?"

"She's a ditz."

"And me?"

"Definitely not a ditz."

Emma laughed, her breath condensing in a vaporous cloud in the frigid air. "Good to know. Now define 'far worse.' "

"Why don't we continue this conversation over brunch," said Logan, holding his hand out to her. "We ran out so fast, we left our coffee."

Logan Crawford wanted to have brunch with her? How weird was that? She didn't know whether to laugh or bolt for her car. *Option Two*, she ordered herself. *Run. Now. If you know what's good for you.* But instead of mouthing an excuse, like a fool who never learns from her mistakes, she accepted his outstretched hand. His fingers curled around hers. Tingly warmth, such a foreign and exciting sensation, spread up her arm. *Idiot. You're behaving like a twitterpated schoolgirl. And look where that got you last time.*

Still, she allowed him to hold her arm as they navigated their way over and around the grimy mounds of frozen snow and the icy ruts that formed a treacherous labyrinth in the street along the top of Chestnut Hill. "Where to?" he asked.

She thought for a moment. "If you like homemade soup and freshly baked bread—"

"Lead the way."

She headed for a small French café tucked at the end of an alley off the main thoroughfare. "Reminds me of something you'd find in a European village," he said.

Emma glanced around as if seeing the café for the first time. "Not exactly what you'd expect in the middle of a big city, is it?"

"No. This entire area of Philadelphia is quite different from what I expected. Cobblestone streets. Quaint little shops. More like parts of Boston than New York or Los Angeles."

"In many ways. Like Brigadoon, a magical place tucked away in the corner of a sea of madness."

"Why madness?"

Damn it, Emma, watch your mouth! "Terrorism? We're not living in the safest of times."

This man was dangerous. He caused her to forget who she was. If she wasn't careful, she'd say too much. She'd spent over sixteen years guarding her secrets, and now she had even more secrets—deadly secrets. "You were telling me about your rabid fans," she said to change the subject.

"I've had the shirt ripped off my back. On more than one occasion."

"Come on. You're Logan Crawford, real estate developer, not Brad Pitt, Hollywood heartthrob."

"The tabloids don't seem to care. And neither do the people who read them. Fame and fortune make for fair game these days, no matter where you gained that fame and fortune. Even Stephen Hawking has his share of groupies, you know."

Emma's life often forced her into the spotlight, but only on a local level. Philadelphians were used to seeing photos of her in *Philadelphia* magazine and the newspapers, but she'd never dealt with national exposure. Outside of the city, she was a nobody and grateful for it. "Why don't you travel with a bodyguard?"

"I have enough of an entourage nipping at my heels most of the time."

She glanced over her shoulder, half expecting to see lurking bodies hovering in the shadows of the café. "So where are they?"

"I needed some space."

"I'm surprised Leslee Howell let you out of her sight."

"Leslee?" His brow creased. Then he snorted a laugh. "Oh, right. The city liaison. You know her?"

Not as well as my husband did. "We've met."

"According to her, everyone in Philadelphia loves her, but you don't sound like you're a member of her fan club."

Wrong sex. Leslee Howell operated a restrictive fan club open only to males with money and power. Logan Crawford would be a plum addition to her trophy case. Hell, she'd probably dedicate an entire wing of her Society Hill penthouse to him. Emma noticed the scowl that had settled across Logan's face.

Maybe the bitch had finally met her match. The thought pleased her. But what did it matter?

"Emma?"

"I'm not the fan club type."

"I take it you don't like her, either."

"I didn't say that."

"If we're going to be friends, you have to stop lying to me."

"Friends? We hardly know each other."

"So tell me all about Emma Wadsworth and we'll get to know each other."

But instead of talking about herself, as they lingered over lobster bisque and thick chunks of sourdough bread, Emma repeatedly turned the conversation back to Logan.

"I'm beginning to think you're a government spy," he said. "You won't tell me anything about yourself."

She brushed off his question with a wave of her hand. "Your life is far more interesting than mine. I don't want to bore you."

"I'm not bored."

"Exactly. Because I'm not talking about myself. Trust me. In five minutes I'd have you snoring in your bisque."

"Humor me."

Emma concentrated her attention on stirring her soup. "I lead a life as dull as the proverbial dishwater. I have two sons, fourteen and fifteen. They attend boarding school. I do some charity work. That's about it."

When stated like that, she suspected she sounded like a pampered socialite who couldn't be bothered to raise her own children. Let him think what he would. She felt more secure knowing her sons were several hundred miles away. Safe from the past. Safe from the unknowns of the future. Hiding secrets was easier when you lived alone and kept for the most part to yourself.

He trapped her in a challenging gaze. "Why do I suspect there's far more you're not telling me?"

Jeez! He looked like he was ready to strip her naked and screw her senseless right there on the tile floor of Chez Colette. *People* had it all wrong. Logan Crawford wasn't one of the sexiest men alive. He was *the* sexiest man alive. Webster must have taken one look at him and invented the damn word.

Logan Crawford could charm Svengali. She didn't stand a chance. She should leave. Now. But she didn't leave. Not then.

And not for some hours.

"Have dinner with me?" he asked when they finally left the café.

Dinner? Hell, she shouldn't have had coffee with him, let alone brunch. "I don't think so . . . I . . ."

He took her glove-clad hands in his. "Don't try to think up an excuse. Just say yes."

Just say yes. She glanced down at their joined hands. Could it really hurt? If she were careful? After all, it was only a dinner. One dinner. One day. A brief respite from the monotony of the rest of her life. Still . . .

"Please?"

"Why not?" This was just all a dream anyway, wasn't it? Tomorrow life would go back to normal. Such as normal was. What difference could one day possibly make?

Chapter 3

Logan arrived at Emma's home shortly before seven. He stepped from the car and reached for the box of long-stemmed roses he'd purchased from the hotel florist. Red roses. With the flowers tucked under his arm, he studied his surroundings. The countrylike setting of the large estate belied its location, a mere half mile from the bustling shopping district where they'd met earlier in the day.

He walked up to the entrance and rang the bell. When Emma opened the door, he handed her the box. Puzzlement washed over her face. "Flowers?"

"Because you won't let me pay your cleaning bill."

Her fingers trembled as she slipped the ribbon from the box and lifted the lid. Her voice faltered. "They're beautiful. Thank you, but you shouldn't have."

"Why not?" When she continued to stare at him without answering, he shrugged. "I have five older sisters. I'm well trained." His gaze raked the length of her body. Damn, she looked good. She wore a simple black wool dress with a short strand of pearls and matching stud earrings. Elegant as hell. And too damn sexy for a widow.

A blush colored her cheeks—as if she could read his thoughts. "I should put these in water." She turned and strode across the tiled foyer to the living room.

Logan followed, stopping short at the entrance to the room. Furnished in garish, ornate French antiques, the interior looked like a paean to bad taste, the complete opposite of the understated woman who lived within its walls.

Emma headed toward an étagère on the other side of the room. He noticed her hesitancy as she reached for a china vase, and he caught the almost imperceptible frown she gave the container as she removed it from the shelf. He followed her down a long hallway, passing an equally ornate dining room, a billiards room, and a library before coming to the kitchen.

She filled the vase with water, then one by one carefully removed the roses, clipped the stems, and placed them in the vase. When she'd finished, she stepped back. Hands on hips, she studied the arrangement. "I'd like to keep them in my studio. I'll be able to enjoy them while I work." She carried the vase down a corridor off to the side of the kitchen. Once again, he followed.

Logan crossed the threshold into her studio and tumbled down a rabbit hole. Emma's studio was the complete opposite of the rest of the rooms he'd seen.

Floor-to-ceiling windows, adorned with hanging baskets of pink and white flowers, covered one wall. Framed needlework and brightly colored, quilted wall hangings dotted the remaining three walls. White wicker bookcases housed an assortment of handmade dolls, books, and bolts of patterned fabrics. A desk in one corner contained a computer monitor and keyboard. A work in progress—some sort of embroidery—sat on a table positioned in the opposite corner.

Off to the side of the table, a door stood slightly ajar. While Emma's back was turned, Logan sneaked a peek, discovering a small, feminine bedroom with a bed showing signs of recent use. The photos of her children, which should have been scattered throughout the house, were crowded onto a dresser and covered most of the wall behind it.

Logan turned his attention back to Emma and found her chewing her bottom lip. If he didn't know better, he'd think she was holding her breath, awaiting his approval of where she'd placed the flowers. When he nodded, she exhaled. Damn! She *had* been holding her breath. He hadn't imagined her apprehension. But what had caused it? Did it have something to do with this strange house? She seemed like a different person within its walls. Hesitant. Nervous. Intimidated. Not the woman who'd entranced and captivated him earlier in the day.

Less than five minutes later, they left the house. As they crossed the cobblestone driveway to his car, Emma craned her neck skyward. Logan followed her gaze. Thousands of stars replaced the massive, dark clouds of earlier in the day.

"What a sky! We don't usually get this many stars. It's like being out in the country."

"I placed a special order."

She chuckled. "I know you keep buying up air rights, but I didn't think your empire stretched *that* high."

The tension he sensed surrounding her inside the house had vanished; the Emma of earlier had returned.

"Now you know."

"Just how much Irish blood runs through your

veins, Logan Crawford?"

"My paternal grandfather was from County Cork. Why?"

"I'm guessing blarney is a dominant gene."

Logan laughed. "Few women have had the temerity to tell me I'm full of shit—"

"I didn't mean—"

"And in such a ladylike manner!"

"But—"

He placed a finger to her lips. "Shh." He suddenly realized he was enjoying himself more than he had in ages. And the evening was still young.

Half an hour later, Logan pulled up to the curb in front of Le Papillion. Two valets sprung into action. One opened Emma's door and offered his hand. The other ran around to the driver's side and opened his door.

Emma stared at the entrance to the building. "Le Papillion?"

"Don't you approve?"

"Of course. I'm just surprised. This is one of the finest restaurants in the country. People wait months for a reservation."

He took her arm and led her up the steps. "I'm not 'people.'"

Logan was used to being greeted by name, but his astonishment surpassed Emma's surprise at his choice of restaurants when the maitre d' extended her a warm, personal welcome. His surprise grew exponentially when the chef and owner of the establishment appeared at their table.

"*Madame* Emma, *ma petit papillion!* It is so good to see you again."

"Hello, Georges. How are you?"

"I am fine. But you!" he admonished in semimock tones. "You do not come visit Georges, and look what happens to you. All skin and bones!" He made a tsking sound and grabbed the menu from her hand. "I will have to remedy this at once. My beautiful butterfly fades before my eyes."

He turned to Logan. "*Monsieur* Crawford, you must see that she eats everything on her plate, down to the last *soupçon*."

As the chef strode back to the kitchen, Emma shook her head. "The man's going to kill me with kindness and cholesterol."

Logan sat back and crossed his arms over his chest. "I take it you're not one of the common folk who wait months for a reservation?"

"No, I suppose I'm not."

Before he could question her further, the sommelier arrived with the wine list. After perusing it briefly, Logan pointed to his selection.

"An excellent choice, *monsieur*."

Logan decided it was time to take the proverbial bull by the horns. "Okay. Out with it. I'm dying of curiosity, and you have my undivided attention, something few people ever get."

"Out with what?"

"Who are you, Emma Wadsworth? I bump into a shy 'butterfly' in a bookstore, and she turns out to inhabit a two-room refuge in the middle of a mausoleum and be on a first-name basis with the owner of a five-star restaurant."

The corners of Emma's mouth turned up slightly, but the smile she gave him didn't mask the sadness that settled in her eyes. "I'm no one special, Logan. Philadelphia is a large city with a small-town mentality. Just about everyone knows everyone else. Georges Matin and I are neighbors. He often catered parties at my home."

Logan found it hard to believe that the gilded crypt

she called home had ever been the setting for anything other than a wake for a Nevada madam. She pointedly sidestepped the other part of his question.

Well, there was more than one way to skin a cat. Or in this case, trap a butterfly. Why was he drawn to this enigmatic woman when he'd never experienced such an intense tug from any other woman? Why her? Why now? Was her allure merely a reaction to last night's revelations and his dissatisfaction with his life?

The woman sitting across from him was the complete opposite of the woman he'd shared a bed with last night. In looks. In personality. In temperament. Maybe he was just looking for variety, but something told Logan it wasn't that simple. From the moment he'd left her earlier in the day, he'd thought of nothing but Emma Wadsworth. He hadn't gotten where he was by letting a challenge get the best of him. He conquered his challenges, and Emma Wadsworth was turning into one very enchanting challenge.

The sommelier reappeared with a bottle of Cristal and poured the champagne. Logan raised his glass in a toast. "To mysterious women and chance meetings." He clicked his glass against hers.

Emma either ignored or was innocent to the challenge in his voice. She merely smiled that sweet, pure smile of hers and took a sip of champagne. Her eyes took on a bittersweet distant expression. Logan wondered what she was thinking. What caused the sadness he saw lurking just beneath the surface? The recently departed Mr. Wadsworth must have been one hell of a lucky bastard.

Logan had never been in love, had always steered clear of that frightening emotion that bound two people for life and beyond. He'd reveled in passion. Been consumed by desire. Exalted in lust. But love? Hell, he'd run from the mere mention of the word. And maybe that had been his biggest mistake in life. Emma's husband was dead, but it was apparent to him that the love that had bound them together would live forever.

A fantasy tiptoed through his mind, and he realized—much to his chagrin—that a part of his body other than his mind now responded to the woman before him.

To hell with propriety!

He set his champagne flute on the table. "I'm having an uncontrollable urge to ask you to dance."

She surprised the hell out of him when she said, "I've heard it can be dangerous to suppress uncontrollable urges."

He'd expected her to decline. Toss him some line about impropriety or some such shit. After all, she was recently widowed—just how recently she hadn't made clear, but her actions up until now had led him to believe her husband's death was fairly recent. The woman was full of surprises.

This is so wrong.

She shouldn't have accepted the dinner invitation, let alone a dance. Obviously some alien had taken possession of her brain. And her mouth.

Logan led her to the dance floor as the string quartet began playing "How Long Has This Been Going On." How long, indeed? When she'd danced with Phillip, she'd danced with two left feet. In Logan's arms she danced like Ginger Rogers. Her body nestled against his. The lyrics to the song so appropriate: *There were chills up my spine, and some thrills I can't define. . . .*

A tingling sensation traversed from her scalp to her toes. Good Lord! Fire ignited her flesh at each place where their bodies met. Such foreign feelings. Too bad nothing could come of it, but she'd allow herself to enjoy the moment.

It's only one evening. One dinner. One dance.

After so many years of hell, wasn't she entitled to a few hours of happiness? Tomorrow life would return to normal, but long after she wasn't even a flicker in Logan Crawford's mind, she'd still have the memories of this day. It would have to be enough. She couldn't risk more. "I feel like Cinderella at the ball."

"You're not going to turn into a pumpkin, are you?"

"The coach changed back into a pumpkin," she reminded him. "Cinderella just returned to her cold hearth."

When they arrived back at her house, Logan walked her to the front door. She unlocked it, then turned to him. "Thank you. I had a wonderful time today."

"Will you join me for dinner tomorrow evening?"

The question took her by surprise. Tomorrow and all tomorrows were out of the question. This had to end now. "I'm sorry. I can't."

"Why not?"

"I have a previous commitment."

"Cancel it."

Chapter 4

"Excuse me?" Who did Logan Crawford think he was?

"I'm sorry. I guess I'm just used to giving orders. I didn't mean it the way it sounded."

"I understand."

"Do you? Do you understand that I want to see you again?"

Hell no. She didn't understand anything. Not the day she'd just spent. Not the feelings this man stirred inside her. But she did recognize the danger he represented.

"Lunch?"

"I'm afraid I'll be tied up the entire day."

He persisted. "Saturday then. I'll cancel my appointments. You plan the day. We'll do whatever you like."

His eyes held sincerity. He really did mean what he was saying. Logan Crawford could spend his Saturday with whomever he chose. And he'd chosen her. Why, she couldn't fathom.

One more day. Would it really matter, or was she

pushing her luck? In the end, the man before her won out over reason, and once again—against her better judgment—she agreed.

"Well, then, until Saturday." He took her face in his hands, lowered his head, and kissed her. Short and sweet. "Pleasant dreams, Cinderella."

Prince Charming closed the door behind him before Emma could react. As she stared out the window watching him stride back to his car, her heart pounded and her legs turned to overcooked linguini. Her lips tingled and burned from their brief encounter with his. One chaste kiss had wreaked havoc.

What the hell is wrong with me? She never should have agreed to see him again. *I've lost my mind.* And if she wasn't careful, she'd lose far worse. She dropped too many defenses around him. And that could prove disastrous.

She turned off the lights and headed for her small refuge at the back of the house and the nightmares that awaited her.

She'd never felt so wonderful.
She'd never felt so miserable.

He'd never felt so wonderful.
He'd never felt so miserable.

Sonofabitch! The woman had burrowed under his skin like a chigger. No, that wasn't fair. The itch he felt for her was anything but unpleasant. She was the most perplexing creature he'd ever met—one moment as skittish as a newborn colt, the next an innocent schoolgirl, totally unaware of her sensuous charms. And bewitching as hell.

He'd made a serious mistake asking her to dance. The bulge in his pants had fought to press against her flat belly. Georges Matin might think she was all skin and bones, but Logan had felt the soft curves hidden under her wool dress. It had taken the vows of a priest to tear him from her door with nothing more than a chaste good-night kiss.

He spent most of the remainder of the night restlessly pacing his suite at the Four Seasons. At the first light of dawn over the Delaware River he reached for the phone. A slurred and fuzzy voice answered.

"Rise and shine, Duchess. There's work to do."

"Logan?"

"You have ten minutes to shower and get in here. I'll order coffee."

"I'll be there in five. Don't forget the croissants."

Beryl Cade was still rubbing the sleep from her eyes when he opened the door at the sound of her knock. She shuffled in, clad in the lime-green sweat suit she'd probably slept in, her gray-streaked brown hair a tangled mess. She plopped into one of the overstuffed chairs and grabbed a chocolate croissant from the plate on the table.

He gave her the once-over and chuckled. "By God, I love you!"

"Of course you do," she mumbled around a mouthful of flaky pastry. "Who else would put up with you the way I do?"

"My mother."

"Yeah, well, I guess that's why Aggie and I get along so well. We're the only two women in the world who can see right through you. Besides, I'm way too old for all that animal sex appeal of yours." She poured herself a cup of coffee and took a quick gulp before continuing. "So what's up, boss?"

Rising from the chair opposite her, he strode to the window. The dawn was a colorful mix of pinks. His thoughts turned to a room in the Chestnut Hill section of the city, a room filled with bright pink flowers and a vase of red roses. "I need you to do some research."

Logan knew Beryl would never betray a confidence. She'd been with him since he graduated and embarked on his first development venture, ever since her husband left her for a male stripper. The experience had soured her to personal relationships of any sort. Like Logan, she lived for her work. She was the only member of his staff who got away with treating him like the unruly, ill-behaved asshole he often was, giving him a swift kick in his reality whenever she felt he needed it.

Still, he kept yesterday a secret, even from her. "I may have stumbled onto something interesting. I want you to find out all you can about an Emma Wadsworth of Philadelphia."

Beryl slammed her coffee cup onto the end table. "For this you got me up at the crack of dawn? The Internet might be available twenty-four/seven, but I'm not. Not even for you, Mr. Bigshot Billionaire!" She grabbed the plate of croissants and coffee pot and stalked to the door. "I'm going back to bed."

Logan spent the remainder of the day shepherded around town by Leslee Howell. Over the past year he'd committed to urban renewal projects in Washington, D.C., Baltimore, Philadelphia, Wilmington, and Camden. Bids were out for parts of New York City, Boston, and Hartford. Since he planned to spend the greater part of the next few years on the East Coast, he'd decided to establish headquarters midway along the Northeast Corridor.

Leslee was competing against possible sites in New Jersey and Delaware. She'd compiled a list of available locations suitable to his needs and insisted upon personally escorting him to each one. She drew out every stop as long as possible, turning each into a photo op for the swarm of local media trailing behind them. He had no doubt she'd faxed their itinerary to every reporter and photographer in the city and all outlying counties.

Her body language told him she fully expected a repeat of their Wednesday night encounter. He found her cloying and did his best to voice his annoyance without being outright rude, but she was either too dense or too calculating to let it bother her. Even when he gave his churlish side free reign and purposely called her Lori, instead of Leslee, she continued her aggressive behavior.

By four o'clock Logan had plummeted beyond his saturation point. "I've had enough for today. Drop Ms. Howell off at City Hall. Then bring me back to the hotel," he told the chauffeur.

"You can't," said Leslee. "I have two more stops planned for today." She affected a sexy pout.

Before yesterday she might have changed his mind with those lips and what he knew she could do with them. But today there was only one woman on his mind, a woman whose innocent mouth and haunting blue-violet eyes hadn't been far from his thoughts all day. "Reschedule. I'm tired."

"Why don't I come back to the hotel with you?" Her hand crept up his thigh. "After all, it's early, and we don't have to be at the auction until eight."

Logan removed her hand from his zipper. "Enough. I'm not interested."

"You were more than interested the other night. As I recall, you were damn eager to screw my brains out."

"Look. We have to work together. Bedrooms and boardrooms don't mix well. It complicates the hell out of things. The other night shouldn't have happened. It was a mistake on my part. I'm sorry."

"You bastard!" Her slap stung as much as the string of insults and accusations she hurled in rapid succession until the limo pulled up in front of City Hall. "A mistake, huh? We'll see about that!" Without waiting for the chauffeur, she jumped from the car, slammed the door, and stalked off into the shadowy arches of the entry.

Logan sighed. It was going to be a long night.

"I don't get it. Did I miss a memo? Have you bought into a production company that makes He-Done-Her-Wrong movies of the week?"

"Hardly," said Logan, absentmindedly shuffling through his phone messages. He looked up and across the room where Beryl lounged on the love seat. Although her hair still looked uncombed, she'd replaced her rumpled sweat suit with a pair of jeans and a flannel shirt. "What's with the asinine questions?"

"Why the sudden interest in the Princess of the Hill?"

"Who?"

Beryl pushed her glasses up onto the bridge of her nose and shot him a sarcastic look. "The lady you asked me to research? Emma Wadsworth? Emma *Brockton* Wadsworth?"

Logan crossed the room, pushed her feet off the love seat, and settled in next to her. "Spill."

"How much do you remember about Colonial history?"

Logan eyed her skeptically. "We kicked British butt back across the Atlantic. Other than that, not much. Why?"

"Well, to begin with, Emma Wadsworth is a Brockton. The last of the Brocktons. The name might not mean anything to you, but to Philadelphians it's as influential as Kennedy is to Bostonians. Only difference is the Brocktons were around from Day One. Back with old Billy Penn. Not nouveau riche immigrants like the Kennedys. And Brockton money came from vast landholdings and shipping, not bootlegging. The lady's ancestors had their own private Manifest Destiny. All profits from their shipping empire were invested in land as the country expanded westward."

"I take it there's more?" He glanced down at the thick file sitting on the glass and marble coffee table in front of them.

"I'll say. The psychologist hidden within me can sum up the lady's life in one sentence: Money doesn't buy happiness."

Over the next half hour Beryl related all she'd learned of the woman the Philadelphia press referred to as "The Princess of the Hill." And because the press had always loved their sad, winsome princess, her life was well documented.

"She was orphaned at five when her parents were killed in a car crash. Her life was taken over by a well-meaning but ill-equipped board of directors who, not knowing what else to do, packed her off to a Swiss boarding school. She met Phillip Wadsworth, eighteen years her senior, during her freshman year of college. He knocked her up. She dropped out of school, and they married." Deep frown lines settled across her face. "Bastard."

"What's that for?"

"She has two sons less than ten months apart."

"So?"

"So that means the bastard forced himself on her right after she gave birth!"

"That's jumping to a pretty big conclusion, even for a man hater like you, isn't it?"

"Shit, Logan. Besides being contrary to doctor's or-

ders, no woman in her right mind would want sex so
soon after giving birth. If you don't believe me, ask
one of your sisters. It's too damn painful."

"Maybe the baby was premature."

Beryl reached for the file and thumbed through
the first few sheets. "Kevin Brockton Wadsworth.
Nine pounds, six ounces. Doesn't sound like a pree-
mie to me."

Logan dismissed her editorial with a wave of his
hand. "Don't read between the lines. Just give me the
facts."

"Fine with me. The lady is a typical Philadelphia
blue blood. She's president of the local embroidery
guild and does charity work. Lots of it. Her handmade dolls and needlework are highly sought-after
collectibles in some circles, shown in galleries and
museums across the country. She donates all the proceeds to charity.

"Her husband took over her finances when they
married and parlayed her billions into a cool gazillion
or two. Rumor has it not all legally gained. Every
once in a while there's an innuendo or two that crops
up in a newspaper clipping. Always about him. Never
her. The press seems to have a hands-off policy when
it comes to their princess."

Beryl wrinkled her nose. Logan wondered whether
the gesture came from jealousy of Emma or Beryl's
disdain for the recently departed Mr. Wadsworth.
"What else haven't you told me?"

"Not much except that Phillip Wadsworth departed for the netherworld last August, and there's
considerable debate about the departure."

"Meaning?"

"Seems he checked out during a bit of, shall we
say, entertaining at his home. The kind of entertaining that goes on between rats when the cat's away."

Logan's patience was shot. His day with Leslee had ill-prepared him for Beryl's revelations. "Let's be a little less cryptic, shall we?"

She shrugged. "Bottom line: The guy stroked out during a pool party. His wife found him buck naked, face down on his bedroom floor when she returned from a trip up to New England to drop the kiddies off at school. There was evidence of a party, but to this day no one has come forth to admit having been at the Wadsworth home that evening. At least that's the tacky tabloid version. The legitimate press makes no mention of his birthday suit or the party."

"Sonofabitch." So much for first impressions concerning the happy marriage and everlasting love between Phillip and Emma Wadsworth.

"Oh, one other thing," said Beryl, handing him the file as she stood to leave. "You're gonna love this. It really confirms my suspicions that the Brockton-Wadsworth match was not one made in heaven."

Logan stared at the file Beryl had shoved into his hands, then looked up at his cocky assistant—his cocky assistant who had an incredible sixth sense about people. "Go on."

"The day after the funeral, Mrs. Wadsworth gave away about a billion dollars to every home for abused women across the country. Rumor has it she only kept her initial fortune from before her marriage."

A knot tightened in Logan's belly. Beryl's disclosures completely destroyed his earlier conception of Emma's relationship with her deceased husband. So why the haunted look of loss in her eyes? If Beryl were correct in her research and analysis—and he had no reason to believe otherwise—under the circumstances, Emma should act more like a merry widow than a melancholy one.

Beryl lumbered across the room, interrupting his ruminations. "Time to get ready. Your public awaits."

"Any chance we can get out of this? I didn't exactly leave Leslee on the best of terms a little while ago."

"Lover's quarrel already?"

"What's that supposed to mean?"

Beryl shrugged. "Nothing." She opened the door to leave, then stopped and motioned across the room before stepping out into the hall. "By the way, lover boy, did you happen to see this morning's paper?"

Chapter 5

Emma woke with a start, her sweat-drenched body springing bolt upright. Her heart pounded wildly against her chest as she gulped for air. *A nightmare. Only a nightmare.* She repeated the mantra a dozen times until her heart slowed to its normal pace.

Rising from the bed, she wandered into her studio and contemplated the roses on her desk. What an odd day she'd had yesterday. Roses from Logan Crawford, of all people. And he wanted to spend tomorrow with her. All day. Her heart sped up again, but this time it wasn't driven by fear, wasn't pounding with anxiety. Her heart fluttered with happiness. Then her gaze fell to the vase.

She never should have brought that gilded monstrosity into her studio, but she'd had no other container for the flowers. How could she have explained placing Logan's flowers in a pitcher when that ugly vase sat on the étagère in plain view? It would have required an explanation she couldn't give.

She remembered all too vividly the day she'd come

home from the hospital to find her mother's furniture
gone, the graceful antique Chippendale pieces replaced
by ornate Rococo better suited to a bordello. While
she'd labored alone through the birth of her first child,
Phillip had stripped the house of every reminder of her
parents, down to the last knickknack and photograph.

For over fifteen years the furnishings had taunted
her, reminding her of her weakness. Now they casti-
gated her for her sin. She'd like nothing better than
to rid the house of every reminder of Phillip, but
she'd been afraid to do so too soon. People might
talk. Talk led to suspicion. Suspicion led to investigation. She had to be careful. So she'd set a timetable
for herself, an appropriate period of mourning prior
to any redecorating. Six months. Too bad Logan
Crawford hadn't waited another few weeks before
showing up in Philadelphia and entering her life.

For now, though, she'd transfer the flowers into a
pitcher. And before heading down to the convention
center, she'd buy herself a new vase.

She picked up the heavy container and headed for
the kitchen. But she only got as far as the hallway before the vase slipped from her hands and shattered
on the marble tile.

Emma stared at the roses in her hands. Somehow
she'd managed to hold on to the flowers, even though
several thorns now gouged her palms and fingers. She
glanced at the puddle of water and broken chunks of
china and laughed. *I guess now I have no choice but
to buy a new vase.* Maybe she should "accidentally"
break a few more of Phillip's whorehouse baubles.

Later that morning, as Emma oversaw the placement
of the artwork, the setting of the tables, the thousand
and one last-minute details of chairing a fund-raiser,
her mind wandered to Saturday.

You plan the day.

A small smile tugged at the corners of her mouth each time she replayed the conversation in her mind.

You plan the day.

The question was, where? What should they do?

"You're awfully preoccupied," said Molly.

"Sorry. I guess I'm just nervous about tonight."

Her friend and cochair squeezed her upper arm. "Relax. It's going to be a huge success. This time tomorrow your scholarship fund for abused women and their children will be rolling in dough, and you and I will be busy planning next year's gala."

"Not tomorrow. I have plans."

"Oh? Anyone I know?"

"What makes you think they're those kind of plans?"

"The dreamy look and goofy smile plastered across your face?"

"Dream on. I'm taking a break. Want anything from the coffee shop?"

"Just some answers."

"When I have some."

At the coffee shop in the convention center lobby Emma grabbed a newspaper from the counter before paying for two cups of coffee. Friday's paper always listed special weekend events. Perhaps something interesting would catch her eye. She'd read the paper this evening before dressing for the auction.

Struggling with his cuff links, Logan gritted his teeth. It was going to be a bitch of an evening. Compounded by the snarling bitch he'd ticked off earlier in the day.

"You'd better make nice to her," said Beryl, taking the recalcitrant cuff link from his hand and adeptly inserting it through the slot.

"I know. Just stick close. I may need you to keep me from strangling her."

"It's your own damn fault." She motioned to the newspaper strewn across the coffee table. "Try keeping your prick zipped in your pants once in awhile."

"Rub it in while you're at it." But she didn't have to. The local headline was seared in his brain: LESLEE REELS IN A BIG ONE. Only a complete idiot could miss the double entendre, and just in case, the accompanying article left little doubt. "I suppose by now the dirty deed's been broadcast over CNN?"

"Not to mention MSNBC and FOX News. Sleep with dogs, wake with fleas." She tossed him a saccharine-sweet smile.

"Some assistant. Where were you Wednesday night when I could have used your pearls of wisdom?"

"In bed. Alone. A totally foreign concept to you, I'm sure."

"Keep it up, sweetheart."

"Come off it, Logan. Why all the angst over a simple lay? It's not like you're some goddamn choir boy suddenly fallen from grace." She made a tsking sound with her tongue. "She must really be something."

"Hardly. She's no more than a hooker on the city payroll."

"Not Leslee. The princess. By the way, where were you all day yesterday? You've been positively twitterpated ever since last night."

"You're not my mother, Beryl. I don't have to account to you for every moment of my time. Twitter what?"

"Look it up, lover boy."

An hour later Beryl and Logan entered the marble-columned convention center ballroom. Beryl cocked her head in Leslee's direction. "Enemy at twelve o'clock," she announced. "Time to circle the wagons, Kimosabe."

Leslee, her long blond hair pulled back and twisted into place with a diamond clasp, was dressed in a very short white cocktail dress adorned with thousands of multifaceted beads that reflected the overhead lights. "Talk about plunging necklines," continued Beryl. "I'll bet she used an entire roll of double-sided tape to keep that baby in place."

"Hmmph. She looks like a goddamn artificial Christmas tree."

As Leslee threaded her way through the crowd, every male head turned, their eyes following in her wake.

"I'll say this for her: The woman definitely knows how to stand out in a crowd. And speaking of standing, how the hell does she walk in those killer stilettos?"

"I wouldn't know," mumbled Logan, "but you're probably the only person in the room looking at her feet."

A moment later, Leslee stood in front of him. She gave Beryl a patronizing smile and latched onto Logan's arm. "It's about time you arrived, darling. Come. Our mayor and his wife are simply dying to meet you."

Logan glanced at Beryl. An amused expression played across her face. She raised her eyebrows. "Don't let me keep you, 'darling.'"

Be nice. He took a deep breath and pasted a congenial smile on his face. "So, are we to be friends, Leslee?"

In her heels the normally five-foot-six Leslee Howell stood nearly eye-to-eye against Logan's six-foot frame. She flashed him a condescending smile, her green eyes gleaming with challenge, before stopping in front of a couple in the center of the room. "Logan, darling, may I present our mayor, Ned Ralston and his wife Molly."

"A pleasure." Logan extricated his arm from Leslee's grasp and extended his hand first to Molly, then Ned.

"The pleasure is ours," responded the mayor. "We're honored that you were able to join us on such short notice."

"I'm always happy to do my part for worthy charities, Mr. Mayor."

"Then I hope you brought your checkbook," said Molly. "I'm looking forward to an autograph accompanied by quite a few zeros."

"Put my money where my mouth is?"

"Sounds good to me."

"I take it you're running this event?"

"Along with my cochair." Molly rose on her toes and scanned the room. "Where the devil did she run off to? I'd like you to meet her. Oh, there she is."

She waved her arms over her head, catching the attention of someone on the other side of the room, a woman with raven hair and haunting eyes. The woman caught Molly's wave and smiled back.

She wore an iridescent black knit that clung to her body like a second skin. It had long sleeves and a high neck, but the left side of the skirt was slit to several inches above her knee, creating the illusion of legs that went on forever. Her hair fell in soft cascading curls, delicately framing her face. At the sight of her, Logan's throat grew dry, and his stomach lurched. "Emma."

The mayor and his wife emitted twin sounds of surprise. Leslee's arms locked possessively around one of his as she plastered herself up against him, her nearly bare breasts hugging his forearm.

Beryl came up from behind him and whispered in his ear. "That, my boy, is twitterpated."

Chapter 6

Emma walked toward them, carrying herself with the regal bearing of a queen. And like a queen, her face showed no emotion. She extended her hand. "Mr. Crawford, how nice to see you again. I had no idea you were joining us this evening."

Her aloof manner and the chill in her voice poleaxed him. Feeling Leslee's tightening grip on his arm, he understood. Shit! Emma had seen the newspaper. He needed massive damage control. Fast.

But before he could speak, Emma said, "I think we're ready to begin." She grabbed Molly's arm and walked away without another glance in Logan's direction.

"What was that all about?" asked Molly. "When did you meet Logan Crawford?"

"Yesterday."

"And?"

"And nothing. He bumped into me at Chapters and Verse. Spilled my coffee. Bought me another. End of story."

"So explain to me why he was staring at you as if you were star-crossed lovers."

Emma spun around. "What?"

"I said—"

"I heard you, Mol." She turned back and continued walking toward the podium. "You're imagining things." However, she wasn't sure whether she was speaking to Molly or herself.

Emma gripped the sides of the wooden podium and struggled to steady her jarred nerves and churning stomach. How could she possibly have thought she could compete with the likes of Leslee Howell? Hadn't sixteen years with Phillip taught her anything?

She'd been so happy earlier in the day as she anticipated tomorrow—so happy until she came across that dreadful article. Even then she'd dismissed it as a Leslee Howell publicity stunt. Hadn't Logan inferred he didn't like Leslee? Apparently, she'd misunderstood, since Leslee was presently draped across Logan like a very contented bitch. If only she'd listened to herself yesterday and walked away. She should have known she'd pay a steep price for a brief few hours of happiness. Life in Emmaville was never happy for long.

Emma took a deep breath and signaled to the band. Gazing across the room, she waited for the crowd to quiet. Leslee smirked at her. And Logan? His face had turned to granite, icy daggers shooting from the cold gray depths of his eyes. But not at her. He directed his murderous glare at Leslee.

Emma cleared her throat, then launched into her prepared speech. "Ladies and gentlemen, physical and sexual abuse of women is at an all-time high in this country. You've seen the statistics. I don't need to bombard you with them. You are here this evening because, like Molly and me, you want to do something to end the abuse. But what can one person do? Not much, I'm afraid."

"Unless that someone is you," shouted out a member of the press.

"Unfortunately, even I don't have that much money, Mr. Frankel." She cleared her throat as a few titters passed through the crowd. "However, if we all join together, we *can* make a difference, and that's what tonight is about.

"One hundred female artists and artisans across the country have generously donated the paintings, sculptures, photographs, and handcrafts you see throughout this room. Bid high tonight, my friends, and together we can make a difference in the lives of battered women and their children. Every dollar spent this evening will go directly into a scholarship fund for victims of abuse."

"You footing the bill for this shindig, Mrs. Wadsworth?" shouted a local television reporter.

"No, Mr. Murdoch. I hope you'll let your viewers know that everything—from the publicity in the papers to the napkins on the tables, and even the tables themselves—was donated by local businesses. This is a group effort on the part of caring Philadelphians."

A ripple of applause wafted across the room.

Molly stepped to the mike and took over for Emma. "Please, everyone, enjoy the evening. There's lots of delicious food to eat, wonderful music to dance to, and beautiful works of art to purchase. Bidding will begin promptly at ten. All major credit cards graciously accepted."

Laughter and applause followed Molly and Emma off the platform.

Emma made a beeline for the ladies' room. She needed a few minutes to sort through her jumbled emotions. Her head told her to forget him. She'd read about Logan Crawford, the man with the huge ego and reputation with women to match. But that wasn't the man who'd held her in his arms yesterday and kissed her so sweetly at her door. That man would never want someone like Leslee Howell. If he did, he wouldn't have looked twice at her. Wouldn't have kissed her. And she wouldn't have fallen in love with him after just one kiss.

Fallen in love? Where the hell had *that* come from? But the thought stopped her dead in her tracks halfway to the powder room. That and the hand that reached out and grabbed her arm from behind.

"Emma, we need to talk."

She squeezed her eyes shut. *No. Not him. Not now. I'm not ready to deal with this.* She opened her eyes and turned to face him.

"About tomorrow," he began.

With those words Emma allowed her brain and not her emotions to rule her actions. "Yes, tomorrow. Actually, something has come up, and I'm afraid I'll have to cancel." She stared coldly down at his hand until he released her.

"Emma, that's not what—"

"If you'll excuse me, Mr. Crawford." She spun on her heel and walked off, hoping he didn't notice that she was shaking like a leaf in a Category Five hurricane.

The very last person in the world she wanted to come across in the ladies' room sat in front of the mirror, touching up her makeup. Leslee laughed. "Really, Emma, you shouldn't try to compete with me. He's so out of your league."

"I don't know what you're talking about."

"Come off it. I saw the way you looked at Logan Crawford. Don't play the naïve innocent with me. I know all your secrets. Phillip loved to talk about them. We both found them quite . . ." She paused for effect, "quite . . . stimulating." She reached for a flute of champagne sitting on the counter and took several sips, never taking her eyes off Emma.

"Anyway, we both know you couldn't satisfy your own husband. What makes you think you could satisfy a man like Logan Crawford?" Her eyes flashed wickedly. "How did Phillip put it? Oh, yes. Sex with Emma is like screwing an iceberg."

Emma reached across the counter, withdrew a tissue from a wicker box and held it out to Leslee. Forcing her voice to remain calm, she finally spoke. "Better wipe your chin, Leslee. Your venom is running."

But again Leslee got the better of her. "That's not venom, darling. That's female honey. I was thinking about all the exciting things Logan can do with his tongue. He's even more adept than Phillip was. I could come just thinking about what he did to me Wednesday night." She rose, shooting off one parting insult before exiting. "But you wouldn't know about that, would you, Emma?"

Collapsing into one of the vanity chairs, Emma lowered her head into her hands. Tears gathered at the corners of her eyes and silently rolled down her cheeks. Leslee's humiliating remarks had torn apart the last threads of her composure. She wished yesterday had never happened. She wished she'd never met Logan Crawford, had never been taken in by his phony, suave charm. He'd robbed her of the steel-plated armor she needed to survive.

"Emma? Are you all right?"

Molly stood over her, a comforting hand on her shoulder. Emma hadn't heard her enter.

"Emma! You're crying! What's wrong? You never cry. Not even when Phillip—"

Emma stopped her midsentence. Shaking her head

fiercely, she sniffed back the remaining tears and brushed at her cheeks with the back of her hand. "I'm fine, Mol. Really."

"No, you're not. What the hell's going on? You've been acting weird all day. Something happened yesterday, didn't it? Something between you and Logan Crawford. Something more than just spilled coffee."

Molly's cheeks and neck grew red, so red that it was hard to tell where her face left off and her flaming Irish curls began. Emma nodded.

"What did that asshole do to you?"

"Calm down. It wasn't like that. He was a perfect gentleman. We had brunch. And dinner. And we danced. And he brought me roses, Mol, and I had to put them in that ugly vase on the étagère because I had nothing else to put them in, and he asked me to spend Saturday with him, and I was so happy, and then I broke the vase this morning, and he's sleeping with Leslee, and . . ."

The words stopped tumbling out. Emma bowed her head and started sobbing.

"My God, you're not falling for him, are you?"

"How should I know? No one falls in love in a day. Besides, I don't even know what love is," she sputtered between gulps. "I feel . . . I . . . oh, God. This is insane. I don't know what I feel."

"Damn him!"

"No, Mol. Don't. He didn't do anything."

"Not Logan. Phillip. I hope he's burning in hell for what he did to you."

"I'm sure he is." Emma paused for several seconds. Her voice was filled with resignation when she finally spoke again. "Anyway, it doesn't matter. I told Logan I couldn't see him again."

"Good. It's for the best." Molly wet a washcloth and handed it to her. "Wash your face." She rooted around in Emma's evening bag and withdrew a compact and lipstick. "Good thing you can get away without much makeup. Otherwise you'd need major repair work to your face."

Emma opened the compact and began to apply powder to her nose. "Molly?"

"Hmm?"

"I'm doing the right thing, aren't I? Not seeing him again?"

"He'd only hurt you in the long run, and you've suffered your share of hurt." She placed her hand on Emma's shoulder. "Forget him."

Emma covered Molly's hand with her own. "He brought me roses, Mol. Two dozen long-stemmed, bloodred roses." She laughed. "Do you believe it?"

"And the wicked queen gave Snow White a big juicy red apple."

"In real life the wicked queen always wins, doesn't she?" She scrutinized her reflection. "Passable?"

"No one will ever know."

"Then let's go. There are several hundred people waiting for us to part them from their money." She stood, raised her chin, threw her shoulders back, and left the room, all traces of her breakdown gone.

Several minutes later Beryl opened the stall where she'd sat in silence since before Emma entered the ladies' room. Walking quickly back into the ballroom, she found Logan and pulled him aside. "We need to talk."

Chapter 7

Acting as auctioneer, Ned Ralston kept the bidding brisk, threatening higher taxes and audits for those who didn't up their bids and various incentives for those who did. When his heavy-handed tactics resulted in good-natured grumbling from the audience, he shrugged and grinned. "All's fair in love and war, and we're here to wage a war against abuse." By halfway through the auction he'd succeeded in prying over a hundred thousand dollars from his constituents.

The last piece of artwork auctioned off was Emma's. She'd designed a quilted and embroidered wall hanging consisting of twelve cross-stitched squares depicting various Philadelphia historic buildings. She'd worked months on the piece, hand stitching each linen square herself, then piecing them together and finishing the wall hanging with intricate hand quilting along the fabric borders.

"I already have a spot for this in my office at City Hall," said Ned. "So if anyone else has designs on it, be prepared to spend big bucks. My wife will bid on my behalf." He nodded toward Molly. "Okay, folks. I'm opening the bidding at five thousand dollars."

"Six."

"Six. Do I hear seven?"

"Seven."

"Seven. Do I hear eight?"

Bidding continued at a furious pace until Molly increased her offer to fifteen thousand dollars, and the other bidders dropped out.

"Fifteen. Do I hear fifteen-five?" asked Ned. Silence met his question. "All right, then. Fifteen. Going once. Going twice—"

"Fifty thousand dollars."

Silence fell at the sound of the deep baritone voice.

From across the room Logan trapped Emma with his steel gray eyes. "Under one condition," he said. "The artist has to spend all day tomorrow with me."

Emma heard Molly gasp. The room filled with buzzing speculation.

"Emma?" Ned turned to her for an answer.

Stunned, she could only nod in agreement to Logan's blackmail. Fifty thousand dollars would go a long way toward helping educate battered women and their children. Whatever his motives, she'd suffer through the day, but she'd make sure he knew it was against her will.

With a huge grin, Ned smacked the gavel on the podium. "Sold to Logan Crawford for fifty thousand dollars and a date with the artist."

The room swelled with applause. A throng of well-wishers immediately surrounded Emma. When she finally broke away to confront Logan, he was nowhere in sight.

Chapter 8

An hour later, clenching and unclenching her fists, Leslee paced back and forth across the deep ivory pile that carpeted her living room. Stopping in front of her coffee table, she grabbed a heavy Lalique candy dish. "Sonofabitch!" With the speed of a major league fastball pitcher, she hurled the crystal across the room. The dish grazed a brass andiron before shattering against the back of her white brick gas hearth. The act did little to appease the bloodcurdling rage churning inside her.

Emma! For years that little bitch of a nobody had been a thorn in her side. By rights Emma should have been six feet under, not Phillip. Or at the very least, she should be locked away in some psycho ward like Phillip had promised.

I can't divorce her. She's my ticket to respectability. With Emma at my side, no one sticks his nose too deep into my business. Trust me, Leslee.

Well, she'd trusted him, and look where it had gotten her. Phillip was dead, and all the excitement and adventure of their secret life had died with him. Worst of all, the Princess of the Hill was still ensconced in her castle. A castle that by rights should belong to her. She, Leslee Howell, had been Phillip Wadsworth's true partner in life. Not that pathetic little bitch.

When Logan Crawford had waltzed into her office, she'd seen an opportunity to forget the past and move on, but once again she'd been thwarted by Emma. How dare he prefer that mouse to her! How dare he humiliate her the way he did at the auction this evening, staring after Emma like some lovestruck basset hound! And in front of the mayor and all those society blue bloods!

But that wasn't enough. How could he bid on that piece of shit? And then demand a date on top of it! Logan Crawford had stabbed her in the heart, then poured salt in the wound. She'd show him.

She reached for another crystal bauble and sent it flying to join the growing pile of expensive broken debris inside the fireplace. She only remembered being this angry one other time in her life—the night she'd discovered Phillip's naked, lifeless body sprawled across the bedroom floor.

How dare he die and leave her!

How dare Logan Crawford play her for a fool!

Leslee stormed over to the fireplace and grabbed a rag doll off the mantel. She pulled a diamond hat pin from the pincushion next to it. Phillip had bought the voodoo doll in Emma's likeness on a trip to Jamaica. Leslee jabbed the pin into the doll. *Too bad voodoo doesn't work.* But there were other ways to screw the bitch.

She sat down at her desk and flipped open her Rolodex. Certain people owed her favors. Big favors.

It was time to collect. If Logan Crawford preferred Emma Wadsworth's company to hers, he'd pay dearly for it, and that little bitch would never know what hit her.

Chapter 9

"Yes!" Marty Bell hung up the phone and high-fived the air. Humming his favorite song, he grabbed the receiver again and punched the speed dial button. Even though it was after one in the morning, he knew his editor would still be at the office. The guy lived there.

"Loomis."

"Hold the presses, boss. I just got a scorcher of a tip from Leslee Howell. I'm on my way to Philly."

"Tip on who?"

"Logan Crawford."

"Again? Jeez! The man can't keep his prick zipped, can he? Actress or model?"

"Neither. He's banging some widow."

"You're kidding!"

"Swear to God. Leslee gave me all the details. The broad is practically royalty down there. Bloodline going back to the Founding Fathers and all that shit."

"What's her name?"

"Emma Wadsworth."

"Phillip Wadsworth's widow?"

"Yeah. You know the chick?"

"Pictures by midnight tomorrow, Bell. Good ones, and you've got yourself that bonus."

"I'm on my way, boss." Marty hung up the phone and grabbed his keys and camera equipment. Flying down the steps of his third-story Brooklyn walk-up, he belted out an off-key version of "I'm in the Money."

Chapter 10

Emma awoke to loud chimes and a steady, heavy pounding. Someone was beating down the door of St. Anthony's during High Mass. No. That wasn't it. St. Anthony's was twelve blocks away. Even if the Second Coming was in full swing, she wouldn't hear it from here. She groaned. The housekeeper must have forgotten her key again. But then she remembered it was Saturday. Now that she was alone in the house, Mavis came only on Thursdays.

Prying open one heavy eyelid, Emma stared at the clock on the nightstand. Six-thirty! Whoever it was could just go away and come back at a less ungodly hour. She pulled the comforter over her head, but the cotton fabric did little to drown out the incessant, repetitive banging, thumping, and chiming. Finally, she dragged herself out of bed, pulled on her robe, and padded barefoot to the front door. Whoever it was had damn well better have a good excuse for getting her up at the crack of dawn. She swung open the door.

"It's about time you answered."

"How dare you! Do you realize what time it is?"

Logan glanced at his watch and shrugged. "I bought you for the day. By my reckoning, that day started six-and-a-half hours ago and doesn't end until midnight."

"You did *not* buy me! I agreed to spend the day with you, and by *my* reckoning the day hasn't started yet."

He ignored her outburst, stepping around her and into the foyer.

"Get out, Logan!"

"Suit yourself, but if you break our agreement, I'll put a stop payment on my check." He turned to leave.

"No! Wait!"

He halted, but kept his back to her. "Yes?"

"Why are you doing this to me?"

He pivoted and trapped her with determined eyes. "It was the only way I could get you to listen to me."

She sighed in resignation. "Go on. I'm listening."

"No. Not like this. Get dressed. Then we'll talk."

She made no effort to move, just continued to stand there glaring at him.

"Emma, please?"

"Apparently, you're leaving me no choice."

"None."

She turned and headed for her bedroom.

And took a long shower. A very long shower. Let him wait. She was furious with him. But she was more furious with herself for caving in to him. For the second time in twenty-four hours her eyes filled with tears.

And she never cried.

Never.

She threw on an old pair of jeans and a faded sweatshirt, not bothering to fix her hair or apply makeup. Glimpsing her reflection in the mirror, she groaned, then reached for her brush and combed the tangles out of her hair. For herself, not him. At least that's what she told herself.

When she threw open her bedroom door, she was hit with the heavy aroma of fresh coffee and . . . and bacon? She stepped into the kitchen to find Logan scrambling eggs at the stove.

"Sit down. Breakfast is almost ready."

Emma stood in the doorway, staring, unable to cover the distance from the hallway to the table. "You're cooking me breakfast?"

"Looks that way, doesn't it?" He served the eggs onto two plates, carried them to the table, and settled himself into one of the chairs. He scooped a forkful of egg into his mouth, then took a sip of his coffee while she continued to stand in the doorway. "Your breakfast is getting cold."

Breakfast? She couldn't force words over the lump in her throat, let alone food. Finally, she managed to make her way to the table and sit down. By sheer concentrated effort she spoke. "What are you doing?"

He stared blankly at the fork that was midway between his plate and mouth. "I think that's rather obvious. I'm eating breakfast."

"That's not what I mean, and you know it."

"Do I?"

"Damn you, Logan Crawford! Stop playing with me."

Placing his fork on the plate, he steepled his fingers. "I'm not playing with you, Emma. Although I must admit, the thought has crossed my mind. Shall we play the kind of games Leslee played with your husband? Or the kind he played with you?"

Emma gasped. "What the hell did she tell you?"

"Tell *me*? Nothing. But Leslee did say some rather despicable things to you last night, didn't she?"

Logan proceeded to summarize her confrontation with Leslee. Each sentence he spoke drove a knife into her heart. "My assistant possesses a rather unique and highly useful talent," he explained. "She remembers nearly everything she hears and reads. I'd say she heard quite an earful in the ladies' room last evening."

Emma trembled. From head to toe her body shook violently. Coffee sloshed over the edge of the cup she clenched between her hands. He knew! His eavesdropping assistant had heard everything. Every humiliating word Leslee had hurled at her. And her confession to Molly. She had heard her tell Molly she might be in love with him. She felt as though he'd raped her soul. Tears she never shed cascaded down her cheeks and splashed onto the table.

When he reached for her hands, she tried to jerk away from his touch but only managed to spill the remainder of her coffee over both of them.

"Look at me."

She refused to acknowledge him. Her blurred gaze remained glued on their hands.

He gently pushed a stray lock of hair from her face and lifted her chin. "There are two things you have to know about me, Emma. I never lie, and I never meant to hurt you."

She spit out her skepticism. "How dare you sit there and say that after what you've just done?"

"Believe me, if there had been any other way—"

"And you never lie?"

"Never."

All right, Logan. Let's see how you answer this one. "Did you . . . Leslee . . . was she telling me the truth about the two of you?"

Logan released her hands and shook his head. He grabbed a napkin and dried his hands. Then he rose from the table and paced back and forth between the refrigerator and the sink, raking his hands through his hair. Finally, he stopped in front of her and shoved his fists into his pockets. "If anyone else had asked me that question, I would have told him it was none of his goddamn business."

Emma wasn't sure she really wanted to know the answer. She dried her own hands, then lowered them to her lap and twisted them around the bunched fabric of her sweatshirt. He was right. It was none of her business. It was his business. His and Leslee's. Brunch, dinner, and a platonic kiss didn't give her proprietary rights over Logan Crawford.

"But you're not just anybody, Emma."

What?

Logan squatted down in front of her, taking her hands in his. "I've made many mistakes in my life. Doozies. Done many things I'm not proud of. If I were given the chance to change only one of them, it would be what happened Wednesday night with Leslee."

Emma tried to push away from him, but he held her hands firmly. His knees pressed up against her, trapping her in her chair. She had started this with her question, now she'd have to suffer through the gory details. She squeezed her eyes shut. *Please! I already know what a great "lay" Leslee Howell is. Don't make me hear this! Not from you!*

But Logan wasn't talking about the glories of Leslee Howell. "I had too much to drink. It's a lame excuse, I know. But she was there. Eager. The whole time I kept thinking, why am I doing this? I don't even like the woman. I was disgusted with myself for taking advantage of the situation and with her for being so easy.

"That's the way it's always been. They throw themselves at me, and I welcome them with open arms because it's easy to walk away afterward. No commitments. No regrets. Slam. Bam. Thank you, ma'am."

Emma opened her eyes. None of what he said made any sense to her. "Then why do you regret Wednesday night?"

"Because Thursday morning I met you."

She lowered her eyes to their joined hands. His thumb rhythmically stroked her wrist. Fire rose up her arm and spread throughout her body. Her toes tingled. She couldn't let this continue. Couldn't walk down that path with him. "Don't do this, Logan. You'd only be disappointed. What Leslee said about me. It's all true. And I won't let you hurt me."

"I would never hurt you, Emma."

Did he mean what he said, or was he just so used to getting his way that he refused to give up until he added her to his list of conquests? And why go to such effort? What could he possibly see in her when he'd bedded some of the world's most beautiful women? Perhaps he was just like Phillip, a man who had to have it all and couldn't stand losing, a man who would go to any length for the sake of the challenge—whether he really wanted whatever the goal or treasure or conquest or not. It didn't matter. "Maybe you don't believe you'd hurt me, but you would."

"You're wrong. And I intend to prove it to you."

Tears formed in her eyes. Again. She was losing count of the number of times he'd made her cry in the past two days. She swiped at a traitorous drop streaking down her cheek. "Why me?"

"I don't know. I can't explain it to myself, let alone you. Nothing like this has ever happened to me before, but from the moment we met, I couldn't get you out of my head. You keep me awake at night." He rose and pulled her into his arms. "And because you're wrong about something else."

She stared at him in confusion.

"It *is* possible to fall in love in a day." He lowered his head and captured her mouth.

With gentle, firm pressure, Logan took his time, coaxing, never forcing. His hands explored her cheeks and stroked her neck while his lips nibbled away from one corner of her mouth to the other. Cupping the back of her head, he wove his fingers through her hair and traced his way up the side of her face with soft, feathery kisses that roamed across her eyelids and back down the other side of her face until he was once again capturing her mouth in his. Slowly, his tongue forayed between her lips, teasing, pleading for an invitation to enter.

Emma's lips parted. When the tip of his tongue kissed the tip of hers, she shivered. As he plunged farther into her mouth, her head spun. In the deepest recesses of her body she felt a painful emptiness and a craving to have him fill it. No one had ever stirred such feelings inside her. Ever.

Finally, he stopped, but the maelstrom of emotion swelling within her only increased. She found it difficult to catch her breath. He held her close against his chest, and the pounding of his heart mingled with the pounding of hers until she couldn't tell where his ended and hers began. All from a kiss. A kiss unlike any she'd ever experienced.

He lowered his head and whispered in her ear. "Definitely not an iceberg."

"Where are you taking me?"

They were in Logan's rented Jaguar an hour later,

driving south on the Blue Route. He pulled a piece of paper from his pocket and consulted it. "Somewhere special." He frowned. "If I can figure out these directions the concierge at the hotel gave me."

"Perhaps if you told me our destination, I could help. I do live here, you know."

"But that would ruin the surprise."

The man confused the hell out of her. Her emotions bounced all over the place, as if she were on some sadistic PMS roller coaster. One moment she was the epitome of joie de vivre, the next on the verge of tears. Maybe that was it. She was just PMS-ing. But the timing was all off. Besides, she wasn't bloated.

A scarier thought hit her. Maybe she'd entered early-onset menopause. She'd read that some women start having symptoms in their early thirties. Crap! That was probably what was causing her irrational behavior. Yet another case of rotten luck she could add to her long list. Welcome to Emmaville: home to rotten luck, twenty-four/seven.

She made a mental note to call her gynecologist and tried to analyze Logan from a more rational perspective. He'd said he loved her. No, he hadn't. She was jumping to conclusions. He'd merely said it was possible to fall in love in a day—not that he had. But then he'd kissed her. A kiss that had rocked her all the way to China and back again at the speed of light.

And he'd told her she wasn't an iceberg.

Big deal. She wasn't the gullible eighteen-year-old she'd been when Phillip entered her life. Experience had taught her that men say anything to get what they want.

Logan said he never lied. Which in itself could be a lie. She couldn't trust him. She knew he sensed the secrets within her. She saw it in the way his eyes searched her face. A man who fought for what he wanted, he'd dig until he found the answers he sought, never realizing until too late that his quest could precipitate her doom.

He shifted into fourth gear, then reached for her hand. "What's bothering you?"

You. This relationship couldn't possibly work. It was doomed before it began. She searched her mind for an answer to appease him. "Your assistant. I can understand why she stayed in the restroom stall. In her place I may have made the same decision. Better to wait until after Leslee exited. But why did she tell you what she overheard?"

"Because she loves me."

Emma pulled her hand from his. "That is so not the answer I wanted to hear. This is insane. I can't compete. Not with Leslee. Not with your assistant. Not with anyone. I don't know what kind of game you're playing, but I refuse to play it with you."

"You're right. This is totally insane. And will continue to be so until you start trusting me." He reached for her hand again and kissed her palm.

Not in this lifetime. I trusted a man once. Look where it got me. She pulled her hand away again and placed it back in her lap.

"Let me tell you about Beryl."

"I don't think so."

Logan chuckled as he squeezed her knee. "Trust, Emma. Trust."

She stared at the hand he left on her knee. "Fine. Tell me about Beryl."

He squeezed her knee again. "As I said, Beryl loves me. And I love her."

"Great. How about if you turn the car around now and take me home?"

"Like a sister. A big sister."

"Oh."

He continued. "I was eight years old. Beryl was fifteen, one of a succession of foster kids my parents took in from time to time. She and my sister Jennifer became the best of friends. My parents eventually adopted her, and I gained another older sister. My fifth. I'm the baby of the family. The only male and terribly spoiled, but I don't suppose you've noticed that."

She chuckled despite herself.

"You should laugh more often."

She felt her cheeks flush. Compliments. She'd received so few in her life that she never knew how to respond to them. Could he really mean what he said, or was he only saying what he thought she wanted to hear? And did it really matter? "You were telling me about Beryl."

"Yes, Beryl." He paused for a moment. "Do you read the comics in the daily papers?"

"Occasionally."

"I'm Dennis the Menace. Or at least I was as a child."

"What does this have to do with Beryl?"

"Everything. Beryl became the big sister who always got me out of trouble. My other sisters pretty much ignored me. I was a pest and an embarrassment to them. Especially around their friends. Beryl took on the job of saving me from myself.

"Several years ago I had the opportunity to pay her back when her marriage failed. She's been with me ever since. Still trying her damnedest to keep me out of trouble."

"And that's what she was doing last night?"

He shrugged. "Her heart's in the right place."

Chapter 11

Logan studied the worry lines etched into Emma's brow. What was it about her that brought out a protective instinct he hadn't even known he possessed? Unused to letting his emotions get the better of him, he tried to understand why she had such an effect on him. Never in his life had he allowed a woman to break through his defenses the way Emma did, let alone at such breakneck speed. And the damn irony of the situation was that she hadn't even tried. She was totally unaware of her power over him. The woman was a puzzle wrapped in an enigma within a mystery—a mystery he felt driven to solve as if his very sanity depended on it.

And damn it, he wanted her. Wanted to bury himself within her and never emerge. The great love-'em-and-leave-'em Crawford had finally fallen and fallen hard—for what seemed to be the only woman in the world immune to all his supposed sex appeal. Boy would the tabloids have a field day with that one!

And what a laugh Aggie would get over it. She always said when he finally failed to dodge Cupid's arrow, he'd feel like he'd been trampled by the bulls at Pamplona. Well, as usual, mixed metaphors be damned, his dear mother was right.

This was much more than a case of testosterone run amok. He could tell Emma wasn't a casual sex kind of woman. That she needed love. Commitment. Two things he'd never given any woman before, had never wanted to give any woman. Yet here he was, the man who never allowed his personal life to impede his headlong race to the top, unable to imagine a future without a woman he'd met forty-eight hours ago. What the hell was happening to him?

And why did he have to fall for a woman who seemed to have an overabundance of inner demons that needed slaying? Demons he suspected he'd have to destroy before she'd ever believe him or trust him. Could he blame her, though, considering his well-documented track record? How could she accept the change that had come over him so suddenly when he himself didn't understand the alien emotions that had taken over his brain and body?

He studied her hands, clenched tightly in her lap. She feared him. Feared herself. Feared what might happen between them. He understood. This was new territory for him as well. He feared making a mistake. Feared losing her before they even had a chance to find each other.

An hour later, after several wrong turns, Logan pulled the Jag into the entrance of Longwood Gardens. Emma smiled. "One of my favorite places."

"Lucky choice on my part."

As they wandered through the indoor gardens, Logan grew increasingly annoyed. He wanted to be alone with Emma, but at every turn someone intruded on their privacy. Tourists from Delaware and New Jersey campaigned to get his headquarters in their states. Others weighed in on whether someone with his fortune and resources should get municipal tax incentives and whether his business practices helped or hurt the economy. And the environment. They all had opinions, and they all voiced them. Some downright obnoxious with their in-your-face attitudes.

Emma hung back, eventually taking refuge on a secluded bench. When Logan finally extricated himself from a crowd of opinionated suburbanites, he found her immersed in a pencil sketch. "May I?" He reached for the small tablet.

She hesitated. "They're very rough. Just quick sketches."

He lifted the book and slowly flipped the pages until he arrived at the last page and saw himself in the center of a large group of people. Head raised, he searched for something beyond the crowd, a look of longing on his face. Dumbstruck, he stared at the drawing. In a few strokes of a pencil she'd succeeded in capturing his innermost thoughts. If only he could see into her soul the way she saw into his.

He closed the book and handed it back to her. "Rough? These are fantastic."

She dismissed his compliment with a shrug of her shoulders and placed the book back in her shoulder bag. "There's nothing special about them."

"Wrong. They're very special. Just like you." Did she know how much he wanted her? Now. Tomorrow. Forever? Yes, the startling realization slammed into him. Forever. He bent his head down, about to kiss her.

"There he is! I told you, Edgar. It's Logan Crawford. Right over there under that palm tree."

Logan groaned. "Let's get out of here."

Chapter 12

Hiding behind a large banana tree, Marty Bell cursed at the missed shot, annoyed by the interrupted kiss. Damn loudmouthed bitch! The look in Crawford's eyes had left no doubt as to what was on his mind, and Marty'd had a perfect bead on it. He grabbed his gear and scurried after them. Crawford and the broad were so engrossed in each other, he didn't even have to worry about being seen. Piece of cake.

After a short drive, his prey stopped at a small country inn that offered Marty no photo opportunities. Afterward they drove down the road to the Brandywine Museum. It was less crowded than the gardens, forcing Marty to keep a low profile. A nearly empty art gallery left little room for maneuvering undetected. He'd built his reputation as the best of the paparazzi on his ability to wait out his quarry. After hours of hiding in the broad's frozen shrubbery early that morning, his perseverance had paid off. Once again he had Crawford in his sights. He'd wait him out in the comfort of his heated Ford Explorer.

Chapter 13

The sign read: PLEASURES A LA MODE. HOME OF THE WORLD'S MOST HEAVENLY SINFUL ICE CREAM. "The world's most heavenly sinful ice cream? This I've got to try." Logan pulled into the small parking lot on the side of the ice cream parlor.

Emma studied the sign. "An oxymoron. How can something in heaven be sinful?"

"Let's find out."

The shop was a tiny gingerbread Victorian painted a rainbow of pastel shades. Inside, an old-fashioned soda fountain covered the back wall. Four small glass-topped wrought-iron tables, each with two matching chairs, took up the available floor space. An elderly woman, engrossed in a paperback, sat hunched on a stool behind the counter. She glanced up briefly when they entered, then returned to her novel.

"Must be a good book," whispered Logan.

"You're just ticked off she didn't recognize you."

He turned his attention to the list of available flavors posted on a chalkboard. The first one whetted both his appetite and his curiosity. "Sex by Chocolate for Two?" He raised an eyebrow at Emma and grinned broadly as the color rose in her cheeks.

"Best damn chocolate you'll ever eat," muttered the old woman.

"We'll take two," he said.

She labored off the stool and shuffled to the freezer, grunting as she bent over and scooped the ice cream from the container, then plopped it into a large cookie cone.

"Three bucks," she said, handing Logan the cone.

He passed the cone to Emma. "We'd like two."

"That is for two," said the woman.

"No. You don't understand," he said, certain the woman was several pistons shy of an engine. "We'd like two cones."

"Can't have two. That one's enough. Share it." She held out her hand. "Three bucks."

Logan gaped at the woman. He turned to Emma. Her eyes wide, she stared at the clerk. Finally, he shrugged and handed over the money. Stuffing the bills in her apron pocket, she grunted before shuffling back to her stool and book.

Sitting at the table closest to the window, Emma and Logan took turns licking the cone.

"Oh, God," moaned Emma. "This *is* sinful."

"Quick! Catch the drip!"

"There's one on your side, too." She laughed between licks, her tongue darting out to lap up the rivers of chocolate.

The sight of that small pink tongue dancing around the side of the dark chocolate ice cream was more than Logan could stand. The tightening in his groin was immediate. Fantasizing about that tongue and what he wished it were doing to him only increased his discomfort. He squeezed his eyes shut and forced the thoughts from his mind. Or at least tried. Too late, he realized they were already branded into his brain, the searing heat spreading throughout his body.

Steam rose from a huge cast-iron radiator against one wall. The heat added to his physical distress and turned the small room into a sauna. The ice cream melted faster than they could consume it. Logan held the cone between them, and they began attacking from both sides at once.

"Sorry," he said, when the cone came too close to Emma's nose.

Emma reached for a napkin. Logan placed his free hand over hers. "It would be a shame to waste perfectly good ice cream," he said. Then he leaned over and kissed the chocolate off her nose.

Ice cream dripped onto his fingers. He held them up to her lips. After the briefest flicker of indecision, she licked them clean, giggling between licks. He fed her more, then feasted on her cream-drenched lips, the cold treat trickling down her chin and over their joined hands.

Logan made quick work of the dribble on her chin, his lips nibbling at the sweet mixture of tastes— bittersweet chocolate and honey-flavored Emma. Then he raised her fingers to his mouth and sucked the chocolate from them one at a time.

When he'd finished with her fingers, Logan captured her mouth with his, his tongue at first flicking, then probing deeply, exploring and caressing.

"So sweet," he moaned, parting just enough to pull air into his lungs before lowering his head once more.

Melting in his arms as quickly as the frozen confection, Emma forgot all but the moment. No guilt. No pain. No past. Only here and now. Her body trembled with need she'd never dared dream possible. Logan unleashed a side of her that had been locked away all her life. Intense emotions ripped through her. Joy. Need. Longing. She didn't understand this power he held over her, how a simple kiss could flip a switch inside her and change her entire life. But there was nothing simple about Logan Crawford's kisses. They were sensual. Masterful. Practiced.

I was thinking about all the exciting things Logan can do with his tongue. He's even more adept than Phillip was. I could come just thinking about what he did to me Wednesday night!

Leslee's words rushed into her brain—along with a dark cloud of anxiety that stripped her of desire and left her naked and raw.

She couldn't breathe.

Her head spun.

Her heart pounded.

Emma abruptly pulled away and stared at Logan, gasping for breath, her eyes filled with fear and uncertainty. He felt her closing off to him, shutting down, as if she were being controlled by some hidden demon. A lurking monster who got his kicks out of jerking her chain each time she dared to come alive. "What is it?"

She reached for a handful of napkins and began cleaning her hands and face. "I . . . we should go."

He knew why *he* wanted to leave. His need for her bordered on desperation. And so did another part of his anatomy. A part that had now succeeded in shrinking his jeans two sizes. He wanted to take her right there in the middle of the ice cream parlor. But somehow he didn't think that was the driving factor in Emma's desperate expression and sudden need to leave.

He shook his head in disgust. He had to slow down. If he pushed, he knew he'd lose her.

He had never needed any woman the way he needed her.

He had never needed a cold shower more in his life.

Pulling her to her feet, he wrapped his arm around her shoulders and led her toward the exit, the remainder of the ice cream cone left forgotten on the table.

Twenty-seven degrees outside with a windchill factor of sixteen, yet sweat dripped from Marty's slicked-back designer haircut and poured in rivulets down the side of his neck. He panted, his hands shaking with excitement as he quickly shot frame after fame. Goddamn triple fucking X. They should give Pulitzers for the shots he was getting.

"Oh, baby!" he coaxed, adjusting the zoom lens. "Give me some tongue. That's it, little mama. Come to daddy!" Salivating from the heady experience, he continued to shoot from his vantage point behind a large black van parked across the street from the ice cream parlor. The chase was over, the fox captured in his crosshairs. Damned if he knew what Leslee had against Crawford and the bitch, but he owed her big time.

Chapter 14

The cold winter sun dipping behind a row of towering evergreens heralded Emma and Logan's arrival back at her house. Logan helped her from the car, then turned to retrieve an overnight bag from the trunk.

Emma's eyes grew wide; her jaw dropped.

He held his arms akimbo and shook his head in frustration. "You don't expect me to take you to dinner in chocolate-splattered jeans, do you?"

Jump to another conclusion, why don't you, Emma? "No. Of course not."

She fumbled with her key, unable to accomplish the simple task of inserting it into the lock. With a loud sigh, Logan closed his hand around hers and guided the metal into the slot. He turned the key, pushed open the door, then removed the key and handed it back to her.

Their eyes met, and she had the distinct feeling she knew what he was thinking. Holy symbolism! When had her brain decided to stray to the gutter? Never in her life had she suffered such erotic thoughts. But no man had ever made love to her with his eyes before, either.

Mechanically, she deactivated the alarm, sensing his gaze on her, certain she felt the touch of those warm gray eyes against her skin.

"Emma?" His voice sounded husky with need.

"Yes?"

"Where should I change?"

"Change?" *Don't change. You're perfect the way you are. Gorgeous and sexy. And I wish I knew what you were doing to me and why.*

"My clothes?"

"Right. Your clothes." She pointed up the stairs. "Any bedroom. Clean towels in the bathroom." Without waiting for him to head up the stairs, she darted toward the safety of her own room.

What was happening to her? She stood in front of her bedroom mirror and stared critically at the image reflected back at her. Gingerly she raised her fingers to her lips, lips still red and swollen from his kisses. What did he see in her? He was a man who could have any woman he wanted with a snap of his fingers.

She wasn't stupid, and she wasn't naïve. She'd been used once by a man, and she wasn't about to let it happen again. And Logan, by his own admission, used women. Lots of them. But when she looked into his eyes, she saw longing, not deviousness. Desire, not cruelty. Sincerity, not callousness. She just couldn't see what he saw in her.

What did it matter, though? Tomorrow he'd be gone. She would hold up her end of the bargain, give him his day, and life would return to normal. Such as normal was in Emmaville. But could it ever be the same again? Logan Crawford had unlocked more than her front door.

A telltale drop of moisture escaped from the corner of her eye and slid down her cheek. *Damn it!* She swiped at the recalcitrant tear and sighed, reminding herself once again that she *never* cried. "Never," she told her disbelieving reflection.

When they returned from dinner later that evening, Logan took the key from Emma's hand before she had a chance to fumble with it. She'd been nervous and edgy throughout the meal, eating little, averting her eyes whenever she found him gazing at her, stiffening in his arms when they danced. She was all too conscious of what she was doing—trying her hardest to keep his eventual departure from hurting any more than she now realized it would.

"I could make some tea or coffee . . . if you'd like," she offered halfheartedly, motioning in the direction of the kitchen.

Logan clasped her wrist and drew her close. When she twisted her head away, he cupped it with his hands and tilted it up to him. "What I'd like is for you to tell me what's going on."

She squeezed her eyes shut. "Nothing."

"You're lying. Closing your eyes doesn't hide it."

"It's over, Logan. You've had your day. You can go now. Have a nice life."

He lowered his hands to her shoulders and shook her gently. "What the hell is that supposed to mean?"

"Please! Stop pretending you care."

He grabbed her hand and cupped it against his groin. "Does this feel like I'm pretending? Damn it, I've been walking around with a two-ton hard-on since Thursday morning because of you."

Emma yanked her hand from his grasp and stepped away from him. "You can't possibly feel that way about me."

Logan shoved his hands through his hair, then slammed the wall in frustration. When he spoke, his voice was low and measured. "Emma, I'm leaving now. Not because I want to, but because if I stay, we're going to wind up doing something you're obviously not ready for. But when I come back tomorrow, I want some answers. I want to know what's got you so frightened of living. I want to know why you have such a low opinion of yourself. And most of all, I want to know what that sonofabitch husband of yours did to you because I think he's the key to all this."

He left without looking back at her, slamming the door behind him.

Emma slumped to the floor. He was asking more than she could give. It frightened her. But as terrified as she was of Logan forcing her secrets from her, five words kept echoing in her head. Five words she'd never expected to hear. Five words that both filled her with euphoria and frightened the hell out of her.

When I come back tomorrow.

Logan hadn't meant to act or sound so harsh. Or crass. But damn, that woman drove him crazy. He didn't want her to think she was nothing more than a casual fuck, but how many cold showers could one grown man stand? And yet he knew he couldn't tell her how he really felt about her. Not yet. She wouldn't believe him. Hell, he didn't believe it himself, but Emma didn't believe even the little he'd divulged. She couldn't even accept a compliment without getting all flustered, for God's sake! Whatever had happened to her, the resulting trauma was deeply imbedded.

"Goddamn sonofabitch!" Logan slammed his hand down on the steering wheel. If her husband weren't already dead, he'd strangle the bastard with his bare hands. Logan laughed. He'd always considered himself a nonviolent man. The woman definitely brought out some interesting sides to his personality.

Chapter 15

Back at the hotel, Logan bypassed his own suite and strode down the hall to Beryl's. An irritable "coming" answered his impatient knock. When she opened the door, he surveyed the room and sighed deeply. *God's in His heaven, and all's right with the world*, he thought, aware that he'd interrupted Beryl's usual Saturday night orgy of pay-per-view and Chinese food. White paper cartons lay strewn across the coffee table and sofa, Mel Gibson's face covered the wide-screen TV, and Beryl stood, hands on hips, furious over the intrusion.

He strode across the room and picked up a carton of Chi-Yang shrimp. Then he slumped into the overstuffed sofa and plopped a hot, spicy prawn into his mouth.

"You look like hell," she said, clicking off Mel and joining him on the couch.

"Thanks, sweetheart. I knew I could count on you to cheer me up."

Beryl laughed. Not a giggle. Not a titter. Not a

chuckle. But a side-splitting, tears-springing-to-the-eyes, can't-catch-your-breath, loud, rip-roaring, hold-down-the-fort belly laugh.

Logan hurled a pillow at her. "I can fire you, you know."

"You wouldn't dare."

"What the hell's so damn funny?"

"You are, you big schmuck. I've been waiting years for some woman to put you in your place." She grabbed the container out of his hand and smiled sweetly at him. "I think I'm really going to like this Emma Wadsworth."

Leaning his elbows on his knees, he lowered his head into his hands. "What's happening to me, Beryl?"

"You're in love, my little Dennis the Menace. Helplessly. Hopelessly. In Love with a capital L."

Logan groaned. "I know."

Beryl patted him on the back. "Ain't it grand?"

He spent the next two hours recounting his day with Emma. "I can't explain it," he said, falling back against the cushions. "I don't really know anything about her. Yet I feel as though I've known her forever—or at least been searching for her that long. God, would you listen to me. I sound like something out of some goddamn romance novel."

His eyes probed Beryl's for answers and understanding. She'd always been there to steady him, and if ever he needed steadying, needed to be set on the right course, it was now. "I know none of this makes any sense."

"Makes perfect sense. The only thing that doesn't make any sense is what you're doing here instead of back in Chestnut Hill."

"I told you why I left her."

"Yeah, I know. For once in your life you were trying to take the high road and control all that raging testosterone." Beryl jumped to her feet and yanked him off the sofa. "For God's sake, you pathetic fool, get the hell back there. Sounds to me like she needs you as much as you need her. You're going to be useless until you two work this out."

She dragged him across the room, opened the door, and pushed him out into the hallway. "Now get out of here. I'm spending my evening with Mel."

Emma sat huddled in the middle of the marble foyer, head in hands. She had last reminded herself that she never cried several hours ago, but the tears continued cascading down her cheeks. She had come to one damning conclusion: She'd fallen in love. For the first time in her life and probably from the moment she met Logan Crawford, her renegade hormones had organized a coup against her. After sixteen years of feeling nothing, the dam had burst, and she found herself drowning in a flood of biblical proportions.

She could no longer deny what her body demanded. It didn't matter how long it lasted. An hour. A night. A week. She wanted Logan to make love to her. She wanted—needed—to experience what it meant to be a woman in the truest sense. And after sixteen years of feeling like a failure, damn it, she was entitled to at least that much. Wasn't she?

She'd reached the age of thirty-four without ever experiencing the love of a man. Sure, she'd had sex. Cold, calculating, unfeeling sex from a cold, calculating, unfeeling bastard. Unsatisfying sex that left her feeling used. If it weren't for her own fingers, she'd never have known any sort of release. Wouldn't have believed such a thing possible had she not first read about orgasms, then given herself one.

Logan wanted to make love to her. He'd made that abundantly clear. And she wanted him. Just once in her life she wanted to experience the passion other women took for granted and not have to resort to satisfying her own body. She wouldn't ask for anything else. If only he would accept what she could give and demand no more.

For a man used to making high-powered decisions, Logan Crawford had never felt so unsure of himself. Killing the engine, he sat at the end of the long driveway, staring at Emma's front door. The house was swathed in darkness except for a dim light glowing behind the small leaded glass foyer window.

He lowered his head onto the steering wheel. For years he'd trusted Beryl's people instincts. They'd never failed him, but this time he wasn't packaging a real estate deal. If a venture failed, he lost money. Lots of money. Not his heart. Not his soul. He'd never before put those on the table. Taking a deep breath, he opened the car door and stepped out into the frigid night air.

As he reached for the doorbell, he noticed the front door standing slightly ajar. He remembered slamming it on his way out, but maybe he'd slammed it so hard, it bounced back open. Either that or an intruder had broken into the house. Logan's pulse already raced with anxiety. Now, fearful for Emma's safety, his adrenaline kicked into overdrive. Cautiously, he pushed the door open a few inches, wincing at the creaking sound from the two hundred-year-old hinges, dreading what he might find on the other side.

Never expecting the sight that confronted him.

Emma raised her head from her drawn-up knees and blinked as if waking from a dream. Her lips parted, but before she said a word, he crossed the foyer and lifted her into his arms. Cupping the back of her head, he filled his hands with her hair. He clasped her against his body, eager to feel skin against skin but satisfied for the moment just to hold her in his arms. He lowered his head, capturing her mouth, reveling in the taste of her.

Logan moaned. Never before had he allowed a woman to capture him. But he was hers. Totally.

"Make love to me," she whispered.

His hunger for her was so intense that with little effort he could have torn the clothes from her body and taken her on the cold marble tiles of the foyer. But gazing into her eyes, he saw a need far greater than his own. Emma was starved for tenderness. That meant putting his own needs on hold. Tonight was for her.

"Are you sure?"

She answered by meeting his lips with hers.

He kicked the door closed with his foot and headed for the stairs. Immediately she stiffened. "No! Not up there!" She clung to his neck, her heart pounding against his chest, but he suspected the rapid beat echoed fear, not desire.

"My bedroom. Next to my studio."

He turned toward the back of the house. What had happened to her in this place? And if the memories were so dreadful, why did she stay?

"I'm sorry," she whispered as they approached her bedroom.

"Don't be." His heart swelled with sympathy, but his head didn't understand. He wanted answers, but he'd wait. After they shared a night of love, she'd open up to him, and in doing so would set herself free. He was convinced of it.

He placed her on the bed and sat down beside her.

Her eyes filled with a strange mixture of innocence and longing. Like a virgin on her wedding night. Her words came back to him. The words she'd spoken in confidence to her friend.

I don't even know what love is.

Suddenly Logan knew one truth above all else. Emma needed to be treated as if this were her first time. He bent down and brushed her lips with his. "If you want me to stop, no matter how far along we are, I will. All you have to do is tell me."

She nodded.

Taking his time, he unfastened the tiny pearl buttons of her silk blouse, kissing each soft curve hidden beneath the folds of fabric. He slid her arms from the sleeves and tossed the garment on the floor. He lifted each arm in turn and traced his lips from her shoulders down to the tips of her fingers and back up again. He sampled each square inch of flesh first with his lips, then his tongue, all the time his fingers strumming across her skin. After making love to each arm, he kissed his way across the lace edge of her bra and buried himself in her cleavage.

Logan unhooked the front clasp of her bra, exposing her breasts. "Beautiful." He cupped one in each hand and planted a kiss on each nub.

Taking a nipple in his mouth, he nursed it to pebbled hardness. She writhed beneath him, her hands combing through his hair, running up and down the length of his arms, his back, urging him to take more of her.

Still savoring her breasts, his hands roamed down her torso, freeing her of her skirt. He slid his palms along her hips, slipped his fingers inside the waistband of her pantyhose, and lifted his head to gaze questioningly at her.

"Don't stop." She raised her hips slightly.

Sitting back on his knees, he began rolling the stockings down her legs, bending forward once again to kiss the sensitive inner flesh of her thighs, the backs of her knees, her ankles.

He bent her legs, parting them slightly. Kneeling between them, he folded his arms over her knees and smiled down at her. A thin wisp of lace was all that separated him from what he wanted. His fingers glided across the fabric. Emma shuddered, her breath growing rapid and shallow.

"Want me to stop?" His fingers teased along the waistband before slipping under the elastic.

Her tongue flicked out and moistened her lips. She shook her head.

"I didn't think so." He played with her waistband. "But one of us is slightly overdressed."

She nodded.

He slipped the panties down her legs and added them to the pile of clothes on the floor. "Much better."

She shook her head.

"No?"

"One of us is still overdressed."

"Well, what are you going to do about it?" he asked.

"Me?"

"You expect me to do all the work?"

She took a deep breath. "No, of course not."

He rolled onto his back and cupped his hands behind his head. "I'm all yours."

Her brain spinning, Emma fumbled with his shirt. Each unfastened button sent a new wave of electricity sweeping through her. Desire empowered her as she combed her fingers through the tight brown curls that dusted his chest, raking her nails lightly against his flesh, following the path of hair from the wide expanse of his pectorals to his waistband. Further emboldened, she lowered her head and flicked her tongue across one of his nipples.

He moaned. "My God! Do you have any idea what you're doing to me?"

"Tell me."

"Undo my pants, and I'll show you."

Emma stared at the belt buckle, her fingers hesitating just above the metal buckle. She looked back up at him. The boldness of the past moment turned to uncertainty. He nodded, coaxing her forward.

Logan sucked in his breath. As she struggled with the zipper, her fingers grazed against the taut fabric encasing his penis, and his moans turned into a low rumbling groan.

Released from its imprisonment, his shaft sprang to life. He fumbled in his pocket and removed a foil packet. In one swift motion he shed his pants and briefs. Then he sheathed himself and pulled her into his arms, trapping her body beneath his.

Heat pooled between Emma's legs, threatening to drive her mad. Arching her back, she offered herself to Logan, but he didn't take her. Instead, he slid down her torso, devouring her with his mouth and hands. He parted her thighs and explored her with his lips and tongue. His fingers slid inside her and began a rhythmic stroking, forcing her heart into her throat. She felt herself falling, colors bursting like fireworks behind her eyes. Whimpering with need, she writhed beneath him.

"Don't fight it," he urged her.

She thrust her pelvis up. Thunder roared inside her head. Lightning exploded behind her eyes. Her body wracked with uncontrollable convulsions, she cried out his name.

Spent with exhaustion and a release like none she'd ever given herself, Emma clung to Logan. She fought to draw air into her lungs as he worked his way back up her torso. He hovered above her, grazing the tip of his penis over her slick, still-throbbing opening.

Wanting more, Emma pulled him closer, arching to meet him. As he slipped inside her, she gasped. Her legs wrapped around him. Slowly he began moving in long rhythmic strokes, producing mini explosions each time he plunged a little deeper. Then, with one incredibly deep thrust, he plummeted them both over the brink.

Complete.

Logan drew Emma closer and kissed her temple. Never in his life had he experienced such satisfaction. But it was far more than sexual gratification. A sense of peace had settled over him. He wasn't sure how it happened or why. He only knew that for the rest of his life he wanted Emma Wadsworth beside him.

Emma tensed, shattering the stillness with a piercing cry. He sighed. Whatever demons haunted her, they followed and attacked even in her dreams. Several times throughout the night he'd awakened to the sounds of her nightmares. Once she had woken up, bathed in sweat and shaking.

"What is it? Tell me what's frightened you."

"Nothing. It's in the past. There's no point."

"The past is prologue, sweetheart. You have to confront those demons of yours in order to slay them. Talk to me. Let me help you."

But she hadn't. She buried her head in his chest and said only, "I can't."

Although determined to set her free, Logan realized he couldn't do it alone. As her breathing grew more even and her sleep once again became peaceful, he formulated a plan.

Chapter 16

Logan brushed the dark tangled waves from Emma's face, bent down and kissed her lips. Her eyelids fluttered open. She smiled, then frowned, her eyes turning black and clouding over with worry. "You're leaving?"

"I have an early meeting."

She flung back the quilt. "I'll make you some breakfast."

He placed his hands on her shoulders, preventing her from rising. "It's a breakfast meeting."

"With Leslee?"

"Don't worry. I'm bringing Beryl the pit bull to run interference." He kissed her once more. "Go back to sleep. I'll see you later."

An hour later Emma leaned against the doorjamb and stared at her unmade bed, reflecting on what had taken place on it since Saturday night. A day and two nights of nonstop lovemaking. And a promise of more to come. Removing her robe, she crossed the room and stretched her naked body on top of the rumpled sheets. She inhaled Logan's scent, a mixture of citrus and sandalwood that hugged the linens. Closing her eyes, she relived every glorious, sensual moment.

She'd spent a lifetime building an impenetrable wall around her emotions. There were no windows, no doors, only a small secret passage for her children. Suddenly, as she lay on the bed, she realized that brick by brick Logan Crawford was tearing down that wall. And as he systematically removed each chunk, Emma came to life in ways she hadn't dared to believe possible.

He'd awakened a latent sexuality in her that she hadn't known existed. Logan had introduced her to the pleasures of her own body. She grew bolder with each encounter, exploring and being explored, enjoying each new discovery. Craving more. Always more.

In the past, she'd found it safer to ignore what others took for granted. Dwelling on what she couldn't have invited insanity. So she denied its existence and lived behind the wall. Logan had given her a precious gift, one she would cherish always, long after he'd gone.

> 'Tis better to have loved and lost
> Than never to have loved at all.

Tennyson. The line drifted within her in a melancholy rhythm. Dim memories of her parents skirted the edges of her mind. So long ago. More a distant dream than reality. Her sons, her only salvation through sixteen years of hell. Four people, two long gone, two safely ensconced in another state, the only loves she had ever known. Until now.

Emma knew the magic Logan brought her wouldn't

last. The pain would be deep, but bittersweet, when he left. She sighed, pushing herself off the bed. And Logan *would* leave. She had no doubt of that.

Convinced Emma's friend held the answers he sought, Logan paced nervously along the corridor outside Molly Ralston's classroom. Through the closed door he heard her wrapping up a talk on symbolism in Medieval painting. As the college students slowly filed from the room, he turned his face to the far wall, not wanting anyone to recognize him.

After the classroom had emptied of students, he entered to find Molly stuffing papers into a bulging briefcase. She looked up, startled to see him. "Logan!"

"I was wondering if we could have lunch."

She shook her head. "I'm sorry. My secretary scheduled a noon appointment for me."

"I know. I'm your appointment."

"You? Why?"

He crossed the room and stood directly in front of her. "Because I need to talk with you."

"I'm not sure that's a good idea." She stepped around him and headed for the door.

"It's about Emma."

She spun around. Her body tensed. Anger spewed from her large emerald green eyes. "Leave her alone. She's been hurt enough."

He closed the gap between them, tentatively placing his hand on her forearm. "I need your help."

She jerked her arm away from him. "To do what? Pick up the pieces after you're through using her?"

"I suppose I deserved that."

"Your reputation precedes you."

"It's not like that. Not this time."

"Words are cheap." She pushed past him, exiting

the classroom, her heels echoing a rapid staccato down the empty corridor.

In desperation he called after her. "Would it matter that I've fallen in love with her?"

Stopping, she slowly turned around and stared at him. He held his breath, watching, waiting for the debate within her to end. Hoping she believed him.

Finally, she walked back toward him. "Maybe we do need to talk."

He took her arm and led her from the building.

They covered the short distance from the University of the Arts to the Bellevue Hotel in silence. Logan waited until they had placed their orders before speaking. Sensing Molly held the answers to the mystery of Emma, he had to win her over. Whatever had happened to her, Emma was too traumatized to open up to him. Until he found a way to scale the wall she had erected between herself and the outside world, there could be no hope of their building a lasting relationship.

He understood Molly's distrust. Gaining her confidence was essential. He cleared his throat. "Have you spoken with Emma since Friday night?"

"This morning."

"Then you know we spent the weekend together?"

She glared at him. "I know everything, Logan—from your eavesdropping assistant to . . . to—"

"To the fact that Emma and I made love?"

Molly leveled a menacing gaze at him. "Right now I feel like gouging your eyes out. Yours *and* your assistant's."

Logan laughed. "You and Beryl have a lot in common. You're both fiercely loyal. I admire that. And I'm glad Emma has someone like you on her side."

"A lot of good it did her." Molly snorted. "It certainly didn't keep you out of her bed, did it?"

She reached for her wineglass, took several sips, then closed her eyes. To Logan it looked as though she were trying to rein in her Irish temper, willing herself to maintain some semblance of control. When she finally spoke again, her voice sounded measured and taut, but he could hear the pleading behind the command. "I want you to leave Emma alone. You have no idea what she's been through."

"Tell me."

"I can't."

"Can't or won't?"

She set her jaw and leaned across the table. "Won't, Logan. I won't do anything that will cause her more pain."

"And what would you do to rid her of that pain?"

Molly lowered her eyes and collapsed back against her chair. "Anything."

Reaching across the table, he covered her hands with his. "Then help me. Please!"

"Do you really love her?"

He found it difficult to speak. To his amazement, his eyes stung with unshed tears. "It's taken me thirty-eight years to fall in love." It was all he could manage to say. The rest of the words stayed trapped inside him. He hoped she could read them in his eyes. Once more he held his breath waiting for her to make a decision.

She stared at him for several minutes, clutching the stem of her wineglass. The waiter brought their food. It sat ignored. The minutes ticked by, and still Molly continued to stare at him. Finally, she broke the silence. "What do you want to know?"

"Everything."

"You don't ask for much, do you?"

"Start with her husband. Did he abuse her?"

"Used, not abused. At least not physically."

"Did she love him?"

"I think she thought she did in the beginning—for a few weeks at least. She was so young. Too young. And so insecure. He played on her need until he got what he wanted."

"If she didn't love him, why did she stay with him?"

Molly fidgeted with her fork, pushing the uneaten food around on her plate. Logan realized he was asking her to betray her friend. He sensed the struggle she faced while she decided what would be best for Emma. "I won't hurt her, Molly."

She sighed. "I believe you, Logan. I don't know why. I shouldn't, but I do." This time her eyes pleaded with him. "You have to understand. This is very difficult for me. I've kept Emma's secrets for a long time. What I'm about to tell you, no one else knows—not the full story, anyway."

She paused, pushed a stray lock of hair behind her ear, knotted her hands in front of her, and took a deep breath. "Phillip Wadsworth was a man who got what he wanted, no matter what he had to do to get it. He plotted his conquest of Emma with the vicious efficiency of a hostile takeover."

Her eyes grew dark with rage. "Emma and I met our freshman year of college and quickly became good friends. One day Phillip called her. Out of the blue. He claimed to have known her parents. They died when she was a child."

"I know."

Molly nodded. "Emma became the poor little rich girl. She had no other living relatives. No one to care about her. No one to love her. She grew up lonely and insecure. Phillip had done his homework. He knew just the right buttons to push, lavishing her with attention until she fell in love with him. Then he got her pregnant, and she dropped out of school to marry him.

"Emma was young and naïve. And easy to manipulate. Phillip took full advantage of her and the situation. He gained control of her fortune in no time."

"Why didn't she leave him?"

"You don't understand. By the time she turned twenty she had two infants, no money, no marketable skills, and worst of all, no self-esteem. He had her right where he wanted her—trapped with no way out."

"There must have been something she could have done. There are always options, Molly. You were her friend. Why didn't you help her?"

She dropped her gaze to her plate. "I was no more than a child myself, Logan. Once Emma dropped out of school, our lives took different paths, and Emma kept pretty much to herself. At the time I had no idea what was going on. Several years passed before I pieced together what had happened. By then Emma had resigned herself to her fate. Phillip still needed her. She gave him prestige and credibility. He forced her into playing the role of devoted wife."

"What are you saying?"

"To the outside world Emma and Phillip lived a storybook life. In public he fawned over her. In private . . ." She hesitated.

"Molly?"

"Emma's children were her life. Her only joy. Phillip made it clear that if she ever left him, he'd see that she never saw her sons again."

"Damn it, Molly! This makes no sense. All she needed was a good lawyer. Why didn't you help her?"

Molly's face grew red. She slapped her hands on the table, rattling the dishes and silverware. "Don't you think I wanted to? She wouldn't let me. She was convinced he'd carry out his threats. For sixteen years she lived in fear of that man. No one knew what was going on, what a devious monster Phillip Wadsworth was."

"But you did."

"At first, only because I knew Emma well enough to sense something was wrong, but every time I brought up the subject, she brushed off my concerns. Told me I was imagining things. Years passed before she admitted the truth. She had little enough self-esteem before she met Phillip. By the time he was finished with her, she had none."

Logan lowered his face into his hands. "My God." Phillip had stolen so much from Emma, and her money was the least of it. Her past read like a Gothic novel. When he looked back up at Molly, there were tears in his eyes. As he blinked them away, one spilled over his lower lid and rolled down his cheek. He scooped it up with his index finger and stared at it. "I've never cried over a woman before." He snorted. "Hell. I haven't cried since I broke my arm in a fall from a tree when I was ten years old."

"No matter what Phillip did to her, Emma refused to cry. She wouldn't give him the satisfaction."

"I've made her cry."

"I know, but maybe those are good tears."

"Are you saying you're on my side, Molly?"

"I'm on Emma's side. Maybe that places us on the same team."

"Tell me something else. Why does she stay in that house? It's obvious she hates the place."

Molly shook her head. "The house has been in Emma's family ever since it was built over two hundred years ago. It's all she has left of her parents."

"Then those garish furnishings belonged to her mother?"

Molly snorted. "Her name was Autumn Summers."

"Emma's mother?"

"No. The 'interior decorator' Phillip hired to redo the house. She was one of his 'friends,' an exotic dancer at a men's club in Center City. She wanted to be a decorator, so Phillip gave her something to decorate while Emma was in the hospital giving birth. Emma came home to find everything gone. All the furniture. The china. The silver. The knickknacks. All the photographs. He took every reminder she had of her parents, including their pictures from her wallet. She has nothing left of them, Logan. Nothing except the house itself. That's why she stays.

"As for the furnishings, she planned to get rid of everything after a respectable period of mourning. You showed up a few weeks too soon."

Logan found it hard to accept that any man could be so brutal, so controlling. Even harder to accept that Emma had lived under such hellish conditions for so long. Her strength in the face of such emotional abuse was hard to fathom. His voice filled with hate for someone he'd never known. "The man was a bastard."

A short time later, Molly and Logan left the restaurant, their meals untouched. Having entered as enemies, they left as friends, united by a shared love. Emma.

"Are you due back at the university?" asked Logan as they headed down South Broad Street.

"No. I'm through for the day. I'm going to hop a train home."

"I'll drive you."

When she agreed, he led her to where he'd parked his rental car. On the way, they passed a newsstand. Stacked in a pile a foot high, the *Daily Tattler* screamed its scandalous headline in three-inch red type. Logan and the *Tattler* had a long history, but always before, he'd shrugged off the gossip rag. Unlike other celebrities who made a second career out of suing the tabloids, he rarely concerned himself with them. Until now.

He stopped dead in his tracks and stared down at the paper, the blood draining from his face at the sight of the damaging photo that accompanied the vile headline.

At his side Molly gasped in horror. "Oh, my God! What have you done?"

Chapter 17

Leslee kicked off her Manolos, sank into the soft ivory leather desk chair, and propped her long legs on her desk. The tight skirt of her raw silk ruby power suit hiked well above her knees. She lifted the newspaper, admiring Marty's handiwork and chuckled at the deliciously vicious headline supplied by his editor. "Nice work." Her lips turned up in an appreciative smile.

Across the room, sprawled on a matching leather couch, Marty sent her a two-fingered salute. Reaching into his jacket pocket, he pulled out a small bag of white powder and tossed it to her. It landed on the desk, skittered across the surface, and dropped into her lap. "A little tip for the tip," he said.

Leslee picked up the bag and made a show of tucking it into her bra. She blew him a kiss.

Marty rose, stretched his lanky frame, and sauntered across the room. He leaned over the back of her chair, dipped his index finger down the front of her jacket, and rubbed the bag against her cleavage. "You keep the tips coming, sugar, and there's more where that came from."

She reached back and stroked his leg. "Don't leave town, Marty. The shit hasn't even begun to hit the fan yet."

Chapter 18

Concentration deserted Emma. She stared at the blank computer screen, unable to focus on the work that had always been her escape. Instead of losing herself in line and color, her mind ricocheted like a shuttlecock, flying between desire and sensibility, the ecstasy Logan had unleashed in her vying against Molly's dire warnings.

Emma regretted having called Molly. She'd expected Molly to be happy for her. Instead, Molly had recited a laundry list of reasons why Emma should end her relationship with Logan. Immediately. And Emma knew Molly was right.

But she also knew what she was doing. Knew the relationship wouldn't last. Had known that going in and accepted it. She'd made a pact with her own personal Mephistopheles, and she had no regrets.

The doorbell chime interrupted her thoughts.

She made her way to the foyer and peered out the window, puzzled by the sight of the local television van parked in front of the house.

"Mr. Murdoch," she said, opening the door.

The reporter greeted her with a nervous smile. In one hand he held a microphone. A rolled-up newspaper was wedged under his arm. Although the temperature hovered at freezing, beads of sweat peppered his forehead, his balding crown shimmering in the early afternoon sunlight. A cameraman hovered behind him, a salacious grin plastered across his face.

William Murdoch shifted his weight from one foot to the other and cleared his throat. "Mrs. Wadsworth, forgive the intrusion, but I was wondering if we could have a statement from you."

"About the auction? Of course."

The cameraman snickered.

Murdoch spun around and glared him into silence. Turning back to Emma, he continued, his tone apologetic. "Actually, it's about the photos in the *Daily Tattler*. With computer technology what it is . . . well, I'm sure the pictures were altered, but—"

"Mr. Murdoch, I have no idea what you're talking about. What photos?"

He pulled the newspaper from under his arm, unfurled it, and handed the tabloid to her. "I'm sorry."

Emma's first reaction was to cringe, but she had the presence of mind to notice the video running. For years the citizens of Philadelphia had believed she lived a fairy-tale existence. Summoning the same strength she'd drawn upon countless times before, she lifted her head, stared into the camera, and calmly said, "I have no comment. Good day, Mr. Murdoch."

She made it as far as the kitchen before her trembling legs gave way, and she collapsed into a chair. THE LADY IS A TRAMP screamed the headline. And there in full color was Emma, dressed only in a bathrobe and a come-hither expression, beckoning

Logan into her home. A boxed subhead surrounded by red, white, and blue banners screamed an equally devastating message: *Billionaire Playboy Adds Descendent of Founding Fathers to his Long List of Conquests (story and photos, page 5).*

Emma flipped through the pages, stunned by the accurate documentation of her erotic encounter with Logan and an ice cream cone. Was that really her? That sensuous-looking woman? She didn't know whether to laugh or cry. She took a deep breath and started to read the short article that accompanied the photographs.

When Philadelphia lost actress Grace Kelly, their homegrown princess, to Prince Rainier of Monaco, the citizens of the City of Brotherly Love had only to look up the road for her successor. Born nearly two decades after Grace traded Philadelphia for Monte Carlo, Emma Brockton Wadsworth descends from family that rubbed elbows with Benjamin Franklin, George Washington, and Thomas Jefferson.

Heir to the massive Brockton fortune and widow of wealthy entrepreneur Phillip Wadsworth, she has always been the darling of the local media, who long ago dubbed her "The Princess of the Hill." But as readers of the Daily Tattler *know, princesses often hide dirty little secrets, and this princess is no exception, her secret affair with billionaire playboy Logan Crawford now exposed, thanks to a reliable source. Only the* Daily Tattler *brings its readers exclusive, provocative pictures and all the sordid details of the steamy fling that has Philadelphia's blue-blood tongues wagging. Read all about it in upcoming issues of the* Daily Tattler.

Emma pushed the paper aside. Rubbish. Unless the *Daily Tattler* had a photographer hidden in her bedroom closet, they'd be hard-pressed to do a follow-up story. Erotic kisses over chocolate ice cream did not a scandal make, and even though plenty could be read into that front-page photo, Emma refused to let it upset her any more than it already had. She'd weathered far worse in her life. Besides, the legitimate press had always been more than kind to her. They wouldn't believe the dirt dished up by this muckraking tabloid anymore than they'd given credence to past innuendoes concerning Phillip's business dealings. Or his death.

No, she wouldn't get upset.

Seconds later the doorbell rang again. Emma rose. Shaking the newspaper images from her thoughts, she walked down the hall to the front door. The sight of half a dozen news vans parked in front of her house quickly challenged her resolve.

Logan and Molly arrived in Chestnut Hill to find a contingent of tabloid print and television reporters camped along Emma's driveway. Several local news stations added to the circus atmosphere. "Fucking vultures," said Logan. "It sure as hell didn't take them long."

"Keep driving," said Molly. "There's a small service road around the next block. It leads to the back door."

"They've probably got that staked out as well."

"Doubtful. It's too well hidden."

They found Emma at the kitchen table. "I guess it's a slow news day," she said, feigning indifference. "You just can't count on the Kennedys or Camilla and Charles for a daily scandal anymore, can you?"

Logan drew her into his arms. "I'm so sorry, sweetheart. They've always attacked me directly. Never gone after anyone I cared about."

"Since you told me you never cared about anyone before, I guess the joke's on me. Kind of gives me a certain notoriety, doesn't it?" She pulled away, motioning to the paper on the table. "Did I really look like that? Seems to me I was yelling at you when you came to the door Saturday morning."

"Well, let's just say your face didn't exactly mirror your words."

"So none of the photos are doctored?" asked Molly.

Emma turned a guilty face to her friend. "Afraid not."

Molly strode from the kitchen. "I think we could all use a drink." A minute later she returned with a decanter and three crystal snifters.

"What do we do?" Emma asked.

"Nothing," answered Logan.

"Nothing?" Emma and Molly gawked at him.

"Trust me. In a day or two they'll move on to a riper scandal. As Emma pointed out, it was probably a slow day in Tabloidville."

"That's easy for you to say, Logan, but after you're gone, Emma still has to live here." Molly jumped up from the table and paced across the kitchen floor. "You have no idea what this town is like. People won't forget. You've totally destroyed her reputation."

She stopped and confronted him. "No. The only way to salvage this situation is to issue a statement that the photos were doctored. Computer-generated forgeries. And you have to keep far away from Emma."

"No!" Emma shot to her feet.

"Think about it," pleaded Molly. "An army of tabloid reporters is camped at your front door. What if they start digging?"

Emma stole a frightened glance toward Logan.

"He knows," said Molly, her words not much more than a whisper.

"You told him?"

Molly studied the floor tiles.

"How much, Mol?"

"Everything."

Emma felt stripped. Raw. He knew. But not everything. Not even Molly knew her darkest secret. But what if Molly were right? What if somehow the press found out the truth about her marriage? What if they started digging? Mephistopheles certainly hadn't waited long to call in his chit.

Logan pulled Emma away from the wall and cradled her in his arms. She'd told him he'd hurt her. No matter what he'd said, she'd known. She wondered what he was thinking. Did he pity her, the spineless victim? Did he regret having gotten involved with her?

As if reading her thoughts, he whispered into her ear. "I'm not going anywhere. I won't desert you."

She wondered if he'd still stick around should the tabloids dig up her worst secret of all.

"I can see there's no use talking sense into either of you." Molly reached for the phone. "At least I can do something about the vultures hovering outside."

"Who are you calling?" asked Logan.

"There are few perks that come with being the mayor's wife, but I *can* call out the cavalry to clear the vermin from the fort. Then, if you don't mind, I'll just walk off into the sunset. Three's a crowd."

"I'll drive you home," offered Logan after Molly completed her call.

"No need. My car's parked at the train station. It's a short walk."

Emma threw her arms around Molly's neck. "I love you, Mol."

"I love you, too. Just be careful."

Emma stood at the back window, arms hugging her chest, watching Molly make her way through the snow-dappled pines along the shoveled path to the service road. Overhead she could hear the raucous sounds of a flock of Canada geese, their familiar "V" formation still visible in the waning light of late afternoon, acting as escort for her friend. Logan came up behind her and slid his arms around her waist. "Regrets?"

"Funny. That was going to be my question to you."

He spun her around and stared into her eyes with an intensity that made her knees go weak and sent her pulse racing. Slowly, he slid his gaze down her body, taking his time, inch by inch. "A million. But none where you're concerned."

"You might. Things could get ugly."

"I can deal with ugly. You did what you had to. If the story comes out, the public will sympathize with you, not castigate you."

Will they? she wondered, when her entire life was served up for all to devour. *Will you, Logan? Or will you turn your back in revulsion? If you're even still here.*

Logan studied the worry lines furrowing Emma's brow. There was more. He sensed it. Another secret she kept hidden away. Something far worse. Could it be something even Molly wasn't aware of? "What is it?"

Turning toward the sink, Emma busied herself rinsing the brandy glasses, ignoring his question. In frustration, he slapped his hands against his thighs.

Every puzzle has a solution, he reminded himself. And he'd always been good at solving puzzles. He couldn't let his talents fail him now, when it mattered most. His future—and Emma's—hung in the balance.

Reaching across the sink, he turned off the tap, removed the glass from her hand, and drew her back into his arms, the simple gesture of comfort as much for himself as for her. If nothing else, maybe he could hug away her demons. He buried his face in her hair, inhaling her sweet scent, exhaling words of comfort and hope. There was only now. Only Emma. Only Logan.

And an unwelcome observer.

A flash of bright light filled the room. Emma stumbled backward out of Logan's arms and screamed.

Marty rushed to snap another shot, but his camera strap caught on a snow shovel leaning against the house. He yanked on the strap to free the camera. The violent jerk caused him to lose his footing on the icy bench under the kitchen window. His legs flew out from under him and off his perch, one heading east, the other west. With one arm flapping in a frenzied effort to regain his balance, the other clutching at both his camera and the slippery window ledge, Marty quickly lost the battle. He flew through the air and landed with a thud and a groan on the hard, cold patio.

Bruised, winded, and nearly choked by the camera strap, he stared up at the figure looming above him. Even in the fast-approaching darkness he had no trouble discerning the anger in Logan Crawford's eyes.

Without a word, Logan bent down and yanked the camera from his hands.

"Hey! That's private property!"

Logan studied the camera for a moment. "Is that

so?" He then removed the memory card and with a flick of his wrist, tossed the camera into the drained swimming pool.

Marty scrambled to his feet and sputtered in outrage as his precious Nikon shattered against the concrete. "That camera cost thousands! I'll see you pay for this, Crawford!"

Logan ignored the outburst. He dropped the memory card to the pavement and ground it under his heel.

"Why you—" Marty lunged for Logan, but both he and his outburst were halted abruptly when Logan sidestepped him. The already bruised Marty landed in the shallow end of the pool on top of his smashed camera and a winter's accumulation of decomposing leaves and assorted muck.

Logan reached into his back pocket for his wallet and withdrew a wad of bills. He tossed them onto Marty's sprawled body. "This should cover the camera. Next time I won't be so nice. You have ten seconds to get out of here before the police arrive."

In the background Marty heard the sound of sirens drawing closer. Clutching the money, he struggled to his feet, raced up the pool steps and across the snow-covered lawn to the safety of his Explorer.

He was still hurling curses at Logan and Emma long after his four-by-four pulled into the parking lot of the Comfort Inn on Delaware Avenue.

Chapter 19

Leslee missed the thrill. She frowned down at the remains of Marty's gift. Nose candy offered a poor substitute for the rush she used to experience from one of Phillip's adventures. Pushing the envelope, thumbing his nose at authority, taking the ultimate risk and always winning. Every time. With Phillip, she'd discovered the ultimate high, a turn-on that paled in comparison to all others.

Now she was reduced to orchestrating from the sidelines and hoping the vicarious pleasure would carry her through. At least she'd have the satisfaction of destroying Emma. That in itself had to be worth a kilo of coke highs.

But how? Tabloid exposés were a short-lived revenge. She had to come up with a plan that would destroy Emma for good, that would bring the bitch to her knees and make sure she never got back up.

Growing up in the seedy neighborhood of Grays Ferry, Leslee Howell was a self-made woman born with enough smarts to know she needed more. A full scholarship to the University of Pennsylvania had given her the education and polish she felt she deserved. Her background had given her a contempt and hatred for anyone with more than she had.

Phillip had understood her needs because he'd come from similar circumstances. Phillip Wadsworth of Newport and Palm Beach started life as Phillip Stanislaw Worchovsky, the only child of impoverished Polish immigrants. Left to fend for himself by the age of twelve, he'd garnered his business degree in murky back rooms of Mafia-controlled Brooklyn neighborhoods, graduating summa cum laude. To the world Phillip had presented himself as well educated and cultured, a savvy entrepreneur. Only Leslee knew the truth of his background. That and his secret life.

Not that Phillip had needed the money. It had never been about the money. It was about the rush that came with screwing the establishment and getting away with it all. Leslee had needed that rush and revenge as much as Phillip. The two had made a perfect team.

The thrill was definitely gone. She flung her arm across the table, scattering the drug paraphernalia across the room. Damn it! She missed Phillip, and it was all Emma's fault.

All Emma's fault.

All Emma's fault.

The idea struck like a thunderbolt, the ultimate revenge quickly formulating inside her head. Leslee jumped to her feet and began pacing across her living room. She threw her head back and laughed. Why hadn't she thought of it sooner? Thanks to Phillip, she had both the means and the necessary skills, not to mention the connections. Her only regret was that Phillip wouldn't be around to enjoy the show.

She hurried over to her desk and switched on her laptop. What she had in mind would take days— maybe even weeks—of careful preparation. And she couldn't afford to make a single mistake.

Chapter 20

District Attorney Roy Harper stared at the contents of the plain brown envelope spread across his desk. Intriguing. But who had slipped the package under the door of his outer office? And why now, so many months after the death of the man in question? Spending taxpayer money to investigate the crimes of a dead man would not endear the D.A. to the voters—voters he was aggressively courting in his bid to secure his party's mayoral nomination in the upcoming primary.

Roy glanced across the room at the rough mock-ups of campaign posters the ad agency had proposed. None appealed to him. If he were going to defeat Ned Ralston next November—and he had no doubt he *would* win the spring primary—he needed a hard-hitting, aggressive campaign. One that proved to the public their beloved mayor was no more than a media-courting wuss.

But lack of an explosive issue hindered Roy's plans. Philadelphia was experiencing a renaissance.

During Ralston's first three years in office, jobs were up, unemployment down. Crime was at an all-time low, tourism at an all-time high. Harper had a network of spies combing through City Hall files in search of anything that would cast doubt on Ralston's platinum reputation. So far they'd come up empty-handed. If the good mayor had any skeletons rattling around in his closet, they were deeply buried.

Unless . . .

His attention drawn back to the photocopies covering his desk, Harper began to weave a connection between the damning circumstantial evidence and his political adversary. Maybe the anonymous gift giver wasn't interested in Harper opening up an investigation on the deceased. Maybe this was the break he'd been looking for. All he had to do was leak the information, then suggest to the public that the mayor had close ties to an alleged criminal. Very close ties. Their wives were the best of friends.

A wicked grin spread across Roy's face, stretching his pencil-thin mustache even thinner. Years ago he'd made a promise to his mother, vowing revenge against the orphaned princess the city had taken to its bosom after the accident that claimed her parents' lives. Ten-year-old Roy had endured stares. Whispers behind his back. Shunning. He and his mother were forced to flee the city that leveled its accusing finger at them, guilty only of association with the wrong man.

Roy twirled his gold Cross pen between his fingers. Faster and faster the pen whirled as his mind raced. Included in the package he'd found yesterday's and today's *Daily Tattler*. Roy placed them side by side, his gaze shifting between the two photos. Emma Wadsworth and Logan Crawford. Molly Ralston and Logan Crawford. Only days before Crawford had been linked to Leslee Howell. The guy was on a one-man crusade to conquer every broad in the whole goddamn city.

Some pricks had all the luck.

But Crawford's involvement with Emma had cast doubt on her lily-white reputation, doubt that Roy could now build on, killing the proverbial two birds with one stone. By the time he finished with her, Emma Wadsworth would be as despised as he'd once been, and *his* Gucci leathers, not Ralston's, would rest on the big mahogany desk in City Hall. All he had to do was tie Emma to her deceased husband's clandestine activities.

Harper studied the list included in the envelope, a dossier of dates and cities around the world, spanning more than five years. On each of those dates a priceless piece of jewelry had disappeared, a holographic calling card left in its place.

None of this was news to Roy Harper. The exploits of Korat were well documented by the media. Speculation ran rampant as to the true identity of the elusive international jewel thief. Korat, a breed of cat thought to bring good luck, was the perfect alias for a cat burglar of such extraordinary talents.

Publishing houses churned out at least one book a year espousing theories as to Korat's identity, and Web sites around the world constantly spewed forth additional conjecture. Interesting how the physical description of the animal perfectly described Phillip Wadsworth—muscular, medium build with short silver-gray hair and green eyes.

But what fascinated the district attorney was the additional information adjacent to each date on the sheet of paper. According to his anonymous donor, each time Korat struck, Mr. and Mrs. Phillip Wadsworth were in that particular city.

The implication was obvious. The elusive cat burglar had been unusually quiet the last six months. Too quiet. Was it because he was dead? Could Phillip Wadsworth have had a secret life as the papers in front of him implied? And how had his widow fit into that life? Of course, it could all be coincidence. But Roy Harper didn't believe in coincidence.

He clicked open the pen, grabbed a yellow legal pad from a stack on the corner of his desk, and began making a list.

Chapter 21

Stretching contentedly, Emma draped a bare leg over Logan's torso. When he made love to her, the world disappeared. She forgot her anxieties and fears. Forgot Phillip. Forgot the tabloids. Being loved by Logan was a heady experience. Decadent. Like feasting on champagne and Godiva chocolates. Never would she have believed she was capable of such feelings or acting with such wild abandon. He'd unleashed a side of her she hadn't known existed.

She liked this new Emma, liked her very much. She smiled at Logan, wishing she could put into words how grateful she felt for all he'd given her.

How different he was from the way the press portrayed him! This was not the arrogant, spoiled man-child she'd read about over the years, a man obsessed with success, never satisfied with what he had. This was a man filled with kindness and love, more concerned with her needs than his own. A man who gave from the depths of his heart and asked nothing in return. She leaned over and kissed his cheek. "Each time is more wonderful than the last."

"That's because you're letting go of your fear and learning to trust." He drew her naked body on top of him, lifted his head from the pillow, and planted a kiss on the tip of her nose.

Emma propped her elbows on his chest. "Chapter One from Professor Crawford's study of female psychology?"

"Sorry, but I can't take the credit. Chalk it up to another of Aggie Crawford's life lessons: Confronting fear defeats it."

"Your mother sounds wonderful," she said, the words catching in her throat.

Flipping her onto her back, Logan straddled her, capturing her head with both his hands. "Talk to me, Emma."

She hesitated.

"Don't shut me out."

"I remember so little of my parents. Sometimes I'm not sure whether I'm recalling memories or dreams. It's all a murky haze."

"Tell me about them."

She closed her eyes. "I remember the last time we were together. The night before they died. I sat between them at the piano. We were singing . . . and laughing."

Emma opened her eyes and blinked away the unshed tears that had gathered. "I fell asleep in my father's arms. He was singing 'Summertime'." She hummed a few bars, then sang softly, " 'Your daddy's rich, and your ma is good looking. So hush little baby. Don't you cry. . . .' " She paused, taking a deep breath to steady the tremor in her voice. "It was his favorite song. They left the next morning before I woke up. They were only supposed to be gone a few hours. I never saw them again."

"How did it happen?"

"A drunk driver." Emma shuddered slightly, then stiffened. "Years later I learned he had several prior citations for driving while intoxicated. Each time he'd walked away with a modest fine and a slap on the wrist."

"Sonofabitch. And your life went downhill from there."

She didn't want his pity. Pushing away from him, she sat at the edge of the bed, her bare feet shuffling the pile of the carpet, her fingers twisting the top sheet into a tight knot. "It hasn't been all bad. I have my sons." A small smile played at the corners of her mouth as she remembered the boys' reaction to the *Tattler* story. Their only concern was her happiness.

James and Kevin were smart boys. Since she couldn't shield them from their father's indifference, she did her best to make up for it. A protective bond had grown between her and the boys. Annoyed and feeling his authority challenged, Phillip had retaliated by shipping them off to boarding school before they'd reached adolescence.

"Why not bring them home?" asked Logan.

"My sons?"

"Surely there are fine private schools in the area. And you've been so lonely. So isolated. Why keep them away? Phillip can't hurt you anymore."

But he could. Even though he was no longer alive, Phillip was still very much a threat to her and the boys if certain secrets were uncovered. And now with the tabloids sniffing at her door, she knew she'd made the right decision in keeping her sons in New England. "It's an excellent school. They do well

there. They have friends. A life of their own." Feeble
excuses, she knew, but she feared revealing anything
more to Logan. He knew too much already.

"Well, at least you now have me."

For a brief moment in time. One that she'd cherish
long after he left.

Chapter 22

Emma turned the key in the ignition, eased down on the gas, and slowly backed the silver Mercedes out of the garage behind the house. The tabloid press remained camped at the end of both her driveway and the service road, the vultures waiting to pounce the moment she exited her property. Her only recourse was to stay within the confines of her home twenty-four/seven, but that was driving her crazy. She wasn't going to let them turn her into a caged animal. Having only too recently acquired her freedom, she wasn't about to relinquish it. Besides, she missed her morning mocha latte.

She slowed as she rounded the last bend of the winding driveway and approached the street, bracing herself for the onslaught. Relentlessly, the reporters and photographers pounced on the car, blocking her escape. She shifted the car into park and gunned the engine. The unexpected action startled the press and caused them to jump back, at which point Emma shifted into drive and turned onto the street. From her rearview mirror she watched as the reporters and photographers scampered to their own vehicles. The chase was on.

Logan had been wrong. No new scandals had drawn the press from her steps. The situation grew worse by the day. Smelling blood, the paparazzi were in for the long haul.

She fought the overwhelming urge to floor the gas pedal and kept the car at the posted speed limit, visions of another victim hounded by paparazzi never far from her mind lately. Who would have thought that she and the tragic Princess of Wales would have had anything in common other than philandering husbands? As much as she detested the stalking, Emma had no intention of winding up a corpse in a mangled Mercedes. Not when she'd just begun to live.

Today was her normal errand day, and come hell or high water, that was exactly what she intended to do. She drove up Germantown Avenue and slipped the car into a metered parking space in front of the bakery. The merchants of Chestnut Hill had known her since her birth. Seeing her hounded brought out the guardian angel in many of them. They took their cue from their princess and ignored the invasive reporters and their cameramen. Unfortunately, the press refused to take the hint and continued their pursuit.

But the tabloids didn't know Emma, didn't know that she'd survived for sixteen years by willing herself out of her body and into another plane of existence. She was a survivor. She'd survived Phillip. She could survive the tabloid bastards. As she went about her errands, she stared straight ahead, silently reciting everything she'd ever been required to memorize in school. The mind trick successfully blocked the onslaught of microphones and camcorders.

Wheninthecourseofhumaneventstobeornottobe-thatisthequestionalaspoorYorickfourscoreandseven-yearsagoIamtheverymodelofamodernmajorgeneral-wethepeopleisthisadaggerIholdbeforemeettuBrute.

The various speeches and text became a jumble within her brain, but as in the past, the silent recitation provided her with the necessary means of escape. The more she tried to concentrate on remembering all of Hamlet's soliloquy or the preamble to the Constitution, the less aware she became of the reporters and photographers jockeying for position in front of her.

By the time she'd returned to the house, Caesar had emancipated the slaves and Lady Macbeth had transformed into a black raven lamenting "never-more," but Emma had accomplished her tasks and remained sane.

And so it went, one day spilling into the next, days of hell where each morning Logan reluctantly left her to spend hours with Leslee Howell and other city officials but returned to transform her nights into—pardon the cliché—heaven on earth. She lived for the nights, marking time from the moment he left each morning, filling the hours in any way she could, until she heard the comforting sound of the rented Jag pulling into the garage.

Her needlework and drawing, as they'd always been, remained her salvation. She designed, stitched, or drew all day in an unabated frenzy until her eyesight blurred and her fingers grew stiff.

Logan lifted the baby doll off the counter in Emma's studio and cradled it in his arms, marveling over the lifelike features Emma had created with needle and embroidery floss. Each toe, each eyelash, each feature was defined, down to the dimples in her cheeks and the tiny nail at the end of each finger. He lifted the smocked gown, grinning when Emma raised an eyebrow. "Just checking whether she's got an inny or an outy."

"She has everything."

"Everything?" Logan couldn't resist peeking beneath the diaper. "So she does!"

Guilt stabbed at him as he watched Emma wrap the doll in tissue paper and settle her into a box. Because of him, Emma was a virtual prisoner in her own house. Much like she'd been before Phillip's death. He saw the strain she fought against. Rabid photographers attacked each time she tried to leave. When she remained cloistered, she nearly worked herself to death, accomplishing more in eight hours than most people did in eighty.

No matter what she did, Emma was always fighting to escape some hidden pain, and this time he was the cause of it. Damn it! He'd wanted to free her of her suffering, not cause more.

Not wanting her to see the anger welling up inside him, he turned abruptly and stared at the wall of framed needlework. How many hours, how many days, how many years had she spent escaping into the monotony of each tiny stitch, repeatedly stabbing the needle through the fabric as the design took shape?

"Why did he let you work?" he asked.

"What?"

"Phillip." Logan waved at the wall. "Why did he allow you to do this when he controlled every other part of your life?"

Emma slumped into her desk chair. She lifted a length of silk ribbon off the counter and wove it through her fingers. "Phillip was a collector. He stalked. He captured. Then he put his prey on exhibit for all to admire. I was the crowning jewel in that collection. My talent enhanced my worth." She huffed out a rueful laugh. "And it amused the hell out of him—his long-suffering wife donating the proceeds of her talent to shelters for abused women because there was no way in hell he was going to allow me to keep a dime of what I made."

Damn the perverse sonofabitch! Logan looked down at Emma's lap. Her fingers had never ceased their nervous twisting and weaving of the ribbon. He wasn't sure she was even aware of her actions.

She continued. "Whenever a crafts museum purchased one of my works for their permanent collection, Phillip threw a huge party in my honor. The bigger the museum, the grander the affair." She stiffened. Her eyes squeezed shut, and she bit down on her lower lip.

"Emma?"

She opened her eyes. "What a sham! And I was so weak. Such a fool. Phillip was right about that."

"Stop punishing yourself. You survived the only way you could."

She stared at him, her eyes full of defeat, but Logan refused to be deterred. Donning his mental armor, he drew his imaginary sword, steeling himself to slay a cowardly demon. What that demon didn't know was that Logan Crawford had never lost at anything in his life—at least nothing that mattered—and he sure as hell wasn't going to let Phillip Wadsworth's ghost break that record.

"Go throw a few things in an overnight bag. We're getting out of here."

"They'll follow us."

"It's dark. We'll lose them."

Emma hesitated. "Where are we going?"

Where? Logan didn't have a clue. All he knew was that he had to get her out of this house, away from the constant reminders of pain trapped between the walls and written on every stick of furniture.

His gaze fell on a flat piece of glazed clay hanging by a ribbon on the wall above her computer. Embedded in the surface were two sets of tiny handprints. Two names and a date were spelled out in crooked block letters underneath. Logan placed his hand over the imprints, both sets of hands covered by his massive palm.

"James and Kevin made that for me when they were in nursery school. For Mother's Day."

"I'd like to meet them. Let's drive up to New England."

"No! The press has left them alone so far. I won't risk tempting fate. I don't want my children dragged into this scandal."

Logan refused to give up. "Then somewhere else. Somewhere they'd never think to look for us."

"The idea of escaping does sound appealing. How about a deserted island? One that doesn't allow reporters and photographers."

"Know any within the tri-state area?"

"Unfortunately, no." She grew thoughtful, then her face brightened. "Cape May. The Jersey shore is all but deserted this time of year. It's bleak and desolate, and no one would ever think to look for us there."

Bleak and desolate wasn't exactly what he had in mind, but there was something to be said for miles of empty beach with only the two of them and the sound of the surf pounding against the jetties. "Start packing."

Few of the countless Victorian bed-and-breakfast inns that lined the streets of Cape May were open at the end of February. Logan drove slowly up and down the deserted roads, searching for a small, out-of-the-way inn not shuttered for the winter. The hour was late. Even those open for business looked closed up for the night.

"There!" Emma pointed down a side street. "Christmas lights."

Logan backed up and turned down the street they'd just passed. "Must be members of the Procrastinator's Club."

"Or maybe not," said Emma as they pulled up in front of The Christmas Inn. Underneath the name a welcoming message read, OPEN ALL YEAR, and under that, suspended from two hooks, a smaller VACANCY sign swung to and fro in the icy wind.

As they stepped into the lobby, they were greeted by the pleasant aroma of apples and cinnamon. Handel's "Messiah" played softly in the background, the notes drifting along the currents of the warm, fragrant air.

"Welcome, folks!" A jolly-looking, white-bearded gentleman in a tartan plaid flannel shirt, maroon corduroy pants, and forest-green suspenders bounced into the lobby. He extended a work-worn hand. "I'm Nicholas Christmas, proprietor of The Christmas Inn, and—" He stopped abruptly and squinted at Logan. "Well, I'll be! You're—"

"Fred T. Ferguson," said Logan in an affected Southern drawl. "From the Macon Fergusons." He gave the proprietor an overly hearty handshake. With his left arm, he softly squeezed Emma's shoulders. "And this here's my wife, Maybelle Sue. Say hello to Mr. Christmas, sugar pie."

Emma offered her hand to Nicholas Christmas, and in a voice dripping of Georgia peaches and pecan pie, said, "A pleasure to meet you, sir."

"Nick, please."

Emma smiled. "All right. A pleasure to meet you, Nick."

Turning his attention back to Logan, Nick Christmas whistled under his breath. "Anyone ever tell you you're a dead ringer for that bigwig tycoon, what's-his-name?"

Logan chuckled. "Happens all the time. Gets Maybelle Sue and me some mighty fine seats at fancy restaurants."

"Until he opens his mouth." Emma smiled sweetly and batted her eyelashes.

Logan roared with laughter.

Nick grabbed a guest register and pen from under a counter and placed it on the desk in front of Logan. "How long you folks plan on staying?"

"Just the weekend," said Logan, filling out the form for Mr. and Mrs. Frederick T. Ferguson of 110 Honeysuckle Drive, Macon, Georgia, and paying in cash.

"Well, you being our only guests right now, you've got yourselves the pick of the inn. There's the Angel Suite, the Gingerbread Suite, the Santa Suite, the—"

"I think my angel here deserves the Angel Suite."

"That's my Sophie's favorite," said Nick. "Sophie's my wife. Retired for the night. Poor thing was all tuckered out from baking a mess of apple pies for the church soup kitchen. I guess you can smell them."

Emma nodded. "I'm sure they taste as delicious as they smell."

"Better," said Nick. "Sophie made a few extra for any guests that might show up. Guess you folks are in luck." He handed Logan a key and stifled a yawn. "I'm pretty pooped myself. Clean-up detail, you know. Anyways, the Angel Suite is second door on the left, top of the stairs. Breakfast's at nine. Sweet dreams."

They thanked Nick and headed up the winding oak staircase. Once inside the suite, Emma gasped with pleasure. "How beautiful!"

The room, furnished in a plethora of Victorian antiques, boasted a four-poster bed with a white lace canopy. The walls were papered in a pastel blue and white stripe with a border of Victorian cherubs around the perimeter, several inches below the ceiling. Sheltered within the arch of a large bay window at the far end of the room stood an eight-foot angel-adorned artificial Christmas tree. Several appliquéd angel pillows were strewn across the bed and needlepoint ones in various sizes and shapes dotted the blue damask-covered love seat and matching armchairs in the sitting area.

On either side of the gas-fired hearth, built-in shelves housed several dozen angel books and assorted angel-decorated bric-a-brac—vases, candy dishes, candles, and crystal statues. A painted wooden sign asked visitors to PLEASE BE AN ANGEL AND DON'T SMOKE. Assorted angel dolls lined the mantelpiece.

Logan took in the room and groaned. "I think I died and went to froufrou hell."

"Don't be a humbug."

"Me?" He scooped her into his arms and captured her mouth. "How do you feel about sinning in front of a room full of angels, Mrs. Ferguson?"

Before she could answer, there was a knock at the door. Logan opened it to find Nick Christmas holding a tray laden with two large slices of apple pie, a teapot, and two cups.

"Don't know where my manners ran off to," he apologized. "Sophie'd have a fit if she found out I hadn't offered you something to warm you up before bedtime."

"Why, that's right kind of you, Nick," drawled Logan, taking the tray from him. "The missus and I've been drooling for a taste of that there apple pie ever since we got us a whiff."

Logan closed the door behind Nick. Turning back to Emma, he shrugged. "I did have something else in mind to warm us up."

"How am I ever going to get through the weekend with that accent? You keep bouncing from drawl to twang with a dash of Texas spice."

"Not convincing?"

"Maybe to a deaf person."

"Or an innkeeper who wants to keep his customers happy?"

"Let's hope so," she answered, offering him a forkful of pie.

Marty Bell was out for blood. This time he planned to catch them in the act. On video. And the hell with Loomis and the *Tattler*. He knew a cable show that would pay plenty for the X-rated tape he intended on shooting tonight. And the special infrared equipment guaranteed him sharp images without the lights that exposed him last time. The way Marty saw it, the video would be just compensation for the pain and suffering he'd sustained at Crawford's hands.

All he had to do was keep out of sight until they returned. He'd already cased out the house and discovered—to his luck—they were using a downstairs bedroom. And to add to that luck, he found a spot between the edge of the blinds and the window frame that afforded him an unobstructed view of the bed. Dressed for an arctic expedition, Marty thumbed his nose at the freezing temperatures and settled in. It was nearly midnight. How much longer could they stay out?

An hour later Marty heard the unmistakable muffled crunch of a pair of boots on hard-packed snow. Cautiously peering around the corner of the house, he spied a figure clad in tight-fitting black spandex. In one hand the trespasser held a small flashlight. The other hand slipped a key into the lock. Without a second's hesitation, Marty raised the camcorder and started shooting.

The intruder slipped into the house and closed the door. Marty quietly made his way to the foyer window and watched through the viewfinder as the burglar deactivated the house alarm, then headed down a corridor to the left of the foyer. Marty followed along the outside of the house.

He soon realized this wasn't any ordinary break-in. This thief had an agenda, and when the intruder sat down at the computer in the study, Marty kept the tape running.

He knew he'd really hit pay dirt when the burglar's ski mask came off.

Chapter 23

Stopped for a red light, Logan glanced to his right and smiled down at the woman sleeping in the seat next to him. He reached over and caressed her cheek. Emma stirred and clasped her hand over his.

"Go back to sleep, sweetheart. We have a way to go yet."

"Not sleeping," she murmured.

Logan chuckled. "And I'm the Prince of Wales."

"No." She murmured another soft, almost indiscernible reply. "Don't want to be a princess." Her body drifted to the left, draping across the console. Her head nestled against his right shoulder.

It was then that Logan realized she was talking in her sleep. Trying not to disturb her, he reached for the gearshift as the light turned green.

Don't want to be a princess. What had she meant by that? He found it hard to fathom the role fate had forced on her. How different their lives had been. Two children born into privilege and wealth. One destined to a life of family love, the other devoid of it.

If the truth came out, Logan feared many people would label Emma a classic abuse victim—or worse yet, a masochist—for staying with Phillip Wadsworth. They'd call her weak. After all, women with far fewer advantages took their children and left intolerable marriages all the time. They built new lives for themselves and their children out of nothing. But the people who would condemn Emma for her weakness didn't understand the power of wealth. Logan did. Emma did.

She wouldn't have stood a chance against Phillip and the battalion of overpaid lawyers he'd hire to fight her. And that was the great power he held over her, the threat that kept her at his side. Accepting and surviving under such circumstances took even greater courage than leaving.

Logan saw beyond the obvious to a woman with remarkable inner strength, a woman who'd weathered the worst and made the most out of the miserable hand dealt her. Emma had rescued him from himself. Could he do any less than rescue her from her past?

Over the preceding weeks he'd tried to analyze his feelings toward her. Accepting the fact that he was in love, he wanted to know why. Why now, after so many years? Why Emma? She certainly wasn't the most gorgeous woman he'd ever met. Or the sexiest. And if he were honest with himself, she wasn't at all the type of woman who usually enticed him. But none of that mattered. He now realized that he'd been attracted to the wrong women for the wrong reasons. Shallow women. Sexual reasons. That's why he'd never fallen in love. He'd never looked in the right places for the right things. Had never wanted to.

She stirred once more, burrowing deeper into his shoulder, and it occurred to him that the entire weekend she hadn't suffered one nightmare. Her sleep had remained free of demons each of the two nights. Were they gone forever, or had they merely chosen to stay in Philadelphia?

At the next traffic light he bent down and brushed his lips across hers. Her lids fluttered open. "We're almost home," he said.

Emma yawned and rubbed the sleep from her eyes. "Sorry. I didn't mean to drift off like that."

He reached for her hand and held it under his while he shifted the stick. "I wore you out."

"Right. Must have been that long walk on the beach this afternoon."

"Among other things."

As they drew closer to Chestnut Hill, Logan felt her tension return. Her body grew rigid, as though anticipating a blow. It came the moment the car turned into the driveway.

Emma drew in a sharp breath. "Someone's here."

Logan pulled up behind the late-model Buick. The occupant killed the engine and stepped out.

"It's about time you got back!" she said, her breath creating clouds of steam in the icy night air. "I've been waiting over two hours! You want a frozen corpse on your conscience?"

Logan laughed and gave Emma's hand a reassuring squeeze. "It's only Beryl."

Beryl! His sneaky assistant who liked to eavesdrop on private conversations. What was she doing here? Emma had a queasy feeling she wouldn't like the reason. Avoiding eye contact with the woman in question, she stepped from the Jaguar and fumbled for her house key.

"I've been trying to reach you all day," said Beryl, as the three of them entered the foyer and Emma headed for the control panel to disarm the security system. "Your cell phone battery must be dead."

"Must be," said Logan. He offered Emma a conspiratorial grin, but she didn't grin back, didn't answer him. She stared in puzzlement at the alarm control panel. "Emma?"

"I *know* I set the alarm before we left."

She glanced around the foyer. Nothing appeared disturbed. Phillip's collection of antique Spanish swords and eighteenth-century pistols still hung over the fireplace. The gilt-trimmed rococo urns with their erotic nudes still stood sentry at either end of the mantel.

Logan strode across the thick burgundy pile carpeting and grabbed one of the swords. "Stay here," he said. "Both of you." Then he crept up the front staircase.

"I'm sure there's nothing to worry about," said Beryl. "You probably just forgot to set the alarm."

Emma looked at her for the first time, studying the woman's eyes. Beryl's held concern, and that confused Emma. This was a woman who'd committed a heinous act against her, and here she stood, offering comfort. She shook her head, dismissing Beryl's remark. She *never* forgot to set the alarm. *Never*.

Beryl placed her hand on Emma's forearm. "Look. I know you must think I'm some kind of freaking monster, but I want you to know I think you're the best thing that's ever happened to him."

Before Emma could respond, Logan returned. "No signs of forced entry. Nothing appears disturbed, but you should be a bit more careful with your jewelry." He opened his hand to reveal an earring. "I stepped on this in the study."

Emma and Beryl both gaped at the contents of his extended palm.

"Holy shit!" gasped Beryl.

Emma stared blankly at the earring, a drop containing at least half a dozen very large, flawless diamonds. "That's not my earring. I've never seen it before."

"Then you'd better have a talk with your housekeeper. Someone must have lost this the last time you had a party here, and obviously, the carpet hasn't been vacuumed since." He took hold of her hand and dropped the earring into her palm, closing her fingers around it.

The touch of the diamonds against her skin sent a wave of fear rocketing up Emma's arm. She opened her fingers and peered at the brilliant stones. A sudden urge to fling the piece from her hand overwhelmed her. She wanted no reminder of the last party held in this house, and she knew the owner, whomever she might be, would never surface to claim her missing bauble. No matter how valuable.

Her head began to throb. She rubbed her temples. She couldn't think. In the background, rising over her panic, she heard Logan asking Beryl what was so important that it couldn't wait until morning.

"Because at seven tomorrow morning we're booked on a flight to L.A.," she explained.

Emma's head whipped around.

"What for?" demanded Logan.

"Apparently Anita planted some doubt in Takamora's head," said Beryl. "He's off to Hong Kong in a few days and wants this deal settled one way or the other before he leaves. Either you hightail it out to L.A. to get things back on track, or the deal's off."

"Anita," repeated Logan, raking his hands through his hair. His face contorted in disgust.

"Hell hath no fury," said Beryl.

Logan glared at her. "That's ancient history. Anita or no Anita, Takamora knows he doesn't have the resources to go into Watts on his own. I won't allow her to sabotage this joint venture."

"It would have been a done deal by now except for her. You know she's doing this out of spite."

"Damn her. I wasn't happy when Takamora brought her in as a consultant, but what choice did I have? I hoped she'd have enough sense to keep things on a professional level, considering what's at stake. Guess I was wrong."

"Anita doesn't care about the money. She has other motives."

"All right. We'll figure out a way to salvage the project with or without her cooperation." Logan wrapped his arm around Emma's waist and drew her close. "Call the airline. Book an additional seat."

Beryl offered him a cocky smile as she headed for the door. "I already did. The limo will be here at four-thirty, and I've made arrangements for the rental agency to pick up the car. Leave the keys under the seat. I'll see you both at the airport."

Logan walked Beryl to her car. When he reentered the house, Emma was no longer in the foyer. He found her in her studio, her arms hugging her torso, her head pressed against the window. His gut twisted into a knot. "You're not coming with me, are you?"

"I can't."

"Why the hell not?"

She turned to face him. "There's no point in . . . in prolonging the inevitable."

He didn't understand what she was saying. He placed his hands on her shoulders. "What the hell is that supposed to mean?"

Emma shrugged from his grasp. "I don't belong in your world. We both know that."

Logan reached out for her once more. "My world? Emma, this is crazy. A few days of California sun is exactly what you need. You won't want to leave once you're there."

Her arguments were irrational, but he couldn't dissuade her. She had made up her mind. Silently, he stood next to her, his hands stuffed in his pockets, and stared past the frost-covered window.

Outside the world looked peaceful. Inside his world reeled in turmoil. He felt her drifting from him, pulling further into herself, and he couldn't understand why. Grasping for straws, he finally blurted out, "I can't change my past. You can't expect that."

Emma tilted her head, her expression blank.

"Once," he said, "about three years ago, Anita Vincent and I spent one night together—one night too many, but she had other ideas. She's had it in for me ever since."

"What are you talking about?"

"You were wondering if I'd slept with her."

"I didn't ask. It's none of my business."

"But it bothers you. Admit it."

"All right. Yes. It bothers me!" Her voice crescendoed. "How many have there been, Logan? Dozens? Hundreds? Am I just the latest in a long line? Logan Crawford's current dalliance? Someone to warm your bed during a brief winter stopover in Philadelphia?"

"Is that all you think this is?"

Sinking down into the chair, Emma propped her elbows on her knees and buried her head in her hands. "I always knew that's all it would be. I thought I could accept it. I didn't want to fall in love with you."

As awful as Logan felt at that moment, his heart began to dance as her words took root. Sinking to his knees, he lifted her face from her hands. Tears gathered in her eyes. One escaped and traveled down her cheek. "I always seem to make you cry." With the pad of his thumb he brushed the moisture from her face.

She sniffed. "I never cry."

"Right. I forgot." God, how he loved her. "So you think we're just two ships passing in the night? Maybe we'll occasionally dock in the same harbor for a few days of great sex?" Emma tried to shrug from his grip, but he held firm. "That's it, isn't it?"

"Yes."

"And you can't handle that, can you?"

She averted her eyes. "No."

"Well, let me tell you something. Neither can I." He forced her to look at him. "Do you remember me telling you I never lie?"

She nodded.

"Then listen, and listen well." He paused, taking a deep breath, slowly exhaling before continuing. "I love you, Emma Brockton Wadsworth. I've never said those words to another living soul—other than blood relatives and Beryl, whom I consider a blood relative—and I never expect to say them to anyone else." He shook his head. "I don't know how it happened or why. Frankly, I don't care.

"You don't want to come to the coast with me? Fine. But you better believe I'll be back. From there or anywhere else I have to go. From now on. Because I have no intention of giving you up. Have I made myself clear?"

Before she had a chance to answer him, he scooped her into his arms and headed for the bedroom.

He loved her! Lying in his arms, Emma still couldn't believe the words she'd heard. No man had ever said those words to her before. And this was no ordinary man. What did Logan Crawford see in her? She wasn't deserving of his love, of anyone's love. Not after what she'd done.

She closed her eyes, exhausted from the emotional tempest of the last several hours, yet too keyed up to fall asleep. Something on the edge of her brain kept annoying her like a mosquito attacking in the dark. Something was very wrong, but the key to the mystery darted elusively out of reach, always one step beyond her grasp.

Finally, overcome by fatigue, she succumbed to a restless sleep. The demons were lying in wait.

She loved him! He felt as giddy as a schoolboy with a crush on a supermodel. He pulled her closer as she tossed fitfully. The demons were back and attacking with a vengeance. He stroked her hair and whispered soothing words that he hoped might penetrate her subconscious and ease her pain. All night he kept her close to him, watching her, protecting her from he knew not what. He'd sleep tomorrow on the long plane ride away from her.

Logan fidgeted restlessly in his seat. Several times he tried to sleep, but an image of Emma's haunted face invaded his mind each time he closed his eyes. What the hell continued to frighten her? Phillip Wadsworth was dead. Yet, even in death the bastard continued to torment her, like a circling vulture, waiting to swoop down and attack at any moment.

The flight attendant removed the empty mimosa glass from his tray and offered him another. Logan accepted, eager for the alcohol to numb him. He polished off the second glass of champagne and orange juice as quickly as he had the first.

"Starting on a bender?" asked Beryl.

"Just fortifying myself against Anita."

"Right. Remember who you're talking to."

He threw his head back against the seat and squeezed his eyes shut. "I'm waiting."

"For what?"

"Your damn words of advice."

Beryl rubbed his upper arm. "Wish I had some, champ."

Logan opened his eyes and turned to face her. "You're enjoying this, aren't you? Logan Crawford, world's greatest lover, finally brought to his knees."

Beryl glared at him. "Damn it! Get a grip, Logan! Stop feeling sorry for yourself."

The words stung, but as always, Beryl was right. He was acting like a blubbering fool. He leaned over and pecked her cheek. "Thanks, Mom. I needed that."

"No shit." She squeezed his hand. "I do like her, you know."

"High praise coming from the woman who's never had a kind word for anyone I've dated."

"Maybe that's because you've never dated anyone worthy of praise before."

"Ouch!"

Chapter 24

As he stared at the cryptic note, Roy Harper weighed his options. He didn't have grounds for a search warrant. He could argue probable cause, but his suspicions were based on an anonymous note and questionable evidence. No judge would sign a warrant under those circumstances—especially against a pillar of the community. But what if his unknown benefactor was correct? If proof existed, exposing her guaranteed him the election.

On the other hand, his benefactor could actually be someone out to sabotage his campaign, the evidence a carefully staged ruse to make a public fool of him. Roy had taken pains to safeguard his true identity, having legally taken his mother's maiden name before returning to Philadelphia. Yet there still existed a slim chance that someone knew the truth, that Roy Harper was in fact Royce Stephens, Jr. And the citizens of Philadelphia would forever associate the Stephens name with a drunken murderer.

Having fled the City of Brotherly Love once, Roy

had no intention of allowing his plans to backfire on him. He'd returned to Philadelphia seeking revenge. This town and the Brocktons ruined his family. Like a phoenix, he intended to rise from the ashes of shame and humiliation and conquer the city that had driven him away. Retribution was at hand. He would have his vengeance in the name of his broken mother and dead father.

Deciding it was worth the risk, Harper picked up his phone and placed a call to Judge Franklin P. Calhoun. Of all the available judges, his best shot at success lay with the doddering old fool who was pushing ninety and suffering from a multitude of ailments.

An hour later Roy stood in the judge's study. "I just can't believe it," said the old man. He shook his head. His liver-spotted, arthritic hand reached for a pen. "Are you certain, Roy?"

"Absolutely, sir."

The judge sighed deeply, dividing his attention between the Affidavit of Probable Cause Roy had presented to him and the document awaiting his signature. With a trembling hand he scratched his signature in the appropriate place. "Think you know someone. Known the family all my life . . ."

His rheumy eyes squinting over thick trifocals, Judge Calhoun dropped his pen and lifted the warrant from his desk. He hesitated before handing it over to the district attorney. "What's this world coming to, Roy?"

The district attorney whipped the papers from the old man's hand and bowed his head in commiseration. "I just don't know, sir."

With the search warrant tucked into his breast pocket, the D.A. took his leave of the judge. On the short drive back to his Center City apartment, he plotted the following morning's events. Although unusual for a district attorney to deliver a search warrant, it was not unheard of, and Roy Harper had no intention of denying himself the pleasure. On this particular case, he intended to be present at every phase, savoring each step of the princess's downfall.

After a restless night, Emma was slipping on a pair of faded jeans when the doorbell rang at eight-thirty. Shrugging into an oversized Phillies sweatshirt, outgrown by one of her sons, she strode to the front of the house, her anger growing with each barefoot step she took. Damned relentless press! Logan was three thousand miles away. Why wouldn't they leave her alone? A scathing lecture about a person's right to privacy on the tip of her tongue, she flung open the door.

"Emma Brockton Wadsworth?"

Two men in dark suits and a woman wearing a police uniform stood in front of her. The taller man and the woman wore grim expressions. Emma recognized the shorter of the two men as Roy Harper, the district attorney who wanted to run against Ned in the next mayoral election. He had a smirk plastered across his face.

"Yes," she replied to the taller man who had asked the question.

"I'm Detective Delgado from the D.A.'s office. This is Officer Johnson and Mr. Harper, the district attorney." He motioned to the woman and other man. "We have a warrant to search your home, ma'am."

She stared at them blankly. "A warrant? For what?"

Detective Delgado handed her an envelope. "It's all spelled out in the warrant, Mrs. Wadsworth."

Roy Harper shouldered his way past the detective and into the foyer. "Let's get on with it, Delgado."

The detective scowled at Harper behind his back, then gave Emma an apologetic look. "May we come in, Mrs. Wadsworth?"

Numbly, she nodded, standing aside to allow the detective and Officer Johnson entry. After closing the door behind them, she opened the envelope and turned her attention to the search warrant. "Stolen jewels? Assorted implements and items used in the course of committing burglary and smuggling of said jewels?" She stared at the paper in bewilderment. "I don't understand. Why would you think there are stolen jewels here?"

"Quit the innocent act," sneered Harper. "We know all about your little European adventures. Just lead us to the study and open the safe."

Emma was taken aback by Harper's arrogance, puzzled by his words. "European adventures? I haven't been to Europe since I was eighteen."

She glanced over at his companions. The detective again looked apologetic. The female officer's expressionless face was set in granite. Good cop, bad cop, and a deaf-mute. Emma had watched enough police shows on television to recognize the dynamics. What she failed to comprehend was why she was involved in their little drama. Shrugging her shoulders, she led them down the hall to Phillip's study.

At the entrance Emma hesitated, her hand on the brass doorknob. The study had been Phillip's sanctum, a room she rarely entered. Even since his death, she'd only crossed the threshold once—in search of the various financial records he'd kept hidden from her.

Harper jerked Emma's hand away and pushed open the door. His eyes made one quick sweep of the room before he strode across the carpet to the opposite end of the room. Flipping aside a gilt-framed antique map of sixteenth-century France, secured to the wall with hinges on one side, he spun around and glared at her. "Open it."

Emma didn't move. Anger churned in her stomach, mixing with the uneasiness and apprehension already present. *Calm down*, she told herself. "How did you know the safe was there?"

Without trying to mask the contempt in his voice, the D.A. gloated. "I have my sources." He jerked his head in the direction of the safe. "Either you open it, or I'll have it drilled."

Sources? Who knew she had a safe? Perplexed, Emma glanced at the good cop and the deaf-mute as she made her way across the room. Both stared at their shoes. She weighed her options. Pretend not to know the combination? Refuse to open the safe until she'd contacted her attorney? She quickly dismissed both options. She had nothing to hide. When the vault, built into the wall by an early ancestor, was opened, they'd see their mistake.

Emma knew the contents of the safe. She'd already searched through it the day after Phillip's death. Other than a few thousand dollars in emergency cash, the vault contained nothing but papers. Birth certificates. The deed to the house. Her will and insurance policy.

What the hell is going on here? She spun the dial right-left-right until the combination clicked into place.

At the sound of the third set of tumblers falling in line, Harper pushed her aside and swung open the door. He peered into the safe, blocking the opening with his body to prevent the others from viewing the safe's contents.

He reached inside and removed a purple velvet pouch. With dramatic fanfare he spilled the contents into his outstretched hand. Emma gasped at the sight of the emerald and sapphire necklace. Harper raised a blond eyebrow in her direction. "Yours?"

Emma stared at the jewels, unable to speak. She'd never seen them before. She didn't own any jewelry. Phillip had taken all of her mother's jewels when he removed the furniture years ago.

Whenever anyone had questioned her lack of adornment, Phillip had said his wife was too precious a jewel herself to risk tempting a thief with expensive gems. But it was just another of the many lies that had created the phony fairy-tale world of Mr. and Mrs. Phillip Wadsworth. She had no jewelry because Phillip allowed her nothing of value by which she might finance an escape. A necklace like that could have bought herself and her sons new identities far enough away that Phillip would never have been able to find them.

So how had it gotten into her safe?

Harper dropped the pouch onto the desk and withdrew a snapshot from his breast pocket. Studying the photo for a second, he then held both it and the necklace up for the detective and officer to see. "No, I think not," he said, turning his attention back to Emma. "This is the Fires of India, stolen from the Duchess of Abruzzia at the Villa Fiorelli in Capri last June."

Handing the necklace to Delgado, he removed a passport from the safe. One by one he flipped the pages, his sneer growing broader with each successive sheet until it stretched from ear to ear. Harper raised his head, leveling two ice gray eyes at her. "You say you haven't been to Europe in over sixteen years, Mrs. Wadsworth?"

"That's correct."

He flipped the passport back to the photo and

waved it under her nose. "Your passport says otherwise. As a matter of fact, it states you arrived in Italy two days before the Fires of India was stolen."

He nodded toward Johnson. "Cuff her, and read her her rights."

Dazed, Emma clung to the edge of Phillip's ornate cherry desk and squeezed her eyes shut to keep the room from spinning. She barely heard Officer Johnson as she recited the Miranda warnings. Her passport? Her passport had expired years ago. Shortly after her marriage. She never bothered to renew it. How could Harper be holding her passport?

"You have the right to remain silent."

Her eyes sprang open, focusing on Officer Johnson. "You're arresting me?"

"If you give up the right to remain silent, anything you say can and will be used against you in a court of law."

Emma's voice took on an edge of hysteria. "Why? On what grounds?"

"Possession of stolen goods for starters," said Harper. "But I'm sure we'll be adding quite a few other charges."

"You have the right to speak with an attorney and to have the attorney present during questioning. If you so desire and cannot afford one, an attorney will be appointed for you without charge before the questioning begins."

Behind her, Emma heard Harper snicker.

"Do you understand your rights as I have read them to you?"

Emma nodded.

"Do you waive and give up those rights?"

Delgado cleared his throat. "You have the mate to this?" he asked Harper.

"No. That was it."

Emma glanced over her shoulder in time to see him place a diamond earring into a plastic evidence bag. A diamond earring that exactly matched the one Logan had found on the carpet. Three additional plastic bags sat on the desk. One contained the purple velvet pouch with the Fires of India. One contained a pair of platform shoes. The third bag held a gold business card case. A cat curling around a stylized K was etched into its lid. Two small emeralds served as the cat's eyes.

"Don't forget this," said Harper, withdrawing a computer disk from the safe. "And box up the computer. The warrant covers that as well."

Emma felt her legs giving out. A huge knot began to grow in her stomach and move upward, threatening to suffocate her. She slumped into the upholstered chair across from the desk and fought to make sense of what was happening. None of those items had been in her safe after Phillip's death. None. And where were the papers and money that should have been there? From where she sat Emma could see that the vault was now empty.

She was in deep shit.

"Do you waive and give up those rights?" repeated the female officer.

Snapping her head around to face Officer Johnson, Emma drew deep within herself for the courage she needed. "Absolutely not!" She had enough sense to know not to say anything else until she figured out what was going on and spoke to her attorney.

Officer Johnson removed a pair of handcuffs hanging from her belt.

Emma cringed at the sight of the metal restraints. "Is that necessary?"

Johnson glanced over at the D.A.

"You think you deserve special treatment, Mrs.

Wadsworth? Or should I address you as Mrs. Korat?" spat Harper.

"Korat?" The name sounded vaguely familiar to Emma, but she couldn't place it and had no idea why Roy Harper should refer to her in that manner.

"In this city we treat all criminals the same." Harper glared at Johnson. "Cuff her."

Officer Johnson reached for Emma's left arm.

"I . . . I have no shoes on," said Emma, motioning down to her feet as the metal was snapped onto her wrist.

Johnson again turned to Harper. He checked his watch. "Go with her. We have a few minutes."

After unlocking the one fastened cuff, Johnson followed Emma down the hall.

"What did he mean by having a few minutes?" asked Emma as she entered the bedroom.

The officer ignored her question.

Emma sighed. She motioned toward the dresser. "The socks are in the top left drawer. Do you want to check it out first to make sure there are no concealed weapons?"

Ignoring Emma's sarcasm, Johnson yanked the drawer open and searched through the neatly folded socks before allowing Emma to select a pair.

Perched on the edge of the unmade bed, Emma struggled with the socks and then her sneakers, the task made difficult by her trembling hands. When she'd finally finished tying the second lace, she stood and motioned toward the closet. "May I get a coat?"

Officer Johnson opened the closet door, removed a navy stadium coat, and handed it to Emma. Before leaving the room, she snapped the handcuffs in place, securing Emma's hands behind her body, then led her to the front foyer where the men waited. Delgado hugged a large box to his chest. Emma assumed it contained the computer hard drive. A smaller box sat at his feet.

Speaking to Johnson, Harper motioned toward the second box. "Get that one." Then he scanned Emma from head to toe, a look of satisfaction in his eyes. "Finally," he whispered, offering her a malicious smile.

Finally what? Nothing made sense to her. With each breath her fear escalated, her control slipped, and panic held her in a viselike grip.

Harper swung the door open, and Emma froze, blinded by the glare of television cameras and flashing strobes.

Fourscoreandsevenyearsago . . .

Whenithecourseofhumaneventsalaspoor Yorick . . .

"Out of the way!" Harper pushed Emma through the crowd toward a squad car. Flashing lights and shouted questions surrounded them. He placed her in the backseat while Delgado and Johnson loaded the cartons of evidence into the trunk of a black sedan.

Off to the side of her house in front of several large hemlocks, Emma spied a makeshift podium. She watched as Harper made his way to the platform and positioned himself in front of the half dozen microphones lining its top.

The reporters and photographers ignored him, concentrating on her. Shouting rapid-fire questions, they circled the vehicle. Camera lenses pressed up against the closed windows, their bright lights bouncing off the glass. Out of the corner of her eye, Emma recognized one of the more aggressive photographers as Marty Bell, the man whose intrusive photographs had wreaked such havoc on her life over the past few weeks.

Emma fought to maintain what little composure

she had left. She sat perfectly still as Delgado and Johnson shouldered their way through the crowd of vultures and into the police car, Johnson at the wheel, Delgado in the passenger seat.

"I can't believe that asshole scheduled a press conference," muttered Delgado as the vehicle made its way down the driveway and out onto the street.

Johnson turned to him, speaking for the first time. "Aren't you the naïve soul? It's an election year, Detective, and your sleazeball of a boss wants to be our next mayor."

Delgado glanced over his shoulder at Emma. "Looks like he hooked himself some prize publicity."

"Yeah, well if this case winds up getting him elected, the city's the big loser."

"Where are you taking me?" asked Emma.

"North Detective Division," answered Delgado.

"What happens there?"

"You'll be booked and have a bail hearing."

"Then what?"

"You post bail. Or maybe being who you are, the judge will release you on your own recognizance."

Emma leaned back and mulled this information over for a few minutes as the squad car sped down Germantown Avenue.

"Detective?" Her voice was high-pitched and shaky, on the verge of cracking.

Delgado shifted in his seat to look at her. "Yes?"

"Do . . . do you have any idea why Mr. Harper called me Mrs. Kro . . . Kor . . . something?"

Delgado stared at Emma.

Johnson slowed to a stop at a traffic light and turned to face Delgado. "Is she for real?"

"Korat," said the detective, still staring at Emma.

"Yes, that was it. Korat. Why did he refer to me as Mrs. Korat?"

"You really don't know?"

Emma shook her head. "The name sounds familiar, but I can't place it."

"Jeez!" Johnson stepped on the gas and sped down the street. "Korat. The international jewel thief and cat burglar? The D.A. has evidence your husband was Korat, and you were his accomplice. So cut the innocent act, lady. When Harper gets through with you—"

"Enough, Officer!" Delgado speared Johnson with a glare that cut her off midsentence.

Neither one of them said another word the rest of the drive, and Emma was too shocked to ask any more questions.

Chapter 25

Standing on the fringes of the pack of reporters, Marty Bell listened to the Philadelphia district attorney spin a fabulous tale of greed and intrigue concerning one of the city's most respected citizens. The news journalists ate it up. Effusing a combination of charismatic charm and a frenzied zeal for the law, Roy Harper set about guaranteeing himself the lead spot on the six o'clock news and the positive publicity he needed to give one of the most popular mayors in the city's history a run for his money.

Marty scanned the faces in the crowd. These were not just local newspeople and the rat pack from the tabloids. Harper had called out the big guns for this press conference. The man wanted national exposure. Today the mayor's office, tomorrow the White House? A political career built on the destruction of an innocent woman. It certainly wouldn't be the first time a politico made his way up the ladder at the expense of others.

Marty shrugged. Why should he care about the

bitch? Especially after what Crawford had done to him. Let the bastard squirm as he got sucked up in a criminal investigation. Serve them both right.

Whistling his off-key rendition of "I'm in the Money," Marty cut through the crowd and headed for his Explorer. CNN and *Newsweek* could have Harper's table scraps. Marty knew where the filet mignon was hidden, and someone was going to pay big time for his silence, or he'd have the journalistic coup of the decade.

Emma heard the alarm masked behind the firm immediacy of her attorney's words. "You need a criminal attorney, Emma. A good one. Don't talk to *anyone* until we get representation for you. Do you understand?"

"Uncle" William Abbott had been one of the trust lawyers appointed as guardian to the orphaned Emma Brockton. The trust lawyers, all former associates of her father, were the closest thing she'd had to family after her parents' death. She'd grown up calling them all "uncle."

Although she'd had little contact with any of them once Phillip wrested control of her finances from the board of directors, Uncle William had helped sort through the massive paperwork after Phillip's death. She hadn't thought twice when allowed to place her one phone call. Uncle William would know what to do. "I understand."

Emma hung up the phone, leaned against the station wall, and closed her eyes. The only criminal attorneys she knew of were the ones she saw on the local news—men who represented South Philadelphia Mafia bosses and North Philadelphia drug dealers. As far as she was concerned, the only difference between them and their clients was that the lawyers were smart enough not to get caught. Sometimes. If she hired counsel noted for representing criminals, wasn't that an admission of guilt in itself? She needed Perry Mason. And a miracle.

Wheninthecourse . . . wheninthecourse . . .

The memorized speeches, her mental savior throughout the years, began to fail her. They no longer blocked out the fear as she underwent the rituals of mug shots and fingerprinting. And they did little to obliterate the degrading humiliation of the body search.

The police treated her like a common criminal.

Wheninthecourse . . .

The looks on their faces told her they already believed her guilty. She suffered dozens of accusing, laserlike stares. Clerks and police officers alike spoke as if she were no more than an animal, incapable of understanding their words, not bothering to mask their contempt for her.

Wheninthecourse . . . wheninthecourse . . .

They pointed her out to each other, their comments cutting, stabbing.

Wheninthecourse . . .

Never had she felt so exposed, so stripped of every defense mechanism she possessed. Emma slumped to the floor next to the wall-mounted phone, cowering from the evil surrounding her. "I don't belong here. This is all a mistake," she told the officer who yanked her to her feet.

"That's what they all say, lady." He half led, half dragged her to another room and sat her down on a chair in front of a large conference table.

As the room filled with people, Emma tried to regain her composure. She tried taking deep calming breaths. They were ragged and shaky and did little to calm her. She forced more air into her lungs, slowly exhaling. All she needed to do was maintain control until after the bail hearing. Then she could go home.

Home.

Back to where all the nightmares had begun.

She rubbed nervously at her fingers as she waited for the hearing to commence. No residue of black ink soiled them. The police used an inkless, computerized fingerprinting system, but she still felt as though a murky stain blanketed her.

He's won, she thought, surrendering to the dark depression. *I have no way of proving my innocence. After sixteen years of trying to destroy me, he's finally won.* Deep in the bowels of hell Phillip Wadsworth was having the last laugh.

Doublebubbletoilandtrouble . . .

Chapter 26

"Bail denied."

Emma stared in disbelief at the closed-circuit television monitor. Her fingers twisted nervously in her lap. The bail commissioner had believed every lie the D.A. fed him, agreeing with Harper that someone of Emma's means might easily skip bail and buy her way out of the country.

Like I'd know how to do that. But even though she had no idea how such things were done, Korat and his accomplice would know, and both the D.A. and the judge were convinced she was that accomplice. So much for being innocent until proven guilty.

Having been advised by Uncle William not to speak until a lawyer arrived to represent her, she hadn't said a word throughout the hearing. Well, damn it! Where the hell was he? And why had they allowed the bail hearing to take place without him?

Staring at the table of evidence, Emma focused on the platform shoes, the hollow heels swung aside to reveal the secret compartments in which Harper claimed the jewels had been smuggled through customs. *Those aren't my shoes! I've never seen them before today. I don't know how they got in my safe. That's not my passport! I don't know anything about cat burglars and fancy jewels and smuggling.*

"What happens now?" she asked the officer leading her from the room.

"You become a guest of the city until the trial."

"What do you mean you can't access the information?" Roy Harper jumped to his feet, knocking over his desk chair. "It's a goddamn computer! Just turn it on, and print out the fucking files!"

"It's password protected, sir."

"Jeez!" Roy leaned across his desk and shouted at his assistant. "Is everyone in this department totally incompetent? Get in your car, Dixon. Take a drive up the interstate. Get off at the Cottman Avenue exit. Head over to State Road. Pay a little visit to the defendant at the Industrial Corrections Facility, and *get the goddamn password!*"

"Umm . . . we already drove over there, sir. She claims she doesn't know it."

"And you believed her? Of course she knows it, fool. She just won't give it to you." Roy picked up his electric pencil sharpener and hurled it across the room, missing the assistant district attorney's head by no more than a few inches.

Dixon jumped. "Hey!"

The sharpener hit the opposite wall. The plastic casing shattered, raining pencil shavings and powdered carbon across the threadbare carpet.

"Then find a hacker who can break into the system. I want that information within forty-eight hours or your ass is on the line. Do I make myself clear, pinhead?"

The assistant D.A. backed toward the door. "Yes, sir. Within forty-eight hours, sir."

Spinning around, LeRoy Dixon raced from the room.

"Oh, my God! You can't be serious." Emma stared at the large cell. Two dozen women, none of whom Emma would want to meet in broad daylight—let alone in a dark alley—crowded inside the cinder-block holding pen. Her body tensed. She dug her nails into the palms of her hands and shrank back against the guard. "This is inhumane."

"Hey, get a load of the new kid on the block!" cackled one of the inmates, pointing through the bars at Emma. "Yo, Miss Fancy Pants! You's expecting the Ritz?"

Emma turned pleading eyes to the guard. "Please!"

"Sorry, honey. We don't have separate facilities for the hoity-toity of Chestnut Hill. You stay here until they finish processing you."

Emma bit her lower lip and glanced back over her shoulder at the cell of hardened women. "How long?"

"Two days tops. Then you get a double." She unfastened Emma's handcuffs. "Remove your shoelaces and belt."

Emma stared at her in disbelief. "Two days? In there? What am I supposed to sleep on?"

"The floor like the rest of the riffraff." She held out her hand. "Belt and laces. Now, princess!"

Emma complied. A moment later the metal clang of the cell door closing behind her echoed the hopelessness consuming her. She glanced about the cramped space. A dozen mean-looking faces with churlish expressions and sullen, angry eyes glowered back at her. The remaining occupants of the cell paced the confined quarters or sprawled across the floor too drunk or strung out to care about the newest arrival.

An enormous woman wearing leather jeans and a T-shirt three sizes too small for her broke from the pack and sauntered up to Emma. Emma retreated until she had backed into the wall and had nowhere else to go. She held her breath, afraid to move even an eyelash. The woman kept coming, stopping only when her chest was an inch from Emma's face, the slogan on her shirt blurring in front of Emma's eyes: BIG IS BEAUTIFUL.

Big was an understatement of epic proportions for the six-foot, two hundred-pound Amazon who had trapped her. Emma swallowed the lump of panic that had lodged in her throat and fought to keep down the bile churning in her stomach. The woman raised her hand, placed it on the wall over Emma's head, and leaned down until they were nose to nose. Squeezing her eyes tight, Emma braced herself for the imminent attack.

"I know you," said the woman.

Slowly Emma opened her eyes. The woman was smiling. Her head bobbed up and down, frizzy drugstore orange hair bouncing on quarterback shoulders. Her dark eyes, the whites veined with red, twinkled. The huge grin, spanning her weathered face, revealed a mouthful of rotting teeth and gaping holes.

"You're the lady who works down at the Eighth Street Women's Shelter. The one who's always bringing extra blankets and toys for the kids."

Emma slowly released her breath and nodded slightly. "Yes," she whispered.

The woman grabbed Emma's right hand with both of her massive paws and pumped away. "I'm Jessie.

Jessie McCoy. You saved my life, ya know. If it wasn't for that shelter of yours, my old man woulda ended up killing me. The shrinks there gave me the courage to stand up for myself, ya know?"

Emma gave Jessie a weak smile and tried unsuccessfully to withdraw her hand. If the woman kept up her vigorous handshake much longer, Emma feared her shoulder might dislocate. "Why . . . why are you here, Jessie?"

Jessie's grin turned sheepish. "I guess I stood up a little too much, you know? Big Jim come around one night wanting to, you know, make up and like start over? Only he started over, all right, just like old times. Only I fought back and beat the shit out of him. Turned his face to Jell-O." Jessie finally released Emma's hand and gave a nonrepentant shrug. "Guess he's trying to make nice to his maker right about now."

"You killed him?"

"Beat his brains to a pulp. Couldn't have happened to a more deserving piece of shit." Jessie stared down at two enormous feet. "I suppose I shouldn't feel so damn good about it, ya know? But Big Jim McCoy deserved to die for what he done to me and my babies." Jessie looked back at Emma. "I guess a lady like you wouldn't understand a lowlife like Big Jim and how he could make you do something like that, huh?"

You'd be surprised, thought Emma.

Jessie's face clouded over. "What's a nice lady like you doin' in a puke hole like this?"

Tears sprang to Emma's eyes. Her limbs began to tremble. Jessie wrapped a massive arm around her and guided her across the cell to a bench on the far wall. "Move it," she barked at the junkie sprawled across the wooden slab. When the semicomatose body made no effort to move, Jessie swept her off the bench and sat Emma down. The woman coughed up a ball of phlegm, muttered an indiscernible word of protest, then resumed her snoring. Emma gaped at her, then at Jessie.

"Pay no attention to her," said Jessie, dismissing the woman at her feet. "Old Suzy Sunshine's so wasted she don't feel a thing. The floor's good enough for that candy mama."

A wiry girl in her late teens sauntered up to the bench. "Hey, Jessie! Who's your new friend?"

"This here's Miss Emma. She's a lady. Not like you losers. So's you better treat her with respect or yous'll answer to me. Understand, Honey-bunch?"

"Yeah, sure, Jess. Whatever ya say, girl. Only if she's such a lady, how come she's in the tank?"

Jessie gave the young girl a withering look. "'Cause the dicks don't know jack. Ain't they ever locked you up for something you never did, Honey?"

"Yeah. All the time. I go out for a bottle of Pepsi and they claim I'm walkin' the streets. But I gotta stay 'cause I ain't got no bail money, and my old man's too stoned to know I'm gone." Honey jutted her chin at Emma. "What's your excuse for spending the night in the presidential suite?"

"The D.A. wants to be the next mayor," mumbled Emma.

Honey gave a loud hoot. "Whatever she's on, I want some. What a trip! Pretty Boy Roy as mayor? That'll be the day."

Honey wandered away, still chortling over the joke. Jessie turned to Emma. "So why are ya here?"

Leaning her head back against the wall, Emma closed her eyes and inhaled deeply. "He claims I was part of a series of jewel thefts."

"Were you?"

Emma's eyes sprang open, glaring at Jessie.

The big woman averted her eyes like a child caught stealing candy. "Sorry. That was a dumb question. 'Course you weren't. Why would a rich lady like you need to take someone else's stuff?" Her face lit up. "Hey, I know! You ain't got nothing to worry about. With all your money and everything, all you gotta do is hire some big-shot fancy lawyer, and he'll pulverize that creep Harper."

Emma reached over and patted the woman's hand. If only it were that simple.

That night Jessie stationed herself on the floor in front of the bench, not allowing any of the others near Emma. But Emma was too frightened to sleep. She sat with her back against the wall, hugging her knees to her chest and staring into the darkness at the restless shadows pacing the lockup.

For all her frightening looks, Jessie had turned out to be a Ferdinand the Bull, her overpowering exterior hiding a heart of gold. Honey was a frightened kid forced to grow up too quickly on the streets of Kensington where she sold her body to pay for her boyfriend's drugs and booze. But many of the other women were hardened criminals for whom jail was a second home. Women who would sooner stab you than give you the time of day. They openly glared at Emma, occasionally hurling graphic threats. Only Jessie's presence kept them at bay.

Emma knew she embodied all they detested. All they felt they deserved but would never acquire. Wealth. Position. Respect. *If only they knew*, she thought. *What a tangled web we weave when first we practice to deceive.*

"Plea bargain?" Emma couldn't believe her ears. Every muscle in her body tensed with rage. What good was an attorney who didn't believe in his own client's innocence? "Only guilty people plea bargain," she insisted. "I'm not guilty."

"The district attorney has a mountain of evidence against you, Mrs. Wadsworth. You have no defense. The way I see it, a plea bargain is your best option."

"Well, that's not the way I see it! I won't admit to a crime I didn't commit! Why should I?" Emma crossed her arms over her chest and glared at him.

The lawyer scrutinized the sparse notes he'd taken during their meeting. "If you insist on pleading not guilty, you have to give me something to work with to prove your innocence. Your word doesn't stack up against the D.A.'s evidence. You can't expect a jury to buy it."

Emma slammed her fists down on the table, then buried her head in her hands. The situation was hopeless. The lawyer was right. She had no defense, no evidence to prove she wasn't the criminal the D.A. claimed. No witnesses. No alibi. At least none anyone would believe. Phillip had seen to that. "Go away. Just go away and leave me alone."

Chapter 27

For the second day in a row, Logan sat at the head of the long mahogany conference table and tried to salvage the multimillion-dollar project that had headed south thanks to a woman with a grudge. He was tired of arguing and ready to cancel the deal. His plate was full. He stood to lose a sizable chunk of money, but screw it. He didn't need another project, and he certainly didn't need the aggravation. Takamora needed him more than he needed the Japanese developer who'd overextended himself in the States and was now in need of a partner to bail him out.

His concentration wandered from the heated discussion flying across the table. He missed Emma. In finding her he had finally found himself. All the prestige, the money—none of it mattered. Only Emma had filled the emptiness inside him, and Logan couldn't bear a continent's worth of separation much longer.

Since awakening this morning, he'd tried phoning her at least a dozen times. With each passing hour, his apprehension grew, his mind unable to focus on the reason he was in Los Angeles. He pushed back his chair and strode from the table. Forty stories up in a smog-shrouded office building, he stared past the hazy landscape and swore under his breath. He glanced at his watch. Where the hell was she? It was already six o'clock back east.

Out of the corner of his eye he saw his secretary enter. After whispering something in Beryl's ear, she glanced at him, then left the conference room with Beryl in tow. *Now what?* He filled his lungs, expelling the air forcefully as he headed back to the table.

When Beryl opened the door a short time later, Logan knew something was wrong. Nothing shook the pit bull, but as she beckoned to him from the doorway, he could see the color had drained from her face.

He excused himself and followed her into his private office. The television in the corner of the room was tuned to CNN. Logan listened as the reporter recapped the breaking events, then cut to a scene shot earlier in the day, a scene that filled him with rage.

He now knew why Emma hadn't answered the phone all day. She was in jail.

Beryl reached for him, placing her hand on his shoulder. "It can't be true."

"Of course it's not true!"

He started rattling off orders. "Get me on the next flight to Philadelphia," he told his secretary.

"What about Takamora?"

"Either he signs in the next five minutes, or the deal's off." He headed back to the conference room.

Logan strode to the head of the table and tossed a pen to Takamora. "I've had enough of this shit. The deal goes through as initially negotiated, or I'm pulling out. Sign now or leave."

Anita Vincent jumped to her feet. "You can't do that!"

"Get the hell out of here, Anita. This is between me and Takamora. I won't have your petty vendettas interfering with my business."

"How dare you!"

"I dare." He turned to Takamora. "I wouldn't put much stock in any advice she gave you. She's more interested in screwing me over than helping you." Takamora shifted his gaze from Logan to Anita, then back to Logan. "What's it going to be, Lee? In or out?"

Lee Takamora picked up the pen and signed the contract.

Anita snatched her briefcase off the table and rose, piercing Logan with an icy glare. "This isn't over. Expect to hear from my attorney. I'm suing you for slander and defamation of character."

"Just try it." Logan pushed past her as he headed out the door.

Much to Logan's frustration, there wasn't an empty seat on a flight from L.A. to Philadelphia until late that night. The next morning, he alighted from the red-eye, hopped into a waiting limo, and headed straight for City Hall. Less than an hour after arriving in Philadelphia, he stormed past the district attorney's startled secretary and barged unannounced into Roy Harper's office, slamming the door behind him.

Harper jumped to his feet. "What the hell!"

Logan leaned over Harper's desk, his nose inches from the district attorney's reddened face. "I want Emma Wadsworth released on bail within the hour."

Harper sat back down in his chair and folded his hands over his chest. His lips curled in a nasty smirk.

"You may have people jumping to your demands on Wall Street, Mr. Crawford, but it doesn't work that way here. This is my turf, and I keep my criminals locked up."

"She's no criminal, you sonofabitch!"

"I have evidence that proves otherwise."

"She has a right to bail!"

Roy picked up a pencil from his desk and drummed the eraser end in the palm of his hand. Concentrating on the pencil's movement for several beats, he deliberately ignored Logan. "Bail was denied because the suspect is a flight risk."

Logan glared at the D.A., sizing him up with one word—smarmy. Lowlifes of every persuasion—from drug dealers to rapists—were routinely granted bail. Emma was hardly a flight risk, and that wiry, lipless little shit damn well knew it. There was something else going on here.

Backing away from the desk, Logan glanced around the room, noting the campaign mock-ups pinned to the walls. Taking his time, he sauntered over to them, studying the signage and posters. Now he understood. Roy Harper planned to use Emma to defeat Ned Ralston, sacrificing her on the altar of political ambition. "You're running for mayor?"

"Not that it's any of your business."

"Oh, but it is, Mr. Harper." Keeping his back to Roy, Logan continued. "Do you have any idea how much revenue my redevelopment projects will bring to this city? How many more jobs will be created if I decide to relocate my headquarters here?"

"Your point, Crawford?"

Turning to face him, Logan continued. "According to Leslee Howell, the three major corporations that relocated to Philadelphia last year resulted in an eight percent reduction in residential property taxes.

All three together aren't as large as my enterprise, and I'm very good friends with the CEOs of two other Fortune Five Hundred businesses considering Philadelphia. *Very* good friends." He stepped back and watched the arrogance drain from Roy Harper's smug face.

"That's blackmail!"

Logan ignored the accusation. "I can't imagine Philadelphians voting for a candidate responsible for a tax increase."

Harper snapped the pencil in half. His eyes narrowed. A pulse throbbed on the side of his neck, the blue vein standing out against skin growing crimson.

Striding back across the room, Logan grabbed the phone on the desk, extending the receiver toward the district attorney. "Bail, Mr. Harper. In one hour."

The district attorney made no effort to take the phone. He glared at Logan.

"Suit yourself." Logan punched a series of numbers into the phone. Halfway through the sequence, he paused and glanced over at Harper. "Just ringing up Ms. Howell. To let her know I've changed my mind about Philadelphia as a prospective site for my upcoming projects. And my new headquarters."

Roy jumped out of his chair and yanked the receiver from Logan's hand. He slammed the phone down into its cradle. His entire body shook. Beads of sweat gathered across his forehead. Indecision echoed in his voice. "I can't revoke my request to deny bail. The judge won't buy it."

"Find a way."

When Harper stole a glance across the room at his posters and banners, Logan knew he'd won.

"Wadsworth!"

Curled up into a tight ball on the narrow bench,

Emma raised her head off her crossed arms and focused her bleary eyes across the cell to the guard unlocking the door.

"Let's go. Someone's posted your bail." The female officer swung open the metal bars.

"Bail?" Emma rose from the bench, grabbing for the wall when her legs faltered.

Jessie offered an arm in support. "Guess Harper had a change of heart, huh?"

"I didn't think he had a heart." Led by Jessie, Emma walked across the cement floor, her progress followed by countless envious eyes.

"Hey, don't question it," said her new friend.

But Emma couldn't help wondering about this sudden reversal. Nothing in Roy Harper's attitude toward her had revealed the slightest sympathy for her predicament. Quite the opposite. He did nothing to hide the loathing and contempt she saw in his face each time he'd looked at her.

The D.A. had convicted and sentenced her before she'd even opened the safe. He was so sure of himself. But how could he have known the contents of the safe when Emma herself hadn't? For two days now that question had gnawed at her along with something else that kept darting around the edges of her brain—something important that she couldn't remember.

"I know. Maybe he wants your vote," said Honey, breaking into her thoughts.

Before leaving the cell, Emma turned one last time to Jessie and grasped her hand. "Thank you."

"Good luck," said Jessie.

"To you, too."

After threading the laces through her sneakers and slipping on her belt and coat, Emma was led down a labyrinth of corridors to a waiting area.

I'm dreaming, she told herself, pausing in the doorway. *This can't be real. He's in California.*

At the far end of the room Logan stood engrossed in conversation with several uniformed policemen. When he saw her, relief flooded his face, quickly erasing deeply etched lines of worry. He covered the distance to her in half a dozen long strides. Cupping her face with his hands, he spoke only with his eyes. Silently, she nodded her answer, fearing that if she spoke, she'd break the spell, awaken, and find herself back in the cell.

Logan wrapped his arm around her shoulders and led her to the policemen. "The place is crawling with reporters. These kind officers have agreed to escort us to the car."

Emma sucked in her breath. Vultures. Not reporters. Birds of prey hovering overhead, waiting to pick her carcass clean with their dagger-sharp words and speculative innuendoes.

HOW THE MIGHTY DO FALL! One of the guards in the cell block had shown her the day's headline from the *Daily Tattler*. The three-inch-high type sat beneath a full-color photo of a handcuffed Emma as she was ushered into the waiting police cruiser.

Logan squeezed her shoulders. "Ready?"

She nodded. Lifting her head, she stared straight ahead as she walked from the room, silently reciting her mantra. *WheninthecourseofhumaneventsalaspoorYorick . . .*

"Mrs. Wadsworth! Mrs. Wadsworth!" Cameras flashed in rapid succession. Reporters jostled each other like hyenas after a kill.

Fourscoreandsevenyearsago . . .

"Was Phillip really Korat? Or was it you?"

Emma stared through the reporter, a silicone-injected Barbie doll from one of the tabloid television shows. *Iamtheverymodelofamodernmajorgeneral* . . .

"Is this how the rich get their kicks? Cat burgling by the rich and famous?" Barbie continued her taunting barrage, a camcorder shoved in Emma's face.

WethepeopleisthisadaggerIholdbeforemeettu-Brute . . .

One of the officers inserted his massive body between Barbie and Emma, cutting off the verbal assault. Before another reporter broke from the pack to take Barbie's place, Emma was whisked inside a dark sedan.

Climbing in beside her, Logan wrapped his arm around her. Her hands clenched in her lap, she sat perfectly still. "Everything's going to be all right," he said.

She didn't speak. She hadn't spoken a word since entering the waiting room, but she knew everything wasn't going to be all right. How could it? Logan had gotten her released on bail, but that was only a temporary reprieve. She still had no proof to refute Harper's evidence.

The car sped across town and onto the Schuylkill Expressway. It headed toward the airport but shot off at the South Street exit and began zigzagging through West Philadelphia. After ten minutes, the car cut across the river and headed east back into Center City along the Benjamin Franklin Parkway.

"I think we've lost them," said the driver, referring to the convoy of reporters who'd attempted to follow them. Turning into the service entrance behind the Four Seasons, he stopped the vehicle, then stepped out and opened the back door for Emma and Logan.

After exiting, Logan reached into his pocket and withdrew a hundred dollar bill. "You never saw us." He tucked the money into the man's breast pocket.

The driver tipped his hat. "No, sir."

"Why are we here?" asked Emma as a security guard led them to a service elevator that transported them to a suite of rooms on the top floor.

Logan unlocked the door. "Would you prefer going back to a house swarming with reporters?"

She shook her head.

Before ushering her into the room, he tipped the guard with another large bill and issued the same stern warning he'd given the chauffeur.

Once inside the suite, Logan headed for a well-stocked bar at the far end of the combination living/dining area. "Level with me, Emma," he said, as he poured them each a drink. "Did you know Phillip was Korat? Is that what causes your nightmares?" He offered her one of the glasses.

Emma reached for the drink. Clutching it in both hands, she stared down at the amber liquid and shook her head.

"CNN claims you and Phillip were in each city every time Korat struck."

Again Emma shook her head. "Maybe Phillip was. I wasn't." Bone tired, she collapsed onto the overstuffed sectional that wrapped around one corner of the large room. She lifted the heavy tumbler to her lips and took a tentative sip. "I haven't been out of the country since I completed boarding school in Switzerland."

Logan stared at her, his expression dumbstruck. "The police confiscated your passport. They have proof you were with Phillip."

"That wasn't my passport."

"What do you mean?"

Lacking the strength to hold the tumbler, Emma rested the glass precariously in her lap. Her life with Phillip had been such a sham. But she'd helped create that false picture. Like the little boy who cried wolf, when she finally told the truth, no one believed her. The police hadn't. The district attorney hadn't. Nor had her own attorney. Why would a jury? She had no way of proving her innocence, and the authorities had some pretty damning evidence to prove her guilt.

How do I explain my whereabouts when the evidence claims I was elsewhere? Struck by the irony of the situation, Emma realized she might pay the price for a sin she hadn't committed as punishment for the one she had.

She looked back up at Logan. He towered over her, waiting for an explanation she couldn't give. Guilt muscled itself in alongside fear and panic, the three emotions swirling within her like a vortex sucking the life from her. She was so tired. Tired of the nightmares. Tired of the lies. Her head pounded. Her body ached.

She closed her eyes. When she opened them, Logan was gone. Somewhere in the distance she heard the sound of running water. She closed her eyes once more, wishing she could shut out the world.

Logan returned and sat down beside her. "You're exhausted." He took the glass from her lap and offered his hand. "I've drawn you a bath." Helping her to her feet, he led her toward the bathroom.

Alone, Emma stared down at the tub of steaming water. She'd evaded his questions, yet instead of getting angry with her or walking out, he'd drawn her a bath. Instead of running from her at the first signs of trouble, he'd flown across the country to rescue her.

She owed him an explanation.

The thought of reliving the past sent a new wave of pain up her neck and into her head, the intensity so severe that tears filled her eyes. With shaking hands, she rummaged through the basket of complimentary toiletries and sundries on the vanity counter until she found a bottle of Tylenol. Her vision blurred from the headache, she struggled with the childproof cap, dropping the bottle and spilling the tablets across the sink. She picked several pills off the counter and gulped them down dry.

Emma stepped out of her clothes, turned off the lights, and lowered herself into the tub. Activating the Jacuzzi, she leaned her head back, and placed a warm washcloth over her eyes.

She didn't see or hear Logan when he entered the bathroom. He kneeled down at the head of the tub and began to massage her temples and neck. She reached back and placed her hand over one of his. "I'm sorry," she whispered.

"Don't be. We're going to get through this."

"If you were smart, you'd run like hell. This could ruin your reputation."

"Why not let me worry about that? Besides, my reputation was never very sterling to begin with."

"Layer on enough tarnish, and you eventually pit the silver."

"I've always thought the pits add character." He shrugged out of his clothes and slid into the tub behind her.

She leaned back and nestled against his chest. His arms wrapped around her. "There are things you need to know," she said. "And I'm not sure how to tell you."

"Take your time. I'm not going anywhere."

Emma crossed her wrists around his forearms. The water bubbled around them, massaging their bodies. She breathed in the warm steam, searching for the courage she needed, hoping he'd believe her. Not knowing what she would do if he didn't.

Finally, she spoke. "My passport expired years ago.

I never renewed it. I haven't been out of the country since I returned for the last time from La Chaux-de-Fonds. I was eighteen."

"But there are records of your trips. The D.A. has copies of airline tickets. Hotel registrations. Credit card receipts for items you purchased in Europe."

"The D.A. might have proof, but I wasn't there. I swear it." She twisted her body, turning pleading eyes on him. "You have to believe me."

Logan brushed his lips against her ear. "I do."

Her body went limp against his chest. The worst was yet to come.

Logan scooped warm water over her shoulders and breasts. "This isn't as bad as it looks," he said. "Actually, it's far better than I first feared."

"No. You don't understand."

"Of course I do. If you weren't in Europe with Phillip, someone else was, posing as you. All we have to do is prove where you were each time Phillip left the country. How hard can that be?"

Breaking away from him, Emma stepped from the tub and wrapped herself in an oversized terry towel. "Not hard. Just impossible."

Chapter 28

Logan jumped from the tub. He grabbed her by the shoulders and spun her around to face him. "What do you mean?"

"I can't prove where I was. I can't refute the charges."

"Of course you can. You're just not thinking straight. You're exhausted."

Emma left the bathroom and walked across the bedroom to the windows at the far end. From behind the sheer curtains, she stared out at the city. An icy late-winter rain pelted the near-empty sidewalks. Those few brave souls daring enough to venture out scurried along at a jogging pace, darting from one sheltered area to the next. Any one of them, she realized, might be a prospective juror, chosen to sit in judgment of her. Would any of those men or women believe her? She doubted it.

She dropped the towel at her feet and slipped into the robe the hotel supplied. Clutching the lapels tightly around her, she motioned to Logan. "You'd better sit down."

He shrugged into the second robe and perched on the edge of the mattress. She paced back and forth, sorting through the pain and helplessness of the past, trying yet again to understand her life. But as always, she couldn't. Little of the past sixteen years ever made any sense to her.

Her pacing continued unabated, but the words wouldn't come. Finally, Logan jumped to his feet and forced her to stop. "*You* sit."

Not having the strength to argue, she complied. With Logan seated beside her, his arm wrapped around her shoulders, she stared into her lap and slowly, haltingly, began to spin her bizarre tale. "About six years ago Phillip came home from work one evening. We sat down to dinner. The next thing I remember is waking up in a strange cabin. Alone."

"What about the children?"

"They were already in boarding school. I only saw them on holidays."

"Sonofabitch."

"No. It was better that way." She paused for a moment, steeling herself to the nightmarish memories her tale unleashed. "I guess I was drugged. I have no memory of getting to the cabin. No idea where it was or how long the trip took. Within minutes I realized I was trapped. The door was locked from the outside. The windows were bolted shut, the glass panes replaced with thick black Plexiglas that I couldn't break or see through.

"The cabin contained plenty of food, heat, and running water. A few pieces of furniture. Not much else. No clock. No radio. No television. Not even a book or magazine. He'd even removed my wristwatch."

"He was trying to drive you mad?"

"I wouldn't give him the satisfaction! He'd taken everything else from me. I wasn't going to let him steal my mind. I exercised a lot, played word games in my head. . . ." She threw him a devilish smile. "Plotted revenge scenarios, visualizing Phillip in a vat of boiling oil, tied to stakes in the desert with fire ants crawling all over him. Things like that."

"How long were you kept there?"

"That time, a week."

"That time? It happened more than once?"

"Two, three times a year. Sometimes more. I had no way of knowing ahead of time, no way of preventing it, and no way of getting out. The length of stay varied from as short as a few days to as long as a couple of weeks. I was never really sure how long I'd been locked up until I was brought home. Judging time was difficult."

"My God! Why didn't you go to the police? Tell someone what the sonofabitch was doing to you?"

"You have no idea what he was capable of, the people he knew, the power he wielded."

"Are you telling me he controlled the police in this town?"

Emma shook her head. "Phillip had powerful connections in all the wrong places, connections he kept well hidden from the respectable side of his life. When I threatened to go to the police, he said it would be a shame if something happened to the kids. I got the message." She knew she came across as seeming weak, the abused spouse who believes the abuse is her fault. Nothing could have been further from the truth. She never believed she deserved what Phillip had done to her.

Emma rose and began pacing again, twisting the fabric belt of the robe into a tight knot. "Even when I saw the contents of the safe, I didn't make the connection. I had no idea Phillip was a jewel thief. Why would I? I didn't know he left the country each time he locked me away. Besides, we had more money than he could spend in several lifetimes. Why would he risk everything he had to steal jewelry he could well afford to purchase?"

"For the thrill," Logan suggested. "Some people get addicted to the adrenaline rush of putting themselves in dangerous situations. Bungee jumping or burglary. It's all the same. The stronger the chance of something going wrong, the greater the high when it doesn't."

"Maybe. I really haven't had the luxury of speculating on Phillip's motivation, but that makes as much sense as anything. Phillip was always a thrill seeker. When I met him, he owned a racecar. After we married, he bought a plane and took up flying. Next came skydiving. I guess even that became too tame after awhile."

She laughed and threw her arms wide. "Korat! The entire world knows of Korat, and I hardly knew the name! Why would I? Each time he struck I was locked up somewhere. Now I learn the police have proof that Phillip was Korat. And they think I'm his accomplice."

She turned away, once again staring out across the rain-drenched city. "Phillip said he could refute any allegations I made about being locked up in that cabin. Now I understand how. He had proof I was traveling with him during each of those periods."

"But it wasn't you," said Logan.

"No. It was someone posing as me." She paused for a moment. Her face brightened. "But maybe not posing well enough."

"What do you mean?"

"What if there are security tapes of Phillip and my

doppelganger during those trips? From the airport or other places. I could prove it wasn't me."

"There won't be any tapes," said Logan.

"There has to be, at least at the airport. Doesn't Homeland Security have cameras everywhere?"

"Phillip's last trip was too long ago. Even if he and his companion were caught on film, those surveillance tapes would have been recorded over long ago."

She sighed. "Of course. What was I thinking? I've watched enough *Law & Order* to know that. And now you know why I can't prove I wasn't in Europe during those robberies."

Emma jumped at the sound of a loud knock on the outer door of the suite.

Logan rose. "It's just room service. I ordered some dinner for us." He grabbed his wallet and headed for the door. Over his shoulder he added, "Get in bed. You're too tired to sit at a table."

Emma wasn't about to argue with him.

A few minutes later, he returned with a wheeled cart and placed a bed tray over her lap. Then he removed the metal dish covers to reveal two large platters of scrambled eggs and mashed potatoes. Emma gave the odd combination a curious once-over.

"Comfort food," he explained, buttering a slice of toast for her. "When I was a little boy, my mother always made me scrambled eggs and mashed potatoes when I wasn't feeling well. I thought you could use some." He arranged a tray for himself, and settled in beside her.

"I remember my mother bringing me tomato soup and tuna fish sandwiches." Her voice quaked. "It's been a long time since anyone did something so nice for me."

Logan kissed her. "You'd better get used to it."

"Will you bring me scrambled eggs and mashed potatoes when I'm in prison?"

He slammed his fork onto his plate. "You're not going to prison."

As confident as he appeared, inwardly Logan's fears for Emma mounted. Long after she'd fallen into an exhausted sleep, he lay awake puzzling through her strange tale. Coming to one irrefutable conclusion, he slipped out of bed to place a series of phone calls. He hadn't a clue as to how he could prove his theory, but his gut told him he was right. And that gut instinct had never failed him.

Chapter 29

Leslee clicked on the evening news. Stretching out on her bed, she settled in to watch the results of her handiwork. A satisfied smile spread across her face when the camera zoomed in on a haggard-looking Logan Crawford entering the Industrial Corrections Facility. She raised a glass of bourbon to the television screen in a mock toast. "Touché, lover boy! That'll teach you to mess with Leslee Howell."

Although it was the top story on the evening news, the sound bites left her hungry for more. She picked up the morning papers strewn across her white satin comforter and once again devoured the headline stories, reveling in Emma's fall from grace. She laughed out loud at the front-page photos. With her hands shackled behind her back, Emma looked pathetic, hardly the image of the crown princess of the city. Leslee savored the moment, knowing the best was yet to come.

The buzzing of the lobby intercom shattered the pleasure of the moment. With a scowl she rose from her bed, grabbed a short silk robe off the bedpost, and headed into the living room. She wasn't expecting anyone and disliked surprise visits.

She stabbed the speaker button. "Who is it?"

"Leslee, baby, why so angry?"

"Go away, Marty. I'm not in the mood."

"I've got something that'll put you in the mood."

She thought for a moment. If Marty had candy with him, the evening could only get better. And two always celebrated better than one. She pressed the button releasing the inner lobby door lock and waited.

A few minutes later Marty rapped at her apartment door. "I hope I didn't interrupt anything important," he said, when she let him in. With a wolf whistle, he ogled her scantily clad figure. His lips curled into an appreciative smile.

Marty withdrew a small plastic bag from his jacket pocket and stroked it against her breast. Her nipple puckered and strained against the fabric of the lace teddy she wore under her silk robe. She grabbed for the packet, but Marty swiftly palmed the coke and tucked it back in his pocket. "Let's talk first." He reached for the glass of bourbon she still held and polished it off in one long swig. Then he sauntered across the carpet to her bar and poured himself another.

"Make yourself right at home, why don't you?"

"Don't mind if I do." He eyed her living room, nodding his approval before stretching out on the leather sectional and settling his feet on the glass-topped coffee table. "Nice digs, babe. I had no idea Philadelphia's civil servants were so well-paid."

Leslee removed a razor blade and small hand mirror from a lacquered box on the mantel and pushing Marty's feet out of the way, placed them on the table. She settled in alongside him, tucking her bare legs up under her body. "There's lots you don't know, Marty."

"And lots more I do. You've been a naughty girl, Leslee, and Papa Marty knows all about it." He nodded toward the drug paraphernalia. "We'll leave that for later. To seal our partnership."

"What are you talking about?"

"About a million or two." Reaching inside his jacket, he removed an envelope and handed it to her. "These are just a few stills from a video I shot the other night during a stakeout. I don't think you'll have any trouble recognizing the place. Or the person."

Leslee opened the envelope and removed the contents. A moment later panic rose inside her as she scrutinized each of the half dozen eight-by-ten glossies. "What do you want?"

"I know who you are and what you've done. I don't care about Crawford or the broad, but my silence has a price." He surveyed his surroundings once more. "Like you, I enjoy the finer things in life."

She dropped the photos onto her lap. "So you're blackmailing me?"

"Leslee, baby, you've got it all wrong. You and me, we're gonna be partners."

After contemplating her predicament for a moment or two, Leslee concluded she had no choice but to agree to whatever terms he suggested. Marty had caught her red-handed planting the evidence against Emma. She tossed him a wicked grin. "Bring out the candy, partner."

She'd find a way to rid herself of this annoying complication later.

Chapter 30

A narrow shaft of bright sunlight streamed in through a break in the room-darkening drapes and settled over Emma's face. Rolling over, she yawned, ridding herself of the cobwebs of sleep, and focused her eyes on the clock radio. One-thirty! The last thing she remembered was sharing a meal with Logan—nearly twenty hours ago! She reached across the bed, her fingers caressing his pillow. The cotton held no residual body heat. He'd probably risen hours earlier.

Suddenly, Emma became aware of muted voices drifting through the closed door, voices that caused a creeping uneasiness within her. As her mind focused and individual sounds grew discernible, the uneasiness blossomed into full-blown panic. With her heart racing, she threw back the quilt, jumped out of bed, and grabbed her robe.

"No!" she cried as she jerked open the bedroom door. Before she could say anything else, Kevin and James bounded across the room and sandwiched her between them.

She clung to her sons. "I don't want you here! I don't want you involved. Please! Go back to school before anyone sees you."

"We're not going back," James said. "Not until you're cleared of these charges."

"You need our help," added Kevin.

Emma stroked his cheek. In Kevin's face she saw what little she remembered of her mother—crystal blue eyes that danced with life. "There's nothing you can do, darling. Coming to Philadelphia only makes you fodder for those dreadful tabloids."

James took her hand and led her to the sofa. Seated with a son on each side, Emma directed her anger toward Logan. "You brought them here. Damn it, Logan, you knew I didn't want them involved."

"They've been involved, Emma. Right from the start."

She stared first at James, then Kevin. Both nodded in agreement.

"We've been dodging paparazzi for weeks," confirmed James. "We just kept it from you."

"God, I'm so sorry." She buried her head in her hands.

"For what?" asked Kevin. "Finding some happiness at last? You deserve that after what you sacrificed for us."

Her head whipped up. "Don't you *ever* blame yourself for what happened to me, Kevin Wadsworth!"

Kevin's gaze traveled over her head to his brother. Following it, Emma searched her older son's face, hating the guilt she saw hidden behind his eyes.

"We know what he did to you, Mom, and we know you stayed to protect us."

She slumped back against the cushions and closed her eyes. She had tried so hard to shield her sons. But they were bright boys, curious and observant and far wiser than typical fourteen- and fifteen-year-olds. Long ago they'd realized their father didn't love them—any of them.

When she opened her eyes, she found Logan seated on the coffee table in front of her. He reached over and grasped her hand. "Forgive me?"

Emma sighed. "You're not a parent. You can't possibly understand. They're too young to have to deal with this."

"Granted. But as they told you, they're already involved. Isn't it better to have them here where we can keep an eye on them?"

She glanced at James and Kevin. Logan was right. Her sons were better protected in the hotel than on their own up at school. "I suppose."

"Besides," he continued, "I *am* a son, and I know if Aggie were in trouble, I'd be by her side no matter what."

Emma nodded and squeezed his hand. He'd only done what he thought best for her. "Forgiven."

He leaned forward to kiss her. "Logan!" She jerked her head away.

"What? They've never seen their mother kissed before?"

"Well, actually," James said, stifling a chuckle, "we haven't."

"But we'd sure like to," Kevin chimed in.

Logan stood, drawing Emma to her feet. "Can't disappoint the boys, now can we?" Not waiting for an answer, he captured her mouth.

Several hours later, the four of them were joined by Molly and Ned for dinner and a brainstorming session.

"What's your take on Atwell and Rush?" Logan asked Ned.

"In my book they're the best. Both for investigative work and defense."

"Good. I've already spoken with them, and they're willing to sign on. God only knows why Emma's lawyer sent her that sorry excuse for a criminal attorney."

"In his defense," Ned said, "Jim Bronstein's the best in the city when it comes to corporate fraud. Abbott's getting on in years, and Emma was in shock when she called him. Maybe he didn't fully understand the situation."

"Then Bronstein should have found her someone else when he realized the case was out of his league. Not try to convince her to plead out. He gets his walking papers tomorrow."

Emma's fork halted midway to her mouth. "Excuse me? Do I get a say in any of this, or are the two of you running the show from here on?" Both Logan and Ned stared at her as if they'd suddenly realized she was in the room.

She continued. "Ned, I value your opinions and any advice you can give me, but we both know this presents a conflict of interest for you. Merely having dinner with me might jeopardize your office." She turned to Logan. "And you're here on business—your business. Not to handle my defense."

"Emma, they're only trying to help," said Molly.

"I realize that, but this is my problem, and I can't allow any of you to get sucked into it."

Logan slammed his fork onto his plate. "Damn it, Emma! You wouldn't be in this mess if it weren't for me." Five sets of eyes stared at him. "Haven't any of you figured out who's behind this? It's so damn obvious!"

When no one answered, Logan continued. "The only person with the means to plant incriminating evidence in Emma's home was Korat's accomplice."

"But why divulge Korat's identity now?" asked Ned. "Why not continue as a solo act, as if Korat were still alive?"

"And why give up a fortune in jewels to divert blame when no one suspected you in the first place?" added Molly.

Emma stared across the table at Logan. She understood. "Unless revenge was more important than money."

"Precisely," said Logan.

"Leslee." The name strangled in Emma's throat. Suddenly, all the pieces of the puzzle fell into place. Someone *had* been in her home the night Logan found the earring—but not to steal. To set her up for a fall. As Phillip's longtime mistress, Leslee Howell must have been his accomplice. She probably had a key to Emma's house. And knew the alarm code. And the combination to the safe.

"Of course!" said Molly. "With a dark wig and low-heeled pumps Leslee might pass for Emma. Especially in a foreign country where there was little chance of running into someone Emma knew."

"Hell hath no fury like a woman scorned," said Logan.

"Who's Leslee?" asked Kevin and James in unison.

Ignoring their question, Emma stared at her plate of shrimp scampi. The aroma of the food, which had at first tempted her taste buds, now repulsed her. In the background she heard Logan answering her sons, but the words jumbled inside her brain. She was no longer sitting at the table. She had returned to a night nearly seven months ago. Seized with panic, Emma's head pounded with one question. *What else does Leslee know?*

Grabbing her napkin, she bolted from the table.

Chapter 31

"Well?" Annoyed by the interruption, Roy Harper didn't bother to mask his contempt for the overeager assistant district attorney waiting nervously in the doorway.

"Rodriguez broke through. We've got the files."

"All of them?"

"And then some." LeRoy Dixon's face beamed with a sheepish grin that reminded Roy of a cat with feathers sticking out of its mouth. "I think you'll find it was worth the wait, sir."

Harper scowled, reaching for the printouts the assistant D.A. held. "I'll be the judge of that." Without a second glance, he dismissed his underling with a curt, "Close the door on your way out, Dixon."

Before reading through the files, Roy locked his office door and withdrew a folder from a secured drawer in his desk. Spreading out the contents of both sets of printouts, he compared the data obtained from the computer with the list provided by his source. Everything matched up. Korat had kept detailed spreadsheets of each heist—date, place, victim, item stolen.

The final column, omitted from the first set of records, was labeled DISBURSEMENT. Roy whistled under his breath. In his hands he held proof that many of the wealthiest members of the beau monde had defrauded Lloyds of London. No wonder Korat had resisted capture year after year! His victims were his partners in crime, splitting the insurance proceeds with him—minus Korat's sizable fee for acquiring new settings for the stolen gemstones. Wadsworth must have died before completing his last deal. Those stones confiscated from his safe definitely weren't paste.

Drumming his pen on the desk, Harper pondered the list of names. A man without scruples might acquire a very large fortune with such information. Unfortunately, Rodriguez and Dixon had also seen the printout. Roy set the papers aside, deciding to give further consideration to the matter after the election.

A knock on the door brought him out of his reverie. "In a minute," he called. Returning the first set of papers to the locked drawer, he crossed the room and unfastened the latch, allowing Delgado to enter.

"Guess you were right about the Wadsworth dame. Quite a bombshell she had tucked away in that computer," said the detective.

"If that's your way of apologizing, Delgado, accepted. But," added Harper, "Interpol's going to wait in line. I'm not turning her over until I'm through with her."

"Interpol?"

Harper sneered at his detective. "And just how do I prosecute her for insurance fraud committed in Europe against an English agency?"

Delgado shook his head. "You've lost me, boss." He pointed to the stack of papers on Harper's desk. "Obviously, you haven't gotten to the best part yet. I wasn't talking about insurance fraud. I was talking about murder."

Chapter 32

"Probably a bad shrimp," said Emma, brushing aside Logan's concern. They were in the bedroom. Molly and Ned had gone home. James and Kevin had retired to the room at the opposite end of the suite. "I'm fine. Really."

"You look far from fine." He assessed her features. Where once her eyes had sparkled, they now reflected only fear, and her skin had lost its luster. She was shriveling before his eyes. "Fight it, Emma. We're going to get through this. Leslee's going to pay for what she's doing to you."

Emma's shoulders slumped. Picking up the cross-stitch supplies Molly had brought her, she settled into an overstuffed chair in front of the bedroom window and began stitching. Her brow creased, her fingers flying furiously, she concentrated only on the placement of the needle in the linen.

Without looking up she asked, "I don't suppose they'll allow me my needlework in prison, will they?" She lifted the sharp embroidery scissors from her lap and studied them. "I suppose they'd consider this a deadly weapon."

Unable to contain himself or his frustration, Logan ripped the fabric and scissors from her hands and hurled them across the room. "Damn it, woman! Don't you dare give up! I've waited my entire life for you, and if you think for one moment I'm going to let Leslee Howell get away with this, you've gone stark raving mad!"

Emma stared at him, her eyes large and brimming with unshed tears. Her lips trembled. Her hands flew to her mouth, muffling her words. "I'm . . . so . . . scared," she said.

Logan gathered her into his arms, offering himself as a lifeline against her grief and fear. Whispering soothing words of comfort, he ran his fingers through her hair, stroked her back, and rocked her, all the while fighting his own battle against the apprehension growing inside him.

How the hell could they prove Leslee had framed Emma—that she'd committed the crimes Emma was accused of? Going to Harper was useless. They had no proof. And having Emma with her prestigious name and wealth as the prime suspect in a high-profile case placed the district attorney in the national spotlight. Emma's conviction was worth a gold mine of publicity to the man. The question remained: Was he Leslee's accomplice in her quest to destroy Emma, or an unwitting pawn with his own agenda? "Tell me what you know about Roy Harper," he said.

"Not much." Her voice sounded hoarse and ragged. "He appeared on the political scene a few years ago. I think I remember hearing he came from somewhere in the Midwest. Indiana maybe. I met him a few times at social functions, but that's about it. I don't recall ever exchanging more than a few words with him. He always struck me as very aloof."

"Is there any possibility he might have some personal grudge against you? Or Phillip, perhaps?"

Emma shook her head. "Not that I know of, but anything's possible. Why?"

"I don't know. But I have this niggling feeling that a large piece of the puzzle is still missing." He twirled a lock of her hair around his fingers, concentrating on the waves as if the answers he sought lay within the strands. "I'm glad Beryl's due back in town tomorrow. She has a way of seeing things the rest of us miss."

"She also has a way of sticking her nose where it doesn't belong. I'm in enough trouble as it is."

Logan scowled. "Beryl does whatever is necessary. Let's concentrate on getting the proof we need to clear you. As far as I'm concerned, that's all that matters."

Emma's eyes filled with tears.

"What is it?"

She reached up and caressed his cheek, her fingertips traveling across his lips, his cheekbones, his brow as if committing his features to memory. "I can't believe you're real. That you're willing to do this for me."

"I love you."

A tear spilled from her eye and trickled down her cheek. Logan captured it with the tip of his tongue and left a gentle kiss in its place. *I love you*. For him those three words were enough to explain everything, but for her they went far beyond. No man had ever professed love for her before.

Logan had told her he'd considered himself an arrogant cynic, a man incapable of love. She had long ago given up on happy endings. Now, all of a sudden, the cynic believed in fairy tales. Her experiences had taught her "happily ever after" only existed in dreams that never came true.

For Emma there could be no happy ending. She alone knew the past lurked in the shadows, and like a chill wind, it stood ready to extinguish the fragile flame of her happiness—and their love. She was convinced that when Logan learned of her sin, he'd leave. No matter how much he professed to love her. And she wouldn't blame him. She wasn't worthy of his love. Not after what she'd done.

Closing her eyes, she sank deeper into his broad chest, seeking refuge from the harsh realities that plagued her. "I love you, too," she whispered.

With Emma cradled in his arms, Logan rose from the chair and placed her on the bed. He took his time undressing her, rediscovering her body inch by inch. "Honey," he murmured, nuzzling between her breasts. "You taste like honey."

He rolled her onto her stomach and straddled her. Beginning with one hand, he massaged her fingers, methodically giving attention to each digit before moving on to her wrist, then working his way up her arm. Her other arm received an equal amount of care before he traveled to the muscles of her back. As she gave herself over to his ministrations, he felt the stress slowly flow from her body. When he worked his way from her toes up her legs to her thigh muscles, tension of a different sort took hold, and his fingers sensed the urgency growing beyond her control.

His lips replaced his fingers, exploring the supple flesh of her inner thigh as he forged a trail toward the fire burning inside her.

Emma writhed beneath him. "Now, please!"

His hands tore away his clothing, then yanked open the nightstand in search of a foil packet.

Fighting off his own need, he flipped her onto her back, entering her slowly, allowing them both to savor the sensation as long as possible. Emma ran her hands along his torso. She arched her back, her body screaming out its need for release. He increased his thrusts. She matched his movements, clinging to his neck, panting, crying out between gasps as he plunged her over the brink. Her body convulsed, crested, then convulsed again as the spasms erupted inside her.

Sounds of retching woke Logan early the following morning. Rolling over, he found himself alone in the bed. He squinted through unfocused eyes at the fuzzy numbers on the clock radio. Five-fifteen. A pinpoint shaft of light poured from a crack in the bathroom door, slicing across the carpet and onto the bed.

In the next room the toilet flushed. Water flowed into the sink. By the time his sleepy brain processed the noises, the narrow shaft of light widened and filled the room. Emma leaned against the door frame, her face pale.

"Still think it was a bad shrimp?" he asked, after she climbed into bed.

She shook her head before closing her eyes and sinking into the pillows. "Maybe a touch of flu. I probably picked it up in that awful jail." She curled up in his arms and fell back to sleep.

Several hours later, while Emma slept, Logan listened over breakfast as James and Kevin filled him in on their life with Phillip Wadsworth. The tales they told were incomprehensible to a man who had grown up in a home filled with love. While Emma had alluded only to the emotional and psychological abuse she'd suffered at the hands of that bastard, her sons described it in graphic detail. The violence, as seen through the eyes of two helpless boys, took on a grotesqueness that ate away at him.

Logan considered it a miracle that Emma's sons had survived without developing any of their father's traits. He knew that abused children often grew up to become abusers. Against incredible odds, Kevin and James seemed to have inherited nothing of their father's evil ways and all of their mother's strength and love.

"Your mother thinks she hid these things from you," he said after James related one incident that occurred when he was five years old.

"We heard more than we actually saw," Kevin added. "Late at night . . ." His lower lip trembled. "Then he sent us away. He knew how much that would hurt Mom. And us."

Logan squeezed his shoulder. "You were a child. You can't blame yourself. There was nothing you could have done."

"If it hadn't been for us, she could have left him," said James. "He told her if she ever left, he'd sue for custody, and she'd never see us again. She lived through hell to protect us, and now it's like he's come back from the dead to continue hurting her." His eyes pleaded with Logan. "There's got to be something we can do. She doesn't deserve this."

"No, she doesn't," agreed Logan. He pushed aside his coffee and lowered his head into his hands.

"Damn it!" His fist pounded the table, rattling the dishes. He was used to solving problems. He was good at it. His brain analyzed a situation, weighed the various available options, then made the correct decision. Every time. But even he had his limitations. Short of physically torturing Leslee Howell into telling the truth, he had absolutely no idea how to prove Emma's innocence.

A sharp knock on the door brought a smile to his face. Beryl. The cavalry had arrived. Logan rose from his chair, strode across the room, and flung the door open. But instead of a disheveled assistant, grumpy from a six-hour flight, he found a smirking Roy Harper flanked by two officers.

Chapter 33

Harper pushed his way into the room, quickly surveying his surroundings. Without any pleasantries he came right to the point. "Where is she, Crawford?"

"Sleeping. What do you want?"

The district attorney waved an envelope in Logan's face. "I have a warrant here for your girlfriend's arrest. Seems she's one very busy lady. Not only is she a master thief, but she almost got away with murder."

"What!"

"Phillip Wadsworth was murdered." Harper paused. As if playing to an audience, he assumed an insolent attitude, arms crossed over his chest, a sly smile of satisfaction on his lips. "By his wife."

James and Kevin sprang to their feet.

"My father died of a heart attack," shouted Kevin. "Ask the coroner, you shithead!"

"Kevin!" Logan held up his hand to prevent the boy from lunging at the district attorney. James grabbed his brother's arm.

Tamping down his own desire to strangle Harper,

Logan planted himself firmly in front of the man and demanded an explanation, but a growing uneasiness swirled within him. Even Harper, as arrogant as he was, wouldn't be stupid enough to make such an accusation without proof.

Instead of answering Logan, the D.A. turned to Emma's sons. "We found a computer file with your mother's diary. She wrote in great detail about how she planned and carried out the murder, making it look like a coronary. Even bragged about how easy it was."

Harper nodded to the officers. "Get her."

"No! Wait, please." Logan blocked their path. "I'll get her for you."

Harper sneered at him. "Out of the way, Crawford."

"Please, she may not be dressed."

The officers, both male, turned to Harper, discomfort and indecision written across their faces. Harper glared at Logan for several seconds before nodding. "Make it quick."

Standing off to the side, Logan watched Emma's silhouette through the film of steam clouding the shower stall door. Her head raised to the pulsing spray, warm water sluiced over her body. Following the contours of her rounded breasts, the stream cascaded along her flat belly, collecting in the raven silk between her legs before spilling into the soapy puddle swirling at her feet.

Angrily, he fought with the doubt invading his thoughts. Emma was incapable of murder. Or was she? Had Phillip pushed her close enough to the brink of sanity that she'd finally fought back to free herself? Was the murder the source of her nightmares? Closing his eyes, he shook his head in a vain attempt to rout the thought from his brain. When he opened them, she was stepping from the shower.

"What's wrong?" she asked.

"Tell me about the night Phillip died."

The question, coming out of nowhere, poleaxed her. Emma grabbed for a towel, clutching it to her dripping body. She backed into the wall and stared at him, her eyes wide. "No!" She lowered her damp head. "I can't. Please don't ever ask me that again."

Logan lifted her chin, forcing her to look at him. "Tell me!"

"Why are you doing this?"

"Harper's in the next room waiting to arrest you for Phillip's murder."

"Murder?" The word hung in the air, echoing off the tiles. Emma's body went limp, collapsing into his.

Bracing her against the tile wall, Logan cupped her face in his hands. His eyes probed her soul, searching for reassurance. "Emma, tell me you didn't kill Phillip."

"I can't."

Chapter 34

Emma stepped from the air-conditioned Mercedes into a night pregnant with equal combinations of heat and humidity. From within the house she could hear the raucous voices and loud music. A party. Her heart raced. What was Phillip up to now?

She dragged herself to the back of the car and removed her one piece of luggage from the trunk. Tossing the overnight bag over her shoulder, she headed for the house that had been more prison than home for the past sixteen years.

Alone in the foyer, she moved across the polished marble floor to the staircase. The few people congregating in the living room had their backs to her. The sounds of splashing water and laughter traveling down the hallway told her the rest of Phillip's guests were gathered in and around the swimming pool. As she headed up the stairs, the clock chimed nine times. Only nine o'clock. With any luck, by the time the party ended hours from now, Phillip would be too drunk to notice her.

She paused outside her bedroom. Of all the rooms in the house, she hated this one the most. Taking a deep breath, she pushed open the bedroom door and stepped into her private hell.

She gasped at the sight that confronted her. Sprawled on her bed in a seductive pose, her long blond hair cascading across the pillow and off the mattress, slept a nude Leslee Howell. Dropping the overnight bag, Emma turned to flee, but an arm reached out and grabbed her.

"Well, well, look who's back. The little wife." Phillip tightened his grip on her upper arm. "Kiddies all safely tucked away out of reach of the Big Bad Wolf?"

Emma fought to keep the hatred she felt from showing on her face. She stared at her naked husband. She knew from experience not to provoke him. Even in the dim light of the nightstand lamp, she could see his glazed eyes and dilated pupils. With one slightly shaking hand, he lifted a Baccarat crystal tumbler of bourbon to his lips.

Dragging her over to the bed, he nudged Leslee. "Wake up, baby. We have company." She stirred, mumbling something indiscernible. "Too much of a good thing, sugar?" Phillip stroked the crystal tumbler against Leslee's bare buttocks. He laughed, polished off his drink, then tossed the empty glass across the room. It hit the closet door and shattered.

Phillip sat on the edge of the mattress and pulled Emma onto his lap. He scowled at her. "How long has it been since you performed your wifely duty, Emma?" Catching her head in a vicelike grip, he forced his tongue past her lips.

Emma jerked her head away, repulsed by the sight of him and sickened by the thick scent of cigars and alcohol and sex. She broke from his grasp.

"*Get back here!*" He lunged for her.

"*No!*" A second later the full force of his body slammed into her, throwing her to the floor. Then nothing. Phillip didn't move. His arms lay limp on either side of her.

Emma pushed Phillip off her and staggered to her feet. A wave of dizziness washed over her. She reached for the bureau to steady herself, but her hand missed the edge and swept across the surface, knocking a hypodermic needle to the floor.

Across the room, Leslee lay in what was most likely a drug-induced stupor. Stretched out at her feet, Phillip remained in a similar state, his body coated in a sheen of sweat. Emma glanced at the syringe and suspected neither Leslee nor Phillip were likely to wake any time soon.

Chapter 35

"I fled the house," said Emma. "I stayed away for two hours, driving aimlessly around the city. Not knowing what else to do, I finally went back, hoping to hide away in one of the other bedrooms until morning."

She paused, looking up at Logan. A bewildered frown creased her brow. "When I returned, the house was dark. Empty except for Phillip. I found him upstairs. Dead. Someone had gone to the trouble of cleaning up—picking up the broken glass, removing the drug paraphernalia. Even spraying air freshener to mask the stench in the room. I'm sure it was Leslee, but why would she go to all that trouble?"

"To protect herself from getting caught up in a drug scandal? Or worse?"

Emma sat on the edge of the bed, silent for a moment. Her head bent, in a faraway voice she spoke into her lap. "But they left evidence of drugs throughout the house—marijuana butts, empty crack vials, used syringes. I spent several hours clearing it all out before calling the police."

Logan kneeled down in front of her. Whether knowingly or unintentionally, she had strayed from the real problem. "Emma, look at me," he demanded. "Phillip died of a heart attack. You're not to blame."

The abruptness of his tone snapped her back to reality. "Don't you understand?" she cried. "I didn't call for help. I let him die."

"But you didn't realize he'd suffered a coronary."

She shook her head. Damp locks of hair slapped at her face. "I must have known. I wanted him dead. I wished it. Every day of my married life."

He gathered her into his arms. Phillip had mentally abused her to the point she felt responsible for a death he'd brought about by his own arrogance. "The drugs and alcohol killed him. Not you."

"No, it's my fault," she insisted. "I let the hate consume me. I walked away and left him to die. That makes me as much a monster as he was and responsible for his death."

Logan's thoughts raced back to Harper's words. Emma's account of Phillip's death didn't correspond with the district attorney's story of premeditated murder. One of them was lying, and he'd bet his last dime it wasn't Emma. "Can you remember what you wrote in your journal about that night?"

Emma stared at him, her features frozen in puzzlement. "Journal? You mean a diary?"

Logan nodded.

"I don't keep a diary."

"You didn't record anything about Phillip's death in the computer Harper seized?"

"Phillip's computer? I never touched it." She related how one of Harper's assistants had come to the prison demanding the password. "He refused to believe me when I said I didn't know it."

An ominous silence filled the room. Someone pounded at the door.

"Now, Crawford," yelled Harper, "or we're coming in."

"Another minute," Logan yelled back.

"They're taking me back to prison, aren't they?"

He couldn't answer. He'd failed her.

Emma rose from the bed. In a voice devoid of hope, she spoke. "I'd better get dressed."

"Emma Brockton Wadsworth, you're under arrest for the murder of Phillip Wadsworth." The officer's voice, an all-business baritone, filled the still room. Beside him stood Roy Harper, his hate-filled eyes boring into her. A second officer off to the side restrained James and Kevin, preventing them from rushing toward her.

The first officer advanced. Emma clung to Logan's hand, afraid to let go. "Don't let them take me," she pleaded.

"Step aside, sir," ordered the officer with the baritone voice.

Logan squeezed her hand and whispered in her ear, "Be brave," before reluctantly separating himself from her.

"You have the right to remain silent," said the officer, grasping her wrists and whipping them behind her back.

As the first cuff clicked into place, Emma drew in a sharp breath. *Block it out!* She forced her mind to find a speech.

Tomorrowandtomorrowandtommorowcreepsinthispettypacefromdaytodaytothelastsyllableofrecordedtime . . .

"No!" Kevin's cry pierced the air, breaking her concentration.

"If you give up the right to remain silent, anything you say can and will be used against you in a court of law."

A small whimper escaped her lips as the second cuff snapped over her wrist. Squeezing her eyes shut, she willed herself to continue Macbeth's speech, pushing away all sound and thought other than Shakespeare's words.

Andallouryesterdayshavelightedfoolsthewayto-dustydeath.

The officer droned on. "You have the right to speak with an attorney and to have an attorney present during questioning."

Emma's knees weakened. With her balance compromised by manacled wrists, she found it difficult to fight against the dizziness creeping up on her.

Outoutbriefcandle!Life'sbutawalkingshadowa-poorplayerthatstrutsandfretshishouruponthestage-andthenisheardnomore.

"If you so desire and cannot afford one, an attorney will be appointed for you without charge before the questioning begins."

The room grew dark and began to spin. Faster and faster. Emma struggled for air. In the distance she heard screaming.

"Mom!"

"Emma!"

Hands reached for her, but she stumbled and was dragged further into the darkness until everything disappeared, and nothing existed but a dense blackness and the echoing memory of one word, its stabbing cadence repeating over and over in her head.

Finally . . . finally . . . finally.

Harper's sneer broke the silence that fell over the room. "What were you doing in there, Crawford, coaching her on how to faint?" He nodded to the officers. "Get her up. Splash some cold water on her face if you have to, but she's walking out of here."

Logan stooped to shield Emma's body from the policemen. He glared at the district attorney. "Got another sideshow set up downstairs, Harper? Reporters and camera crews waiting for you to appear on cue?" He motioned toward Emma. "Can't you see she's ill?"

Ignoring Logan's plea, Harper yelled at the policemen, "Do as I say!"

The officers looked at one another, each waiting for the other to make the first move. When neither complied, the baritone cleared his throat.

The second officer stammered, "I don't think she's faking, sir."

"James, call an ambulance." Logan lifted Emma against his chest. He cradled her limp, shackled wrists in one hand and turned to the baritone. "Get these goddamn things off her!"

The officer nervously fingered the key hanging from his belt and glanced at Harper for direction.

"She's going to the hospital, Harper, or I go downstairs and start rattling a few skeletons from *your* closet." Logan held his breath. He'd played his trump card. Now all he could do was pray his suspicions about the man were correct, and Harper wouldn't call his bluff.

The color drained from the district attorney's face, and although his tone remained calm, his voice faltered. "Nice try, Crawford, but I don't have any."

"Well, then you have nothing to fear."

The D.A. glowered at him, then glanced at Emma, her body sagging in Logan's arms. "I suppose maybe we'd better have a doctor examine her," he muttered. "Wouldn't want her slapping a lawsuit against the city."

"That's the least of your problems, Harper." When

beads of sweat broke out across the district attorney's brow, Logan knew he'd hit pay dirt.

But what was Harper hiding, and how was Emma connected?

Chapter 36

Marty pushed open the hotel room door, stepped inside, and surveyed the ransacked room. *Damn mess!* Carefully, he reached inside the smashed television and removed a camera, hurled in frustration, no doubt, by the disappointed intruder. Stepping across the overturned mattress, he righted a trash basket and deposited the broken camera in it.

With hands on hips he circled the room, noting the damage. A torn shirt hung from a lopsided lampshade. Another covered the leg of a toppled chair. Upended dresser drawers balanced precariously on top of each other in a corner. Torn newspapers, magazines, and sheets ripped from the Philadelphia Yellow Pages blanketed the carpet.

He poked his head into the bathroom to find toiletries scattered across the tile. Marty laughed. Someone left *extremely* angry and *very* empty-handed. Just as he'd planned.

Expecting a double cross, Marty had rented a safe-deposit box for his video and moved across town to the Doubletree. For the past several days, he'd maintained a watch on his former Comfort Inn room, which he'd furnished with cheap camera equipment and discount store clothing. Today, while he cooled his heels waiting for a press conference that never happened, the intruder struck.

She'd made a big mistake.

"It's all such a damn mess!" Logan paced back and forth across the room, clenching and unclenching his fists.

"Wearing a path in the linoleum isn't going to solve anything," said Beryl. "Sit down, damn it!"

He scowled at her but dropped into a vinyl-covered chair at the side of the hospital bed.

"That's better. Now behave yourself."

Across the room, Kevin fought to muffle a nervous laugh. Beryl leveled a stern warning in his direction.

"Is she always like this?" asked James.

"No." Logan sighed. "Usually she's much worse."

Ignoring the slur on her character, Beryl cut to the heart of the matter. "We've already established that Leslee framed Emma—at least as Korat's accomplice and probably for his murder, but I still can't figure out where Harper fits into the picture. He's got to have some ulterior motive in all this. I've never heard of a D.A. showing up at the scene to serve search or arrest warrants."

"Publicity," said Logan. "He's running for mayor, but I'd bet my last dime he's hiding a secret of his own." He turned to James and Kevin. "Did either of you see how nervous he got after my bluff?"

"You were bluffing?" asked Kevin.

"Unfortunately, yes."

"Hmff! Sounds like we need to do a little dirt

digging ourselves," said Beryl. "What about the lawyers?"

"Waiting to get their hands on Harper's evidence. There's not much they can do until they see what he's got and can interview Emma." He glanced across the room at the figure in the bed. She appeared so frail. Her skin, as white as the stark hospital sheets, created an almost ghoulish contrast against the ebony waves of hair that fanned out across the pillow.

Beryl came up behind him and squeezed his shoulders. "She's a fighter, champ. She's just resting between rounds."

Logan reached up and patted her hand. Beryl. Always there when he needed her—whether it was to kick his ass back into reality or offer a comforting word.

A day had already passed, and Emma still lay comatose. A battery of tests had ruled out any physiological reason—no brain tumors, no head trauma, no problems with her nervous system. Aside from the aftermath of a mild case of what appeared to be food poisoning, Emma seemed perfectly healthy—except she was unconscious.

Maybe Beryl was right. Her words echoed Dr. Greenwald's assertion that Emma's psyche had deliberately shut down as a means of self-preservation. With emotional trauma attacking from all sides and terrified of going back to jail, her subconscious had found the only means of keeping her free.

"Think about it," the doctor had said. "You've just told me this woman, whom we all thought led an idyllic life, has suffered through sixteen years of horrendous psychological abuse. She's finally freed of it, yet she really isn't free. She's consumed with guilt over how she believes that freedom was obtained.

"On top of that, she's framed for crimes her husband committed *and* his murder. Now, factor in the belief she has no way of defending herself against the charges. It's enough to drive anyone over the edge."

"Will she come out of it?" asked Logan.

Dr. Greenwald scratched his gray beard, shrugged his shoulders and raised his hands, palms up, in a noncommittal gesture. "Hopefully. When she's ready."

Once word leaked of Emma's arrest on murder charges, a three-ring circus of paparazzi set up shop outside Thomas Jefferson University Hospital. Round-the-clock shifts of police guarded her door, but their assignment was to prevent the escape of an unconscious prisoner, not keep the press out. Logan worried that one of the officers might succumb to a photographer's bribe.

Due to the nature of Emma's condition, he and her doctors had requested certain concessions not usually allowed under other circumstances. Normally, hospitalized prisoners were permitted visits by immediate family and legal counsel only, with relatives limited to stays of no more than thirty minutes at a time.

At first Harper insisted on adhering to those rules. With Emma carried off to the hospital on a stretcher, he'd reluctantly canceled the press conference scheduled for the Four Seasons. Announcing the arrest of an unconscious woman would vilify him in the public's eye. Annoyed at having his plans thwarted, the D.A. was in no mood to yield to any requests for deferential treatment.

In the corridor outside Emma's hospital room, Dr. Greenwald pressed his argument for open-ended visitation for his patient. "You don't understand. She needs constant verbal stimulation to break through her unconscious state."

The D.A. remained unmoved. "So play twenty-four-hour talk radio for her."

"Familiar voices, loved ones, work best," insisted the doctor.

Only after Logan sought help from Ned Ralston did Harper acquiesce. Reluctantly. And not before hurling a few digs at the incumbent mayor when Ned summoned him to his office. "Better start writing that concession speech, Ralston. You just handed me the election. The voters of Philadelphia won't stand for a mayor who protects a murderer."

"An *alleged* murderer. I'm sure I don't have to remind Philadelphia's district attorney that a person is innocent until proven guilty. Oh, and by the way." He stared down Harper's glare. "In case you hadn't noticed, you haven't even won the primary yet."

Maintaining his smug attitude as he exited the mayor's office, Harper shot Ralston a contemptuous smile and tossed off a parting shot. "Only a matter of time."

"How long do you intend to camp out here?" asked Beryl, nodding in the direction of the cot set up for Logan. He'd maintained a constant vigil, talking to Emma throughout the night, taking only an occasional short nap.

"Until she wakes up."

Beryl crossed over to the cot and stared down at it. With hands on hips she confronted him. "No way, José."

"Sorry?"

"You have a business you've been ignoring for weeks."

"Damn it, Beryl! To hell with the business! Where's your sense of compassion?"

"With your investors and the scores of people

who'll be standing on unemployment lines if you don't pull yourself together and get back to work!"

"I'm not leaving her!"

Beryl pushed her gray-streaked bangs off her forehead and snorted. "Look, Logan, no one wanted you to fall in love more than I did. But moping around a hospital room isn't helping Emma, and it's sure as hell not doing anything for you. A lot of families depend on you for their livelihoods. What would Emma tell you?"

Logan looked across the room at James and Kevin. In their eyes he saw Emma staring back at him.

"She's right," said James. "Besides, we'll be here."

Logan considered Beryl's words, knowing they made sense. He just felt so damn helpless. He threw his head back, rubbed his eyes, and took a weary breath. "All right," he finally agreed, "but I'm still spending my nights here."

Beryl glanced at the makeshift bed. "Fine with me. It's your back. I'll line up a good chiropractor—just in case."

"Always looking out for me, aren't you?"

"Someone has to. Although I wouldn't mind relinquishing the responsibility." Jutting her chin toward Emma, she added, "To the right person, of course."

Then she swung her head around and winked at Kevin and James.

Chapter 37

Leslee smiled across the table at Marty. She wished she could read his mind. The cagey little shit hadn't mentioned a word about his ransacked room. His only complaint all evening? The paltry number of shrimp in his seafood primavera! She clicked her long carmine fingernails against the side of her espresso cup and continued contributing to the evening's small talk.

Marty was definitely up to something. He'd expected someone to come after the videotape and photos. She had to destroy that evidence! Leslee shuddered to think what might happen if the tape surfaced. Marty's pictures would exonerate Emma and implicate her—not only in the thefts but in Phillip's murder.

No one would believe how hard she'd worked to revive Phillip after discovering his lifeless body. She loved him! Her entire life had centered on Phillip Wadsworth. She never could have killed him!

Her plan had been foolproof. After Logan jilted

her, she'd fabricated a diary that implicated Emma as Korat's accomplice and Phillip's murderer. She'd loaded the diary onto Phillip's computer, planted the evidence in his safe. Everything pointing to Emma. Except Leslee hadn't counted on Marty sticking his damn camera where it didn't belong. Now those fake diaries, the jewels, the spreadsheets—all of it meant to finger Emma—could very well boomerang and screw Leslee big time. She couldn't let that happen. The police and D.A. must never suspect anyone other than Emma.

Leslee had worked too long and too hard to let some slimy scumbag of a photographer destroy her. No! She wanted the satisfaction of seeing Emma in prison, and she'd do whatever it took to make certain that happened. If she couldn't get hold of the tape, she'd have to see that Marty Bell never had the opportunity to sell it.

Voices. Distant voices.

"Mr. Crawford?" The voice belonged to a woman, but Emma didn't recognize it. "We need to do a few things in here. Why don't the four of you get something to eat downstairs? It won't take us long."

Someone held her hand. Logan. She recognized his touch. She felt him let go, felt his lips on hers, heard him mumble something. The sounds of footsteps surrounded her, then grew faint.

Finally . . . finally . . . finally.

"So what do you think?" another woman's voice asked.

"About?"

Emma sensed them walking around her, but she couldn't see anything. No matter how hard she concentrated, she couldn't open her eyes. They poked and prodded her body. Something was wrapped around her arm and tightened.

"One hundred over seventy."

Where am I? What's happening? She tried to speak, but the sounds were blocked by a drumming chant that grew louder and louder.

Finally . . . finally . . . finally.

"You think she did what the papers claim?"

Something was stuck in her ear. The incessant repetition increased in tempo, rising to a crescendo pitch.

Finally . . . finally . . . finally.

"Ninety-nine point two."

I'm in a prison hospital! What was the last thing she remembered? Harper. Murder. Someone grabbing her hands behind her back. *Help me!* Feeling sick. Pounding. *I can't breathe!* Spinning.

Mom!

Emma!

Blackness.

And the unrelenting taunt of *Finally . . . finally . . . finally.* The word haunted her, forcing its way into every thought.

"Anything's possible, but I tend to doubt it."

"Why?" A loud grunt punctuated the question. Emma felt the sheet pulled taut under her.

"Look at her. Does she look like a murderer?"

I didn't mean to!

"Did Ted Bundy look like a serial killer?"

"Score one point for the woman in white. So what's your theory?"

"I heard rumors her husband abused her. Maybe he forced her to take part in all those thefts. I'll bet one day she decided she'd had enough and did the guy in."

Emma moaned. *No! That's not what happened!*

"Did you say something?"

"No, I thought it was you."

"I'll get the doctor. Stay here with her."

When Logan, James, Kevin, and Beryl returned from the hospital restaurant, they found Dr. Greenwald bending over Emma. He raised her eyelids one at a time, flashing a small light in her pupils. "I think she's coming out of it," he said, straightening up and facing them. "Talk to her as much as possible."

The doctor left. Logan took Emma's hand in one of his and stroked her hair with his other hand. "Wake up, Emma. We won't let them take you back to prison. I swear."

"Logan!" Beryl elbowed him. "Don't make promises you can't keep!"

"She's not going back there!"

"And just how are you going to prevent it?"

"He'll think of something," answered Kevin. He gazed down at his mother. "He has to."

Logan eyed Beryl. "I have to," he repeated. "I . . ." He stopped abruptly and stared down at his hand. "She can hear me! She squeezed my hand! You can hear me, can't you, Emma? Squeeze my hand again, sweetheart."

"Please, Mom!" James leaned over the bed. "You can do it."

Emma's fingers flickered slightly against Logan's palm. Grabbing her by the shoulders, he lifted her off the pillows and into his arms.

She wrapped her arms around him and whispered, "Finally."

"Yes, finally," repeated Logan, lowering Emma back down. Her eyes opened. He smiled down at her, laughing with relief. "It's about time you woke up."

Emma peered up at the four blurry faces hovering in the black emptiness above her and shook her head, struggling past the cobwebs of confusion. Gradually the darkness faded, and both the images and her mind grew sharper. "No . . . Harper . . ." She grappled with the words. "He—"

"He's not here," Logan reassured her. "You're safe."

Once more Emma shook her head and moaned. "No . . . don't . . . understand." She grasped the bedrails and labored to pull herself upright. The effort proved too much. She collapsed back onto the bed, exhausted by the attempt. Panting for breath, her voice filled with panic, she tried once again. "Harper . . . said . . . 'finally.' "

"She's delirious." Logan placed his hand over her brow. "Get the doctor," he told James.

"No. Wait." Beryl grabbed James's arm, but her eyes never left Emma. "She's trying to tell us something."

"Yes." Emma forced the word out between gasps.

"Take your time," said Beryl.

Gradually Emma's panic subsided, her breathing regulated. She closed her eyes and filled her lungs with air, exhaling slowly. Once. Twice. She tried speaking again. The words came haltingly at first, but as she forced them from her brain to her lips, they began to flow. "I heard you . . . talking . . . but I couldn't see you . . . couldn't speak. I tried, but I . . . I . . . everything was black . . . and I couldn't make any sounds."

Logan stroked her cheek. "You were unconscious."

For the first time Emma surveyed her surroundings, her gaze darting from one end of the room to the other. A subtle pastel print covered the walls. Across from her bed a large picture window, devoid of bars, framed a gray Philadelphia skyline. Assorted floral arrangements lined the sill. A metal pole, holding an IV bag, stood beside her bed. Emma followed the course of the tube that snaked from the bottom of the bag, over the bedrail, and into her arm.

"I'm not in prison?"

"You're in the hospital," he assured her.

She reached for his hand. Clutching it with both of hers, she attempted once more to convey her thoughts, anxious for him to understand the revelation that had come to her in the black void. "A word kept repeating . . . over and over. Like a drum, pounding inside me. It wouldn't stop. And then, when I heard you talking about Harper, the pounding grew faster and louder, and the word screamed inside my head."

"What word?"

"Finally."

"Finally?" Her pronouncement met with puzzlement. Four confused faces stared down at her.

Sensing the importance of the connection, Emma took another deep breath and pushed forward with her explanation. "I know it sounds strange, but . . . when Harper first arrested me . . . at the house . . . before they led me outside . . ." Her voice faltered. Her eyes filled with tears, the memory of the day rekindling her fear.

"Go slowly," whispered Logan.

Swallowing her fear, she proceeded, the words spilling out at an ever-increasing pace as she recounted the event. "He wore a vicious smirk. His eyes were cold . . . mean. They raked over me. I could feel the hate emanating from them.

"Then he said, 'finally.' At first I was confused. I remember thinking, finally what? But now I understand." Emma released her grip on Logan's hand and expelled a long sigh. She studied the four faces hovering above her, anticipating their reaction to her next statement. "I don't know why, but I'm certain Harper had been waiting a very long time for that moment."

For several seconds, no one spoke, the weight of Emma's words settling in on them. Finally, James broke the silence with the one question on everyone's mind. "Why?"

Logan glanced briefly at both boys before shifting his attention to Beryl. "I think it's time we learned more about Mr. Roy Harper," he said.

Beryl nodded in agreement. "Mind if I take along a couple of assistants?"

"As long as it's all right with their mother."

Consternation clouded Emma's features. "You're not going to do anything that could get them in trouble, are you?"

"Strictly recon," Beryl assured her. "An innocent trip to the library, a quiet visit to the newspaper morgue. Maybe a perusal of certain City Hall records. I only ferret it out and dig it up. Then I hand it off to the refined gentlemen standing before you."

Still uncertain as to how she felt about Beryl, Emma hesitated to give her consent. Although she accepted that the woman's heart was in the right place, she still questioned her methods and judgment. Emma didn't want Beryl influencing James and Kevin. She reluctantly agreed only after a fair amount of pleading from both boys—that and Kevin's threat to otherwise personally wring the truth from Harper with his own two hands. One Wadsworth in jail was more than enough.

After Beryl left with the boys in tow, Logan said, "You had me worried there for a while, you know." He lowered the bedrail and perched on the edge of the mattress.

She gazed up at him and smiled. "You're still here."

"Of course I'm still here. Why wouldn't I be?"

Emma closed her eyes and turned her head away from him. "I expected you to leave when you found out what I'd done."

Logan emptied a lungful of frustration. He lowered his face until it was mere inches from hers. His words, although whispered, took on the tone of a general commanding his troops. "You did *nothing* wrong. That damn sonofabitch brought about his own death. If you persist in taking responsibility, he's won. Is that what you want?"

His question hit like a shower of icy water. Had she survived sixteen years of living with Phillip only to succumb once she was free? In death, had Phillip taken from her what she refused to relinquish to him during his life? Had the vulture finally stripped its prey to the bare bones, leaving it devoid of everything save a victim's mentality?

Searching her mind for answers, Emma traveled back to that steamy August night and attempted to view the drama as an impartial observer and not a participant. Had she known at the time that Phillip had suffered a heart attack, or had undeserved guilt planted the idea in her mind afterward?

All she could remember was the desperate need to escape. To run as far from her husband as possible. And later, when she reluctantly returned, she'd feared a confrontation with him. Yet how could she have dreaded a confrontation if she'd known she left him suffering a potentially fatal heart attack?

Because I didn't know!

She had fled, convinced that Phillip had passed out from overindulging in one of his many vices. Which, like Leslee, he probably had. She hadn't seen him collapse. One moment Phillip was flinging curses at her. The next, he was on top of her. But she'd heard no gasp of pain, no moaning sounds to suggest anything was wrong. The coronary may have occurred well after she left the house.

"It's not my fault," she whispered, the realization sinking in and lifting the burden of guilt from her. A light-headed giddiness overcame her. She started laughing. Tears streamed down her face, but they were tears of joy, not of fear or sorrow. "It's not my fault," she repeated, this time louder and more assertive. "It's not my fault!"

Logan lifted her into his arms and held her close to his chest. He released a long sigh of pent-up anxiety. His spunky fighter was back. Major obstacles loomed ahead. Emma still faced felony indictments, but he was convinced they'd just won the biggest battle.

Chapter 38

Blowing on his hands and stomping his feet to keep warm, Marty huddled under the building overhang and grumbled about the lack of information coming from inside the hospital.

"Quit your bitching, Bell." Derrick Morse, a reporter with *Scoop*, glared at him. "We're all freezing our balls off 'cause of you."

"Like hell!"

"Yeah? Who broke the story about Crawford and the broad? If it weren't for you, we'd all be on the Riviera chasing after Prince Chuckie and Horse Face."

"Or club crawling with the Hiltons in L.A.," broke in a cameraman from *Celebrity Edition*. "But, no. Thanks to the *Daily Tattler*, my dick's getting frostbite in Philadelphia."

"You could just as easily have pulled an assignment staking out Kate Winslet on location in Russia," countered Marty. "You think it's cold in Philadelphia? This is paradise compared to Moscow in March."

Plummeting temperatures swiftly changed an icy drizzle to a light snowfall, but the die-hard core of journalists and photographers remained camped outside the hospital. Each hoped to outscoop the others with breaking news concerning the mysterious and sudden hospitalization of Emma Wadsworth. Speculation among the gossipmongers ran two-to-one in favor of a suicide attempt, with those believing otherwise split evenly between various theories. All were in agreement, however, that the official report of a viral infection was nothing more than a cover-up.

But after freezing their butts off for over a day, Marty and the rest of the tabloid crews had come no closer to uncovering the real reason for Emma's admittance. Crawford remained cloistered inside the hospital with her, and try as they might, no one could pry any information from hospital personnel. When lucrative bribes failed to open any mouths, Marty assumed Crawford had paid mightily for their silence.

Marty concluded nothing monumental was about to happen. And he could do without the blame hurling from jealous colleagues. "I don't need to take this shit from you assholes. I'm outta here." He muscled his way through the pack to the sidewalk. Then, with his face to the ever-increasing wind, he strode briskly down the street to his Explorer.

Once inside, he turned the heater up full blast and waited for the welcoming warmth to penetrate his raw bones. He was about to head back to the Doubletree when he spied Crawford's assistant and the broad's brats exiting through a service door at the rear of the hospital. Marty watched them hail a cab on Walnut Street. He shifted his SUV into drive and peeled away from the curb, speeding around the corner just as the light changed.

A car horn blared, followed closely by the sound of

screeching brakes and a dull, metallic thud. As he slipped into traffic behind the taxi, Marty glanced into his rearview mirror. Passersby were gathering around the aftermath of a minor collision between a red Subaru and a black Jeep Cherokee that had also tried to beat out the light.

"Gotcha!" Marty licked his right index finger and added a mark to an imaginary tally in the air. "Score one for the Bellmeister."

With one hand draped over the steering wheel, the other drumming his thigh to the beat of Roy Orbison singing "Pretty Woman" on the oldies station, Marty followed the cab. The taxi wove through noontime traffic, fought its way around City Hall, and headed west on the Benjamin Franklin Parkway toward the Four Seasons. But instead of pulling up to the hotel entrance as Marty expected, the cab cut across the Parkway toward Vine Street.

When it pulled up in front of an imposing granite building, Marty eased into an illegal spot on the next block. From his passenger side mirror, he watched as the three exited the cab and entered the building. After cutting his engine, Marty grabbed his camera, jumped from his Explorer and hustled down the street after them.

"What the hell?" He stared up at the name spelled out on the building and scratched his jaw. He certainly hadn't expected to find himself at The Free Library of Philadelphia. Puzzled by the turn of events but convinced he was better off on a wild goose chase than waiting for scraps outside the hospital, Marty followed his quarry inside.

By the time he entered the lobby, Crawford's gofer and the brats were nowhere in sight. Methodically moving from room to room, Marty eventually caught up with them on the second floor in the Newspaper

Center. A cavernous room with high ceilings and large windows, the area overflowed with reading tables, metal shelving, and computer terminals.

The broad and the brats sat with their backs to him, hunched over microfilm readers along the far wall. He grabbed a newspaper off a rack and crept across the marble floor to a nearby table, positioning himself out of view but within earshot.

For hours he watched and listened as the bitch moved back and forth from a computer terminal to the microfilm viewer. Periodically she passed slips of paper to a library assistant, who scurried up to the balcony, replaced viewed microfilm, then returned with a fresh batch.

"Hmm," said the bitch. "This is strange." She moved from the microfilm viewer back to the computer terminal. "His official bio states he received a BS from the University of Indiana and a JD from Purdue, but neither school has a record of him."

Both of the brats joined her, leaning over her shoulders to study the information on the monitor.

"So either he really isn't a lawyer and lied about his credentials—" said one of them.

"Or he changed his name," suggested the other. He elbowed the bitch out of her chair. "Let me try something."

"What are you doing?" she asked. The other kid leaned over and whispered something in her ear. "A hacker?"

"Shh!" The kid who'd muscled his way in front of the computer spun around in the chair and glared at the other two. "Announce it to the whole friggin' library, why don't you, Jimbo?" He turned his attention back to the screen, his fingers flying across the keyboard.

"What are you doing?" she asked.

"Trying to access his social security number. Once I have that, I should be able to discover his former identity if he changed his name. Assuming he did it legally. If not, he probably has a new number to go along with the new name, and I strike out."

As he manipulated the keys, the other two hovered close behind him, shielding the monitor from view. Marty was about to change seats in the hope of gaining a glimpse of the screen when the brat at the computer yelled, "Bingo!"

Marty bolted from the table, camera ready, intent on capturing whatever information had popped onto the monitor. He ducked behind a tall shelf, poked his zoom lens through the stacks, and took aim. But before he could shoot, the bitch shifted slightly to the right, blocking his view. "Damn!" he muttered under his breath.

Repositioning himself, he noticed the brothers' exuberant mood had died. The two boys were staring in disbelief at the monitor. "We'd better get back to the hospital," said one of them. He reached across his brother's shoulder and flicked off the monitor before Marty could shoot.

Chapter 39

Gordon Atwell, the senior partner of the prestigious law firm of Atwell and Rush, leaned back in the vinyl hospital chair and studied Emma. He was a tall, imposing man who had made a name for himself as an NBA center before turning his attention to criminal defense. Years of applying expert strategies both on the court and in the courts had given him a much-envied reputation. In his thirty-year professional career he'd never lost a championship game nor a case. Emma prayed his luck would hold out.

"You believe me?" she asked. For the past hour she'd related the tale of her life as Mrs. Phillip Wadsworth, forcing herself to divulge to this stranger secrets she'd kept from everyone else. Throughout the ordeal Logan held her hand, buoying her with a gentle squeeze whenever the memories threatened to overcome her. On more than one occasion she took a deep breath and urged herself forward. *I can do this.* She silently repeated the affirmation each time her voice faltered. *I can do this.* She'd glance over at Logan and see the soundless reply in his eyes and feel it in his touch.

You can do this.

Emma had insisted Logan remain throughout her questioning by the attorney, although Atwell warned her that lawyer/client confidentiality didn't extend to him.

"He could be subpoenaed by the prosecution," said Atwell.

"I'm not telling you anything Logan hasn't already heard." With that Atwell reluctantly agreed.

Emotionally exhausted, Emma collapsed against the pillows propped behind her on the bed and held her breath, waiting for the attorney's answer.

"I believe you," he said. "But keep in mind, without proof we have an uphill battle in front of us. According to the diaries Harper obtained from the computer in your house, you killed your husband with a substance that created the appearance of a massive coronary. I'm assuming that might be a reference to digitalis. At any rate, it's unfortunate you had the body cremated. We can't do toxicology studies on ashes."

"But what about the coroner's report?" asked Logan.

Emma knew the report wouldn't help them. Phillip was twenty pounds overweight. He suffered from high blood pressure, high cholesterol, and high living. With no signs of foul play and a corpse that had obviously succumbed to a heart attack, the coroner had deemed an autopsy unwarranted. Besides, Dr. O'Hara was a close friend of Ned and Molly Ralston. Wanting to protect her friend from the humiliation of a public disclosure of Phillip's drug habits, Molly had persuaded the doctor to forgo the autopsy. Unfortunately, Molly's well-intentioned intercession had backfired. An autopsy would have cleared Emma of murder charges.

"On the other hand," suggested Atwell, "perhaps it's better that we don't have a body to exhume. An autopsy may have revealed that Phillip *was* murdered."

"But I didn't give him anything," insisted Emma.

"I'm not suggesting you did," said Atwell. He rose from his chair, his massive six-foot-seven-inch frame towering over her, "but someone else may have."

"Who?"

"Whoever forged the diaries. Someone may have wanted Phillip out of the way and decided you were the perfect person to frame for his murder."

"Leslee forged the diaries," said Logan.

"Speculation," replied Atwell. "Where's your proof?"

"I'm working on it."

"I wish I could see those diaries," said Emma. "Am I not entitled to that much? How can I prove I didn't write something when I don't have access to it?"

"I'm working on *that*," said Atwell. He stared out the window as if mulling over some detail in his mind. "The D.A. is keeping his evidence close to the cuff right now, but he'll have to turn copies of everything over to us before the preliminary hearing. Meanwhile, I'm going to attempt to get bail for you, arguing that the evidence Harper has is all circumstantial. Since the diaries aren't handwritten, he has no proof that you wrote them."

Within minutes of Emma awakening from her coma, Harper had tried sending her back to prison, but Dr. Greenwald bought her precious time by insisting she remain for several days of observation and additional testing. The D.A. had little choice but to acquiesce.

"Maybe Harper forged the diaries," suggested Emma. Both men stared at her.

"His motive?" asked Atwell.

Emma related the revelation that had come to her earlier. "He hates me," she said. "I don't know why. I've never said more than a half-dozen words to the man, but I see it in his eyes. The intensity of it frightens me."

"And it should," said James, bursting into the room. Kevin and Beryl followed on his heels. He approached his mother's bed and bent over to kiss her cheek.

"What is it?" she asked. "What did you find out?"

"Roy Harper's real name is Royce Stephens, Jr.," James said

Emma gasped. No wonder the man hated her. Twenty-nine years ago a ten-year-old boy had sworn revenge against her family, blaming them for his father's death. He was now fulfilling that vow. "Are you sure?"

Kevin nodded. "Positive. He legally changed his name two years before moving back to Philadelphia."

Emma closed her eyes and rubbed at the stabbing pain invading her temples. She had already relived too many painful memories for one day. Now this. "There's a very good possibility Phillip never was Korat, and Leslee is perfectly innocent," she said, staring at first her attorney, then Logan.

The two men dropped their jaws in unison, gawking at her as if she were speaking in tongues. She ignored the disbelief written across their faces and continued. "Royce Stephens, Sr. was the drunk driver who killed my parents. Two hours after he was indicted for vehicular homicide, he hanged himself in his jail cell.

"His wife and young son publicly blamed the city

and my family. Royce, Jr. vowed to avenge his father's death. Nobody took the rantings of a ten-year-old seriously, though, and within weeks he and his mother left town. No one ever heard from either of them again." She looked up at Logan. "Until now."

After Gordon Atwell departed, Beryl turned to James and Kevin. "Five's a crowd. How about the three of us get a bite over at the Hard Rock?"

"You like the Hard Rock?" asked James.

Beryl lowered her glasses and peered over the rims at him. "Kid, I was rocking to The Beatles when half the world still thought they were misspelled bugs."

"Back in the Stone Age?" asked Kevin.

Beryl whipped her head around and sneered at him. "Just for that I won't tell you about the week I spent in Aruba with Mick Jagger and Keith Richards."

Kevin turned to Logan. "Is she serious?"

"Beryl's led a rather interesting life. You'll have to decide on your own what to believe."

"Awesome!" He grabbed Beryl's hand. "Let's go!" Kevin pushed his brother out in front of him and dragged Beryl from behind. At the door he paused to blow a hasty kiss to his mother.

Emma laughed and waved them out the door. "That was nice of her," she said to Logan after the door closed behind the threesome.

"You're not upset that the boys were so eager to desert you?"

"They weren't deserting me." She smiled up at him. "They were giving us some time alone."

"Thoughtful guys." Logan sat down alongside her on the bed and draped one arm around her shoulders. With his other hand he reached for the television remote and pointed it at the TV suspended from the ceiling. "Let's see what's going on in the rest of the world."

"Good evening, and welcome to the six o'clock news. Our lead story tonight is the attempted suicide of prominent Chestnut Hill socialite Emma Brockton Wadsworth. Unnamed sources tell us that Mrs. Wadsworth, widow of billionaire Phillip Wadsworth and recently linked to flamboyant billionaire developer Logan Crawford, was rushed to Thomas Jefferson University Hospital yesterday, the victim of an apparent overdose of prescription narcotics.

"Although unconfirmed at this time, Channel Ten has learned from a reliable source that Mrs. Wadsworth, out on bail for the alleged possession of stolen goods and suspected as being the accomplice of the notorious jewel thief Korat, was about to be arrested for the murder of her husband.

"Phillip Wadsworth, whom police now believe was Korat, died late last August, presumably from a massive coronary. Sources now tell us the district attorney's office has proof he was murdered, and his wife is the prime suspect in that murder. Stay tuned to Channel Ten for updates on this breaking story.

"On to other news—"

Logan bounded from the bed, stormed across the room, and slammed his fist against the wall. "That sonofabitch! Unnamed sources, my ass!"

He spun around at the sound of a half-stifled sob. Emma sat on the bed, staring wide-eyed at the now darkened screen, the remote still clutched in her hand. "His father stole my parents from me," she said. "Why am I paying for that?"

"Because he's a sick, twisted bastard. But don't worry. There's no way in hell he's getting away with this."

Chapter 40

"I suppose you're the 'reliable source'?" asked Marty. He swirled his glass of Scotch, pretending to concentrate on the ice cubes clinking against the side of the heavy tumbler. Out of the corner of his eye, he studied Leslee's poker-faced expression for any signs of cracks. Although he didn't trust her worth a dime, he was fascinated by this game of cat and mouse she played with him. Far from the fool she took him for, Marty wanted her to go on believing he was—at least until he figured out what she was up to.

Leslee aimed the remote at the screen and clicked off the television. "Of course not. But nonetheless, this is a delicious little twist to events, isn't it?" Her eyes alight with malicious fire, she slowly stroked the tip of her tongue across her lips.

Marty really didn't care about her vendetta against Crawford and the Wadsworth broad. From the start he was in it, as he was in all things, for the money. His photos of the couple had brought him big bucks.

But now the stakes had risen. The photos didn't amount to jack compared to the fat wad he suspected Leslee had stashed away from all those jewel heists. Not to mention the megabucks additional thefts could net with the right new partner. Him.

He pursed his lips and tossed her a loud kiss. Who would have guessed the bleached-blond bimbo had such talents? But Marty played a mean game of poker. He held all the aces, and only *he* knew Leslee's little secret. Unless she cut him in on the hand, she'd soon find herself with nothing but deuces. And they wouldn't be wild.

Leslee stood, stretching languidly. Her large, ripe breasts strained against the buttons of her silk blouse. She smiled a wicked, suggestive smile. "I'm in the mood for Italian, lover. Let's stroll down to South Philly and catch a bite. There's a great little place at Fourth and Bainbridge."

Marty reached up, wrapped his arms around her waist, and pulled her onto his lap. "I'm in the mood for Leslee Howell, baby, and I can get a bite of her right here."

She broke from his grasp and squirmed off his lap. "Later, lover. I really am famished." She grabbed his coat from a side chair where he'd earlier discarded it and tossed it at him. "I'll make it up to you when we get back." She slipped into her sable, hugged the fur to her cheeks, and pouted. "I promise."

"This is going to cost you big time, lady." He shrugged into his coat. "I'll drive. It's too cold to walk."

"A big he-man like you hampered by a little chill? Come now, Marty."

"I thought you were starving. Walking all the way down to Fourth and Bainbridge will take close to half an hour."

Leslee sidled up to him. She rubbed her leg between his and nipped at his ear lobe. "You don't want me to get fat from all that pasta, do you? I need to walk off some calories before I eat."

"I can think of a better way to burn calories, baby." He grabbed for her breast and began massaging it. "Then we can drive to the restaurant."

Leslee bit down on his lobe. Hard.

"Oww!"

"I told you I'm hungry."

"Bitch, you're going to pay for that." He pinched her nipple. "Big time."

"Whatever you say, lover. After we have dinner."

Darkness draped across Society Hill. Only an occasional street lamp or the soft, muted glow coming from behind curtained windows lit their path. Fighting a harsh wind, Marty and Leslee walked south on Third Street. Wispy clouds hid the stars and shrouded a thin crescent moon, creating an eerie backdrop to the deserted streets. Marty pulled his collar up around his neck and complained. "That's it! I'm going back for the car. It's as cold as a witch's tit out here."

She reached over and grabbed his arm. "No. Wait. If you're that cold, we can catch a cab on Pine Street. It'll be faster than going back."

With a grumble, Marty trudged on. Pine Street was still two blocks ahead, but Leslee was right. His Explorer was parked in a lot four blocks in the opposite direction. His toes grew numb. He glanced down at Leslee's feet. A slave to fashion, she was probably turning blue inside her suede stiletto pumps, even with that full-length sable coat wrapped around her. She'd never give him the satisfaction of admitting it, though. Then again, Leslee Howell was such a cold bitch, maybe she was impervious to the frigid temperatures.

Walking with his head bowed to the wind, Marty didn't notice a lone figure wearing a ski mask step from the alley between two town houses until the burly man blocked his path. When he looked up, he came face-to-face with a .357 Magnum. "D . . . Don't shoot," he pleaded. "My wallet's in my pants pocket."

From behind him he heard a hoarse laugh and felt the cold, hard metal of a second gun against the back of his head.

"Yo, man! Butthead here thinks we're gonna rob him." With the ski mask covering his assailant's face, Marty couldn't see the man's expression, but the derision in his voice sent a wave of fear coursing through him.

"I guess he's in for a big surprise," said the man behind him. He jabbed Marty with the barrel of the gun. "Okay, stud, into the car. Nice and easy."

Afraid to comply, but more afraid not to, Marty shifted his eyes from the man in front of him to Leslee. She'd stepped away from him and was standing alongside the first gunman. Too late Marty understood the depths of her depravity.

"Good-bye, Marty," she said, her voice tinged with satisfaction.

"Leslee, please!"

She ignored him. "Get him out of my sight," she told the gunman standing in front of him.

"Make a sound, and you get it right here," said the gruff-voiced man. He grabbed Marty's arm and forced him over to an SUV parked at the curb.

In the dim light cast by a corner street lamp, Marty recognized the car as a black Jeep Cherokee. A black Jeep Cherokee with streaks of red paint imbedded on the dented rear fender. Had Leslee's thugs been following him all day, waiting for the right opportunity to snuff him?

The two goons shoved him into the backseat. One of the gunmen climbed in beside him and pressed the gun against his ribs. Marty cowered. And prayed for a miracle. With nothing to lose, he begged his captors for his life. "Whatever she's paying you," he said, "I'll double it. Triple it. Just let me go. I'll never say a word to anyone."

A snide laugh greeted his offer. "You ain't got that kind of money, pal. Besides, Leslee don't like being double-crossed. Makes her real mean."

Marty was living proof of that. Soon he'd be dead proof if he didn't think of something fast. But thinking wasn't easy when you were speeding down I-95 toward your grave. Marty suspected they were headed for the marshes south of the airport. The swamps, with their reputation as a favorite gangland dumping ground, held many an unsolved mystery. The muddy environs, polluted from years of industrial waste, quickly decomposed any corpse unlucky enough to end up there. By the time the remote area was dredged for his remains, if it ever was, there wouldn't be much of anything to find.

With Gunman Number One zipping around cars at breakneck speed and Gunman Number Two releasing the gun's safety, Marty's options were reduced to praying for a crash—one that left his captors dead and him uninjured. When he heard the distant sound of sirens growing louder by the second, he became a believer in the power of prayer.

"Shit!" The driver pounded the steering wheel and stared into his rearview mirror. "That asshole creeping along at just the speed limit back there was an unmarked car. If he pulls us over, we're toast."

Marty craned his neck. Bright lights rapidly approached from behind them. He prayed harder.

"Turn around!" Gunman Number Two forced the gun deeper into his ribs. "Outrun them," he ordered the driver.

Gunman Number One floored the gas pedal, forcing the Jeep onto two wheels as the vehicle careened around an eighteen-wheeler in the center lane of traffic. The violent maneuver propelled Gunman Number Two into Marty, sandwiching him against the door. A swerve in the opposing direction hurled them back against the opposite door with Marty now on top. Before he could move, he was shoved to the floor and pinned down with two steel-tipped boots, one at his neck, the other at his groin.

His assassin gripped the Magnum in both hands, leaned over him, and held the barrel of the gun to his forehead. "I can just as easily blow you away here, motherfucker. Don't make no difference to me. Dead is dead."

"You'll . . . you'll mess up your car," said Marty, playing for time. In the background he heard two more sirens joining the chase.

"Screw the car! It's hot." He forced his boots farther into Marty, bracing himself against the recoil.

"Wait!" Half-strangled by the foot against his windpipe, rivulets of sweat pouring down his face, Marty tried one last, desperate measure to halt his execution. "Shoot me here, and you'll hit the gas tank. You'll die with me."

It worked! Marty gulped in a lungful of air as the gunman eased up on the pressure against his neck. Every second of life he could buy himself helped—as long as they didn't outrun the cops.

From his position on the floor, he could no longer see the road, but a long, sharp turn convinced him they were exiting the expressway. A moment later, screeching tires, colliding metal, and breaking glass sent his stomach acids into a tailspin. The sirens grew still, and Marty feared his luck had run out.

"Douse the lights, and take the next right," directed Gunman Number Two. Over the next several miles he continued directing the driver, who never let up on the gas, through a series of turns.

Marty wondered how many bodies the gunmen had dumped in the reedy marsh waters surrounding them. In the inky blackness of night he could barely see the gun stuck in his face, yet the driver sped around turns with a frightening familiarity. Were they headed for a favorite burial bog or simply winding back and forth to make sure they'd lost the cops? He strained to hear additional sirens, but an eerie silence, broken only by the sound of the tires speeding along the rutted roadway, filled the night air.

"Pull over up ahead." Gunman Number Two yanked Marty back onto the seat and held the gun to his temple. "We'll off him here."

As the car slowed to a stop along the side of the road, Marty said one final prayer.

The gunman reached across his body to open the door. "Welcome to your eternal resting place," he said. He was about to push Marty out in front of him when a series of lights appeared along the ridge on the road ahead of them.

"Shit! Hang on!" The driver floored the gas pedal, spinning the car around a hundred and eighty degrees. The sudden turn jerked Marty out of the gunman's grip, pitching him from the car.

Tires squealed. As Marty flew through the air, the gunman fired off two shots, one coming within inches of Marty's head, the other grazing his sleeve before he landed face down in a half-frozen pile of decaying muck. Blaring sirens and answering gunfire filled the air around him.

Spitting mud from his mouth, Marty lifted his head in time to see dozens of red and blue lights speed along the road in front of him. As he staggered to his feet, a deafening explosion rocked the ground, engulfing the sky in an enormous orange fireball. The force of the blast hurled him backward into a ditch. He landed with a thud, his head striking something hard.

The world went black.

Chapter 41

When Logan entered Emma's room the following morning, he found her frowning at a newspaper article. Several other dailies and tabloids were spread across the bed. With Emma once again conscious, he'd spent the night at the hotel suite with James and Kevin. She was still uncomfortable having her sons in Philadelphia. Knowing the boys thought themselves impervious to the bloodthirsty press, Logan had offered to keep an eye on them. Now viewing the scandal sheets covering her bed and the deep worry lines set into the corners of her mouth, he wondered if he'd made the right decision. Perhaps he should have stayed at the hospital and let Beryl keep an eye on James and Kevin.

"Where did you get those?"

"One of the nurses brought them for me."

"Why upset yourself?"

She jutted her chin at the front-page story in the *Philadelphia Inquirer* and scowled. "Knowledge is power. I thought if I read the statements coming out of Harper's office, I might find a discrepancy in his story—some clue that could prove he's framing me."

Logan smiled at the feistiness in her voice. Now that she no longer blamed herself for Phillip's death, she was determined not to let Harper destroy her. The fighter was back. He perched on the edge of the mattress. "Find anything?"

Emma shook her head. Her brow furrowed. She swatted the paper. "All reports quote 'reliable, unnamed sources.' The smarmy rat's being very careful." She chewed her lower lip and eyed Logan. "Did you know this was not my first suicide attempt?"

"What!"

"According to yet *another* unnamed source, one close to the accused murderer"—Emma pointed to herself—"*moi*, I've tried on several other occasions to end my life." She threw her hands up in disgust and shrieked, "Do you believe this? I've never tried to kill myself! Where do they get these lies? What gives them the right to do this to me?"

Logan watched as she pummeled the mattress with her fists, allowing her to vent the pent-up frustration. He viewed the anger as a good sign, far better than the guilt she'd worn like a shroud for so long. The anger would empower her, not defeat her the way the guilt had threatened to.

"Talk about fickle!" As she continued her tirade, her voice rose several octaves. "Even the legitimate press has turned against me. Have they seen any proof of these accusations? No! But they're willing to try me and convict me based on nothing more than the speculations and innuendoes of a corrupt D.A.! Damn them all!"

She pounded the mattress one final time for emphasis, then collapsed back against the pillows. Her face red, her lips pursed tight, with narrowed eyes she glared straight ahead. "I'm not a thief! I'm not a murderer! Roy Harper is *not* going to get away with this!"

Then, like a leaky balloon, the fight seeped from her. Sadness shadowed her face, and her misting eyes mirrored her deflated spirits. Rising from the bed, she walked across the room to the window. She pushed aside the partly drawn drapes and silently stared out across the city. Her shoulders slumped in defeat.

Alarmed by the swift reversal of attitude and the sudden change of emotion, Logan joined her at the window. "What is it?"

A short, ironic laugh escaped her lips. "Who am I kidding? Even if I prove my innocence, people will always remember all the horrible things I've been accused of. They'll point and stare and whisper behind my back for the rest of my life, always wondering if the rumors were true. They'll claim I got off because I could afford an expensive attorney. Like O. J. Simpson. Or Michael Jackson." She twisted her neck around and gazed up at him with eyes that were hollow and lifeless. "The rich are different. You know that. At least that's what people believe. There's 'us,' and there's 'them.' Separate and not at all equal. They'll dub me the female O. J."

Logan was at a loss for words. Her fears were a frightening possibility. Their only hope was finding irrefutable proof that Emma was the victim of a vengeful, corrupt district attorney. The press had already stripped her naked. He didn't want to think what both they and Harper would do to her once the case came to trial. He couldn't let that happen. They had to expose Roy Harper before court proceedings began.

Until Emma had entered his life, he'd been self-absorbed, a man incapable of loving anyone but himself. Somehow this vulnerable, delicate woman with her tortured past and nightmarish memories had pierced the Tin Woodsman's armor and uncovered his deeply buried heart. From the first time she'd graced him with that sweet, innocent smile of hers, he'd felt the emptiness leeching from him. Emma had given life to a part of him he'd thought lifeless. Emma had given him his heart. Now he had to save her in order to save them both.

Never had he been so determined. And scared shitless.

Chapter 42

A shrill squawk roused Marty. Prying open one eye, then the other, he regarded the source of the noise. Several feet away a group of large blackbirds perched on a rotating Ferris wheel. Gradually, the wheel slowed to a stop and the flock melded into one bird clawing the skeletal remnants of what was once a mattress. Or maybe a couch. Stuffing-dotted springs were all that remained.

Something small and furry scurried across his outstretched hand. Marty jerked at the sight of the long-tailed rodent scampering into the underbrush. The sudden motion sent a sharp pain up his arm and into his neck, joining the dull throbbing in his brain. He reached behind his head and fingered a goose egg–sized lump at the base of his skull. Shivers wracked his body. He raised his head and scowled at the abandoned green pickup half-buried beside him, its rusted-out carcass the likely source of the swelling.

He glanced down at himself. His soggy Burberry

camelhair coat was torn in half a dozen places and spattered with mud. The pants of his Armani suit were in a far worse state. Blood stained the ragged tatters of fabric stuck to his legs. He gingerly bent his legs and cringed in pain when the fabric pulled away from the still-oozing scabs that covered his knees.

As his body moved into a more wakeful state, the events of last night came flooding back. Marty laughed. He was probably suffering from hypothermia and might be on the verge of pneumonia and who-knew-how-many infections from the sludge seeping into his open wounds, but he was alive. He was alive!

Systematically he moved one limb after another, his relief growing with each flexed muscle. The bullets had missed him; he had no broken bones. All in all, his injuries appeared minor—a major miracle, considering he never expected to see the light of another day.

With the corroded truck as support, Marty pulled himself up to a standing position. The effort sent the earth spinning. He grabbed for a rotting fender. Leaning back against the vehicle's front end, he took several long, deep breaths. His body shuddered from the pain, but the ground stopped moving.

As the sun rose, he scanned his bleak surroundings and fought back a sudden panic attack. He was in the middle of nowhere and freezing his balls off. He needed dry clothes, and he needed them fast. He pulled out his cell phone, not that he had a clue who to call, but it hardly mattered; he may have survived the night, but his phone hadn't.

He patted his pants pocket. When he felt his wallet, the panic subsided. As long as he had his credit cards, he'd be all right. *If* he could find a way out of the swamp. With unsure footing but steady determination, he fought his way up the embankment to the road. He wasn't about to give in to the cold or the pain. He had a score to settle.

Once on the deserted road, he spied the burned-out hull of the Jeep Cherokee. With any luck his captors hadn't survived the fiery crash, and Leslee would never know he was still alive. Marty meant to keep it that way. At least until he figured out how to get even.

A thunderous roar pierced the sky. Craning his head, he saw a jet descending rapidly. Within a matter of moments a second plane followed. Then a third. The red-eyes from the West Coast were starting to land, leaving a trail of bread crumbs for him to follow. Forcing his sore limbs into action, Marty headed down the road in the direction of the airport.

At six-thirty the bedside clock radio clicked on, announcing the morning headlines. Rolling onto her back, Leslee waited for the day's weather report. With half an ear she listened to the solemn-voiced announcer ticking off a night's worth of disasters and mayhem.

"Good morning. Radio Headline News time is six-thirty. In the news this hour—the Philadelphia Housing Authority's governing board begins investigations today into the claims of sexual harassment against its executive director, Edward Schuster.

"In other news—testimony resumes this morning in the trial of ten teenagers charged with assaulting an African-American family in Grays Ferry.

"A gunman fatally shot the owner of a convenience store during an overnight holdup in the seven-hundred block of West Cumberland.

"Gunfire erupted in Tinicum Creek early last night during a high-speed chase between police and the occupants of a stolen Jeep Cherokee. Two men perished when the vehicle flipped over and burst into flames.

"In sports—"

Bolting upright, Leslee slapped the radio off and reached for the television remote. She clicked on the local morning news, hoping for a more in-depth report on the victims of the Cherokee blaze.

She jumped out of bed and began pacing the room in long strides. With fists clenched, her long nails carved deep crescent moons into her palms as her patience was tested by half a dozen breakfast cereal, laundry detergent, and laxative commercials. When the anchor's perky face once again filled the screen, she froze midstride and held her breath, waiting for more information on the story.

After a long, drawn-out report on the sexual harassment investigation, complete with interviews of everyone from Edward Schuster's second-in-command to his barber, the anchor finally got around to the incident in Tinicum Creek.

Two bodies were discovered in the Jeep's charred remains. Two unidentified bodies. No report of survivors. Leslee released a lungful of air. Her hired thugs must have disposed of Marty's body prior to the crash.

She collapsed onto the foot of the bed, her entire body numb from relief. With an unsteady hand she aimed the remote at the screen and consigned the pert anchor to television oblivion. She had nothing to fear. Marty was dead. Her secret was safe.

She walked into the living room and sat down at the Louis XIV desk Phillip had bought her on one of their many trips to France. She opened the gilt-edged center drawer and removed a computer disk. With Marty no longer a threat, she could now continue to enjoy her destruction of Emma.

Leslee had expected Harper to leak the diaries by now. She didn't know what that idiot district attorney was waiting for, but she was getting impatient. She wanted Emma back in jail where she belonged, not mollycoddled in some hospital.

Well, she was no stranger to taking matters into her own hands. If Harper wouldn't act, she would. Then she'd sit back and enjoy the horrified reactions of the public once they learned just how evil their precious princess really was.

"For you, my darling," she said, holding the disk up toward a picture of Phillip. She kissed the disk, then blew one at the photograph sitting in a gold-edged frame. Slipping the disk into an envelope, she slid her tongue across the flap, sealed it, and placed it in her briefcase.

Marty found his way out of the marsh and to the airport. Even at this early hour, the terminal was alive with travelers scurrying to catch flights. As he walked down the concourse, heads snapped around and people pointed at the bruised, limping man in the blood- and mud-encrusted clothing.

When a security guard approached him, he offered a well-rehearsed explanation. Looking as sheepish as he could, he told the man, "My girlfriend's husband caught us together at a motel down the road. He . . . uhm . . . ah . . . decided to give me a little incentive to find a new piece of ass."

The stocky officer folded his arms across his chest and eyed him suspiciously. "Yeah, right." He reached out to grab Marty's arm. "Tell me another, bozo."

Marty took a step away from the man and held his ground. "I haven't done anything wrong."

"Fine. You can tell that to my supervisor."

Afraid of any intensive questioning concerning the previous night, Marty whipped out his wallet. "Look, I can show you ID. I'm no vagrant. I've got plenty of money and credit cards with me." He yanked a wad of twenties and fifties from the billfold and waved them in the guard's face.

The man eased off. He rubbed his chin as he eyed Marty and considered his story. "You plannin' on catchin' a flight lookin' like that?"

Marty shook his head. His teeth chattered when he spoke. "This was the nearest place I could get some clean clothes and a hot cup of coffee. Look, you can stay with me the whole time if you don't trust me, but let me get out of these wet things before I freeze to death."

The guard studied him for a moment longer before motioning down the corridor to a souvenir shop. "You can get some stuff in there. The nearest men's room is to the right."

After profusely thanking the guard and adding in a few "God-bless-you's" for good measure, Marty headed for the neon-lit shop. He purchased some basic toiletries, aspirins, first-aid cream, Band-Aids, an Eagles sweat suit, socks, ski cap, and jacket. Before donning the new garments, he cleaned himself as well as he could in the public restroom. Then, filled with several cups of steaming black coffee, he hailed a cab for the nearest hotel.

Chapter 43

"Goddamn it! Of all the—" Logan was at a loss for words. He paced back and forth across the room, screaming into the phone. "I can't leave now! Do something, Henry! File for an appeal or delay or whatever it is I pay your damn firm for. Just don't bother me. Not now!"

He heard the loud sigh across the continent. "Look, Logan. Anita Vincent isn't going away. She's out for blood. She made good on her threat to sue you for slander and defamation. Don't ask me how she did it, but somehow she managed to get a judge to issue an injunction halting your deal with Takamora and the Watts project until the lawsuit is settled."

Logan's blood pressure soared into the danger zone. He shouted into the phone. "He can't do that! The claim is ridiculous!"

"He already did. Bottom line? The sooner you get your ass back to Los Angeles, the sooner we'll be able to get the case dismissed."

Logan muttered a reluctant agreement, hung up the phone, and turned to Beryl. After filling in the gaps of the conversation she hadn't heard, he added, "Get me on the next flight to L.A. Then call Henry back and make arrangements to have me deposed. See if they'll agree to a meeting near the airport. I want this to take as little time as possible." He grabbed his coat and headed for the door.

"Where are you going?"

"Back to the hospital to break the news to Emma."

Beryl grabbed his arm. "Don't worry, champ. The boys and I are here."

Logan sucked in a lungful of air. "Harper. He may try something."

Beryl patted him on the back. "Not to worry."

He scowled his skepticism.

"Hey! It's me. Your pit bull. Remember? Plus, I've got two pit bulls-in-training to help me."

As morose as Logan felt, he couldn't help but laugh. "Emma warned me you'd corrupt those kids. Just don't let her know." He bent down and kissed her cheek. "What would I do without you?"

"Flounder?"

He shook his head as he left the suite, knowing, as usual, Beryl was right.

On the short cab ride from the hotel to the hospital, Logan's apprehension intensified. The last time he'd flown back to L.A., Harper had arrested Emma. He fought off a growing feeling of foreboding. He had to resolve the situation with Anita as quickly as possible. No matter what it cost.

The taxi pulled up in front of the hospital. A throng of reporters and photographers lunged for the cab like addicts clamoring for their daily fix of gossip. He hated to think how they'd weave his current business problems with Anita Vincent into their destruction of Emma. Once word of the lawsuit leaked, the tabloids would salivate.

First Leslee. Now Anita. Emma certainly didn't need another scandal flung at her. It was all his fault. His past held too much dirt, and it was all flying in Emma's direction. Logan sucked in his breath, jumped from the cab, and ran the gauntlet, dodging shouted questions and flashing cameras as best he could.

Less than ten minutes later Beryl called. "You're booked on a one o'clock flight. Henry got them to agree to take the deposition at six tonight at the Hyatt near the airport. Talk fast. The red-eye leaves a little after ten and gets you back in Philly before six tomorrow morning."

"There isn't a later flight?"

"Nada, pal. You miss that one, and you're stuck in L.A. for the night."

"I'll be on it." He hit the END button on his cell phone, flipped the case closed, and slipped it back into his breast pocket.

Emma sat curled up in a chair in front of the window. Her legs bent snug against her body, crossed arms resting atop her knees, she stared out at the overcast cityscape. Logan leaned over the back of the chair and buried his face in her hair. "I have to leave."

"I know." She reached up and stroked his cheek. "Don't worry about me. I'm safe here."

He glanced over at the closed door and drew in a deep breath. Slowly he released it along with a silent prayer. He drew her into his arms and kissed her. "You mean everything to me."

He reluctantly broke the kiss. She lifted her head, and their eyes met. In hers he saw hopelessness hiding beneath the surface. It tore him apart. How could he leave her to face Harper alone? For all her bravado and vows to beat him, Logan knew she was scared.

And there was something else. Another secret she hid from him. One that should be the source of great joy, not trepidation. Poor Emma. He'd guessed her secret but kept it to himself. If only she'd learn to trust him. But her past still held her back.

Logan knew patience and time were his allies. He refrained from broaching the subject. Emma possessed an inner strength that had sustained her for years. He needed to believe she'd work through her anxieties and find the courage to face him. She must, as much for herself as for him.

"Go," she said, moving out of his embrace. "You'll miss your plane."

Marty sat in a rental car across from the hospital. He kept an eye on the main entrance, waiting for Logan Crawford to leave. He couldn't risk joining the crowd of paparazzi hovering under the portico. If his face showed up on the evening news, Leslee would know he was alive.

He was surprised to see Crawford leave the hospital and hail a taxi shortly after he'd arrived. Pulling into traffic behind the departing cab, Marty followed, planning to confront Crawford when the taxi dropped him off at the hotel. But the cab bypassed the Four Seasons and headed south on the expressway, speeding toward the airport. When it pulled up in front of the terminal, Marty was right behind it. Leaving the motor running, he jumped from the rented Dodge Neon and clambered after his prey. "Crawford!"

Crawford stopped short just inside the terminal.

He spun around, nearly collided with Marty. "You don't learn, do you, Bell?"

"Hear me out. I've got something you need."

Brushing Marty aside, Logan strode off. "In your dreams, Bell."

Marty persisted. He shouted after him. "I've been having some real interesting dreams lately, buddy. The kind that prove your girlfriend's innocence."

Crawford froze.

"Ah." Marty caught up with him. "I see I have your attention."

His face red, Crawford clenched both fists and moved within inches of him. "What you have is five seconds to leave, or I'll have you arrested."

Without flinching, Marty stood his ground. "On what charges?"

"Harassment." He beckoned to an airport patrolman strolling toward them.

"Goddamn bastard! You'll regret this, Crawford!" He spun on his heels and headed back to the rental car. He arrived in time to see a tow truck driving off with it. Flailing his arms, he stood at the curb and swore one obscenity after another at the receding vehicle.

An hour and a half later and several hundred dollars poorer, Marty had retrieved his car and was heading back into Center City. So Crawford wouldn't bite. No matter. Marty was willing to bet he'd get a more positive response from the bitch. He reached into his pocket and pulled out the new cell phone he'd bought when he rented the car.

She answered on the first ring.

Chapter 44

Emma sat poised on the side of the bed. She clutched the phone. *Proof. He had proof!* Her head spun. Dare she hope? She struggled to keep her voice steady. "What kind of proof, Mr. Bell?"

Across the room Beryl jumped out of a chair. Emma motioned her nearer the phone and held it so the two of them could hear his reply.

"The undeniable kind, lady. The kind that will exonerate you beyond a shadow of a doubt, but it's gonna cost you."

Anything, she thought. *I'll pay anything.* "How much?"

"A million bucks."

She stifled a gasp. *Anything. I'll pay anything.* "I'll need some time."

"You've got until four o'clock."

Emma stared at the wall clock. Two hours! How could he expect her to raise that kind of money in such a short period? "That's impossible. I need more time."

"Time is a luxury I can't afford right now, lady. It's four o'clock, or you take your chances with the D.A."

"But—"

"No buts. See ya around, Mrs. Wadsworth." Marty paused, then chuckled. "Or maybe not. I don't take many photos at the state pen."

"Wait! Please don't hang up." Silence greeted her plea. "Mr. Bell! Please!"

"You want the proof, you pay, lady. It's as simple as that. And don't cry poverty. I'm not buying it."

"You don't understand," pleaded Emma. "I'll pay you. I just can't get hold of that much money in two hours. Please! Can't we work something out?" Another long silence followed. She worried the bedsheet into a tight ball. "Mr. Bell? Are you still there?"

"Yeah, I'm listening. What're you offering?"

She sucked in her breath. "Three hundred thousand. I have that in the bank. I could get it by your deadline."

Beryl clamped her hand over the mouthpiece. "Are you nuts? You can't trust that slimeball. He hasn't even told you what kind of proof he has."

Emma glared at her. "I have to do this. It may be my only hope." She yanked the phone away from Beryl. "Mr. Bell?"

"All right," he grumbled. "Three hundred grand. In small bills in a gym bag, understand?"

"Yes. Small bills in a gym bag."

"Meet me in Rittenhouse Square in two hours."

"I . . . I can't. I'm under house arrest. They won't let me leave the hospital." Emma turned pleading eyes to Beryl, who gave her a nodding shrug. "I'll have someone bring it. Mr. Crawford's assistant. Will that be satisfactory?" She held her breath.

"Yeah. Okay. But tell her to keep her mouth shut. And you, too. This is just between us, got it?"

Emma agreed. She hung up the phone, sank back into the pillows, and squeezed her eyes shut.

"I don't like this, Emma," said Beryl. "And Logan sure as hell won't, either."

"I know."

"He's not getting a dime until he shows me this proof of his."

Emma nodded. "I'll call the bank. The president is an old friend of my father's. He'll release the money to you."

Three hundred grand! Marty laughed out loud. He would have settled for half that, but the broad would never know. Damn! She would've paid him a million bucks if he was willing to wait. Too bad cooling his heels another few days in Philadelphia wasn't an option—not with Leslee Howell lurking in the shadows. The sooner he brought her down, the sooner he'd sleep at night. A near-death experience was enough to temper even *his* immense greed.

Worried that Leslee might discover her plan had failed, Marty had decided to hide out across the state line in Delaware. Pacing across the threadbare carpet of his motel room, he alternately checked his watch and glanced over his shoulder at the cheap bedside clock. Back and forth. From closet to door. Check watch. Door to closet. Check clock. Closet to door. Check watch. Waiting for the minutes to tick away.

Each time he passed the wall-mounted mirror, he shuddered at the sight of his reflection. Jeez! He looked like shit. The first thing he planned to do after getting the pay-off money was hop a plane and check himself into some fancy spa somewhere in the Caribbean. A week or two of pampering sounded real good. And a man could get plenty pampered on the bankroll Marty was about to score.

The anticipation of all that dough sent him into a nervous frenzy. He couldn't wait any longer—even if it meant sitting in the cramped Neon until Crawford's gofer showed up. He grabbed his coat and a large brown envelope and raced from the room. Within minutes he was speeding north, heading toward Rittenhouse Square and his money.

After arriving in town, Marty circled the grassy square in search of a parking spot. It was another bitter, dreary day in Philadelphia, and the small park was virtually empty except for the few shoppers scurrying across the diagonal paths from one side to another.

At opposite corners two dark sedans, one navy and one black, sat with their motors running. Each held two male occupants. Expecting one of the cars to leave at any moment, Marty circled a second time, then a third. When both vehicles still remained after his fourth trip around the square, Marty grew suspicious. He'd worked his share of stakeouts in search of a killer photo and encountered plenty of bodyguards and undercover cops throughout his illustrious career. His sixth sense told him these guys weren't waiting for their dates. Had Crawford's bitch set him up?

Marty pulled into traffic and headed north until he found a parking spot near Market Street. He killed the engine. With both eyes fixed on his watch, he waited, willing the minute hand to move from one number to the next. Five minutes passed. Ten. Fifteen. Finally, after twenty, he started up the car and headed back to the square.

The two occupied sedans still sat at each corner, their engines still running.

"Damn!" He slammed his fist against the steering wheel. He wanted his money. He'd earned it. That

Wadsworth bitch wasn't going to get away with this. He'd see to that. He cursed her all the way back to Delaware.

Emma couldn't control her disappointment. Slumped against the pillows, she fought back tears of frustration. "Maybe he had car trouble or something," she said to Beryl. "You should have waited longer."

Beryl threw the gym bag onto the bed. "Damn it! I waited over an hour. He never showed. Don't you think he would have called if he had car trouble?"

"I suppose."

"I knew you couldn't trust that slimeball. Besides, what kind of proof could he possibly have? Face facts, Emma, Bell was toying with you."

Emma clasped her hands over her belly and stared down at them. One nightmare after another. When would it ever end? "I should know not to get my hopes up." She glanced across the room at her sons and forced a smile. "We should all know that."

The phone rang before anyone could respond to her desolate comment.

Emma checked the wall clock before answering. It was too early for a call from Logan unless he was phoning from the plane. She waited a moment before answering to collect herself, not wanting him to hear the unsteadiness in her voice. There was no need to alarm him about Bell's attempted shakedown. Logan had enough on his mind right now. "Hello?"

"You set me up!"

"What? Who—? Mr. Bell? Is that you?"

"How many other patsies did you try to double-cross today, lady?"

"Double-cross? What do you mean? What happened? Why weren't you at Rittenhouse Square?"

"Like you don't know!"

"I don't! Mr. Crawford's assistant waited over an hour for you. I have the money right here. Please! I need that proof, Mr. Bell."

"Then you shouldn't have called the cops."

Confused, Emma looked from her sons to Beryl. "I didn't. I swear."

"Well, someone did, lady, because they were there waiting for me."

"I'm sure you're mistaken, Mr. Bell." She glared at Beryl. "No one notified the police." Silence greeted her statement. "Please. Can't we try this again? Now?"

"You say you have the money with you?"

"Yes, it's right here. Beryl will meet you wherever you say."

"I'll think it over. Maybe you'll hear from me tomorrow. Maybe not."

"But—"

The phone went dead.

Emma glared at Beryl. "You did this. You called the police."

Beryl stared her down. "No. I called the mayor."

"Why?"

"Because Logan asked me to."

For several minutes no one spoke. Kevin cleared his throat. Off to the side she heard James shuffle his feet. "I'd like to be alone," she said.

When the door closed behind them, she turned off the lights. In the darkened room she pulled the blankets around her and rhythmically stroked her belly. She could no longer ignore the symptoms or blame them on stress. Having done the math, there was no denying the fact. As careful as they'd been, something had gone wrong. She *was* pregnant.

After hanging up from the Wadsworth bitch, Marty replayed the conversation in his head. The bitch sure sounded innocent enough. And desperate. Maybe she was right. Maybe he *had* jumped to the wrong conclusion. Or maybe not. She could've been acting. One way or the other, three hundred thousand smackers were sitting in her hospital room at this very minute. He meant to have it all. And then some. Tonight.

Once again, he left the dingy motel room and headed back to Philadelphia.

An hour later Marty was rifling through a large storage room in the hospital's basement. He found a set of scrubs and an assortment of medical paraphernalia that he hoped would fool the guards into thinking he was a lab tech. *If* they didn't notice his lack of an ID badge. He stepped into the green draw-string pants. Discarding his jacket and turtleneck, he slipped the matching V-neck shirt over his head. Before leaving, he hid his clothes behind a row of bedpans on a top shelf.

Marty made his way down the basement corridor, coming to an area containing several vending machines and a counter with a microwave oven. He stopped, listening for voices or footsteps—anything that might alert him to the presence of others, but the only sounds he heard were the whirring of the vending machine motors and the humming of the overhead fluorescent lights. With long, confident strides, he covered the distance across the alcove and grabbed a metal clipboard someone had carelessly left behind.

He climbed the stairs, hugging the clipboard to his chest with one hand. From his other hand he swung a carryall of empty test tubes and bandages. Visions of Andy Jackson, Ulysses S. Grant and Ben Franklin swam before his eyes. As he whistled "I'm in the Money," he began his search of the hospital corridors.

She wouldn't be difficult to find. After all, how many hospital rooms had police guards stationed outside the door?

Alone in her darkened room, Emma fought to shake the despair that threatened to smother her. She tried to convince herself that Beryl was right, that Marty Bell was playing some sick mind game with her—perhaps in retaliation for his smashed camera and shattered pride. But her thoughts were crowded with doubts. What if he *did* have evidence that could clear her? Would he now destroy it, convinced she'd set him up? Had Logan's well-intentioned protection sentenced her to the mercy of a vindictive district attorney bent on destroying her?

She glanced down at the large gym bag full of money. It sat at the foot of her bed where Beryl had tossed it—six thousand fifty-dollar bills bundled together in stacks of one hundred. A small price to pay for freedom. Emma leaned back against the pillows and sighed. All she could do was hope the photographer's greed was greater than his ego or his fear of the police and that he'd contact her in the morning.

She flicked on the light and reached for her bag of needlework supplies, hoping she could lose herself in the mindless busywork of the repetitive stitches. Hours stretched ahead, long and oppressive—a night she knew would not yield to the welcome oblivion of sleep.

On the opposite wall the large, mounted clock mocked her efforts to speed up the hours until daybreak. It was only eight o'clock. Working a bit of quick mental arithmetic, she realized Logan was now in Los Angeles. He would call soon. What would she tell him? Staring down at her lap, she gulped back the lump in her throat.

Secrets. So many secrets in Emmaville. And now

one more. She had to tell him, but how would he react? Her heart told her not to worry; her past experiences filled her with doubts.

Lost in morose thoughts, she failed to hear the soft whoosh of the door opening and closing. Not until he stood looming over the bed did she sense Marty Bell's presence. She looked up and stared down the barrel of a small handgun.

"Not a word above a whisper," he warned her.

Emma nodded. "You've changed your mind?"

Marty gave a noncommittal shrug. "Maybe." He regarded the black gym bag at the foot of the bed. "That the money?"

"Yes."

The gun still pointed at her, Marty jerked the bag open with his free hand and scrutinized the contents. A malicious smile spread across his face. He withdrew a brown envelope from under his shirt, and tossed it at her. "Your proof."

With trembling fingers Emma pried open the metal clasp and withdrew a series of eight-by-ten glossy photographs.

"Those are prints from a video," he said, motioning at the pictures with the gun.

The first showed a black-clad figure hovering at her front door. Emma rifled through the pictures. They catalogued the stranger's progression as he made his way through her house and into the den. In rapid succession Marty's photos captured him unlocking the safe. Opening it. Removing the contents. Placing other items in the emptied vault. Sitting down at the desk. Flicking on the computer. Removing his hooded mask . . .

Emma gasped. *He* was a *she*! "Leslee!" It was Leslee all along. Not Harper. "Thank you, Mr. Bell. Thank you!"

"Not so fast, lady." Marty snatched the photos from her hands and stuffed them in the money bag.

"What are you doing? I need those!"

He smirked. "After the crap I went through today, I decided to take you up on your original offer." He zipped the gym bag and looped the strap over his shoulder. "Three hundred G's buys you a peek at the merchandise. So you know it's for real. When I get the rest, you get to keep the pics. And just to prove what a nice guy I am, I'll throw in the video."

Emma lunged for the bag. Marty swatted her hand away with the gun. She clutched her wrist and pleaded with him. "Please! How do I know you won't just take off?"

Marty cocked his head and shrugged. "You don't."

Emma eyed the duffel tucked under his arm, then stole a glance at the door. Two policemen stood on the other side. All she had to do was scream.

"Don't even think of it," he warned, shoving the gun within inches of her nose. "If you want the proof, I walk out of here free and clear."

Emma lowered her head in resignation.

The phone rang.

Logan! If she could somehow convey her plight to him without Bell realizing it . . . She reached for the receiver.

"Leave it!" he snarled.

She stared at the telephone as it continued to ring. Four. Five. Six. Seven. Ten times. Then, silence. She slumped back against the pillows and closed her eyes in defeat.

Marty Bell slipped from the room as quietly as he'd entered.

Chapter 45

With mounting feelings of déjà vu, Logan hung up the phone and punched in another series of numbers. If Emma wasn't answering the phone, she wasn't in the room, and that could only mean Harper had her. Or Bell. After what Beryl had just related to him, he couldn't rule out the paparazzo. Damn! He should have listened to Bell at the airport. Instead, he'd unwittingly unleashed him on Emma. And in desperate need of a miracle, she'd fallen for the bait.

Ned answered the phone on the first ring. Quickly, Logan caught the mayor up on the situation and conveyed his suspicions.

"Easy, pal. We're on top of it. Emma's safe. I'll get back to you."

Emma flung the blankets aside, jumped out of bed and donned her terry robe. Like a caged animal, she paced back and forth across the darkened hospital room. She silently lectured herself on the counterproductive nature of the depression threatening to consume her. She tried to focus on the positive events of the day rather than the negatives.

At least she now knew there was a witness. An eyewitness! Marty Bell saw Leslee Howell plant the evidence Harper was using to build a case against her. Suddenly she realized that the photos weren't important. Once subpoenaed, Marty had to testify or risk being held in contempt of court. Unless he had something to hide, he would testify.

But why had he been lurking outside her house that night? Had he come in search of more pictures of her and Logan, or was he there for some other reason? Maybe Bell was somehow connected to Leslee, but if so, why was he now willing to sell her out? Had Leslee double-crossed him?

And how did Roy Harper fit in? He'd known what he would find in her safe that day. Was he part of the conspiracy or an unwitting patsy who'd seized upon the opportunity for his own vengeful purposes?

Her head spun with too many unanswered questions. She rubbed her throbbing temples. Leaning against the wall, she stared out the window. Devoid of stars, the night sky draped a heavy quilt over the still-bustling city streets. Late-evening commuters, briefcases in hand, dodged strolling couples. Emma tried to recall the last time she'd walked in silent anonymity on the sidewalks of Philadelphia. Would she ever again know that simple pleasure? Or was her face now such a familiar sight, thanks to the supermarket tabloids, that even when she was cleared of all charges, her notoriety would shadow her every step? "More questions," she whispered to the four walls. "And no answers."

A knock on the door drew her out of her reverie. Emma turned from the window. "Come in."

Light from the corridor flooded the room, silhouetting Ned Ralston. In his right hand he held a large duffel. His left hand reached along the wall until he found the light switch. The sudden bright fluorescent bombardment had little effect on Emma. She stood frozen in place, staring at the bag. Her still bulging gym bag.

"Hey, kiddo, want to blow this joint?"

Emma forced her gaze upward, settling on Ned's face. He grinned from ear to ear, like a little boy incapable of keeping a secret. "Don't tease me, Ned." She pointed to the gym bag. "How did you get that?"

With a loud grunt he tossed the gym bag across the room. It landed with a thud on the bed. "I never knew three hundred thou' could be so heavy! Next time get the guy a cashier's check, will you?"

"Ned! What's going on?"

He scratched his balding head. His face filled with an expression of mock puzzlement. "I could have sworn I told you that already, Emma. One of us must be going senile. Get dressed. You're leaving."

"Leaving? How? I'm under arrest."

"Not anymore." Ned's eyes sparkled with merriment. "You're a free woman. Marty Bell is singing his heart out down at police headquarters."

"And Leslee?"

"Under arrest for the attempted murder of Marty Bell. Among other things."

"Leslee tried to kill Marty?" Emma shook her head in disbelief. Everything was happening so quickly. She wanted to pinch herself. This had to be a dream. "Why? How?"

Ned hugged her, adding a peck to her cheek. "I'll fill in the blanks on the way back to the hotel."

Twenty minutes later Emma sat in the back of the mayor's car. She hung on Ned's every word. After re-

ceiving Beryl's phone call, Ned had convinced the police commissioner to have Marty tailed. Once they
spotted him in Rittenhouse Square, he was never out
of their sights.

"They saw him enter my room?"

Ned nodded.

"He pulled a gun on me!"

"Illegal possession of a firearm. It's one of the
charges the police are holding him on." He gave her
hand a reassuring pat. "Marty's been a bad boy,
Emma, but I don't think you were ever in any physical danger. He's too much of a coward."

"How reassuring. Especially in hindsight. What
about Harper?"

"Bell claims Harper's innocent. Leslee used him to
get at you. She sent him anonymous packages with
detailed proof of Phillip's double life as Korat. Just as
she suspected he would, Harper jumped to the conclusion that you were Korat's accomplice."

"And she made certain of that by hiding the stolen
jewels in my safe and creating a phony diary she
loaded into Phillip's computer."

The mayor's car pulled up in front of the Four Seasons. Through the tinted windows Emma saw a convoy of media vans. She spun around and confronted
Ned. "I don't believe this! How could you!"

Ned raised his hands, palms out. "I didn't. I swear
no one knows you're free yet. Just the police commissioner and the guards at your door. The press
couldn't have found out this fast." He tapped his
driver on the shoulder. "See if you can find out what's
going on, but be discreet."

Nodding, the driver stepped from the car. Within
minutes he returned, resuming his position behind
the wheel. "The D.A. is speaking at a fund-raising
dinner inside, sir. A group of conservative clergy and

a handful of pols. According to a waiter I cornered, he just demanded your resignation."

"What! On what grounds?"

"Aiding and abetting a criminal. You should be able to catch it in a few minutes on the eleven o'clock news."

"What time is it now?" asked Emma.

The driver consulted his watch. "Half past ten."

Emma flung open the car door and leaped out.

Ned followed on her heels. "What are you doing?"

"Stealing a bit of Harper's thunder with a sound bite of my own." She hurried into the hotel lobby and headed for the ballroom. At the entrance, she stopped, turned, and offered Ned a sly grin. "Want to watch?" Before he could stop her, Emma yanked open the large door and slipped inside.

Roy Harper stood at the front of the large room behind a raised dais swathed in spotlights. Beneath the podium a semicircle of cameras recorded the district attorney's fiery oratory. Like a revival preacher, he belted out fire and damnation, accusing the honorable mayor of less than honorable behavior. His audience hung on every word, peppering each invective with murmurs of agreement and applause.

The D.A. continued whipping the crowd into a righteous frenzy. "The Bible says, 'Woe to the bloody city! It is all full of lies and robbery.' I ask you, my fellow citizens, and forgive me the paraphrase— What did the mayor know, and when did he know it? *I* say he has orchestrated a massive cover-up of the truth to protect a thief and murderer, a woman who has walked among us for years, deceiving us all."

Harper paused, allowing his words to take hold before continuing his vitriolic rhetoric. "Jesus said, 'The thief cometh not, but for to steal, and to kill, and to destroy.' It is your duty to inform your congregations of the cancer that has taken hold of the great city of Philadelphia. From your pulpits, the cry will echo into the streets! Ned Ralston must go!"

Behind her, Emma heard Ned groan. She took a deep breath. "This stops right now," she muttered. "I will not stand here and watch him destroy you." Donning the regal demeanor she had cloaked herself in for years, she stepped from the shadows into the center of the room.

The district attorney stopped midsentence, leveling his hate-filled eyes on her. "You!" The room began to buzz. In unison the camera crews shifted their attention to Emma. "Brothers! Sisters!" screamed Harper over the din. "The she-devil walks among us!"

Around her, Emma heard the shouts of "Jezebel" and "harlot" and "murderer." She stood perfectly still, her gaze locked on Harper. His well-orchestrated thunder usurped, his control of the crowd lost, the district attorney became flustered. He sputtered and railed, accusing her of every offense known to God and man. Throughout his verbal stoning, Emma stood firm, her head held high, her face devoid of emotion.

An aide entered the room from a side door and strode to the podium. He whispered into the D.A.'s ear. Harper's face drained of color. A look of dismay spread across his countenance.

"Are you finished?" Emma asked Harper. She kept her words soft, her pain masked. Around her the crowd grew perfectly still. "Because it's time to cut the rhetoric and admit the truth."

"I . . . I don't know what you're talking about," he said, but he'd lost both his bluster and his audience. All eyes focused on Emma.

"Really?" She glanced in the direction of the aide, who stood off to the side of the podium. "Could have fooled me. But if you want to continue spouting biblical quotes, how do you feel about 'He that is without sin among you, let him first cast a stone'?"

Harper's mouth gaped open but no words came out.

Emma turned and scanned the crowd until she found a familiar face. "Reverend Higgenbothom." The man shifted nervously in his seat. "We've served side by side on several committees. Together we've raised money for the poor and homeless of this city. Do you really believe I'm capable of the crimes this man accuses me of?"

The reverend shook his head. He cleared his throat. "I did find the charges hard to fathom, Mrs. Wadsworth."

Emma singled out another member of the audience. "Councilman Hughes, you knew my father. You've known me all my life. Does the name Royce Stephens mean anything to you?" She stole a quick glance at the district attorney. Sweat beads covered his brow.

"Of course, but what does the man responsible for your parents' deaths have to do with the charges against you?"

You'll soon find out, thought Emma. "I'm told that after Stephens committed suicide, his wife and son vowed revenge."

"It wasn't suicide," Harper shouted. "They killed him!" He pointed an accusing finger at Emma. "They killed him for you!"

Councilman Hughes turned to Harper. "The man was found hanging in his cell, a suicide note and a letter of apology in his shirt pocket."

"Which they forced him to write before they murdered him," Harper said.

Emma shook her head. "One of the many distortions of the truth you've nursed for nearly three decades, Mr. Harper. Or should I call you by your real name?"

She faced the audience once more. "I am not a thief. I am not a murderer. The crimes Mr. Harper accuses me of were committed by the person who used Mr. Harper to frame me. Because *she* knew what I have only lately discovered. This man does *not* have our city's best interests at heart. He is here for one purpose, and one purpose only—to carry out his mother's dying wish. To destroy those she blamed for ruining her life. Roy Harper is a sham. Roy Harper is Royce Stephens, Jr."

The room erupted in pandemonium. Within seconds the mayor was at her side. The press swarmed around her, shouting questions, flashing cameras. Emma ignored them all, allowing Ned to lead her from the ballroom to the sanctuary of a waiting elevator.

Emotionally wrung out, she leaned against the back wall of the elevator as it ascended. "Did I really just do what I think I did?"

Ned laughed. "You were magnificent." He wrapped his arm around her shoulders and gave her a brotherly hug. "Thank you. That was quite a courageous performance. I know someone who's going to be sorry he missed it."

Emma chuckled. "With all the video running, I'm sure Logan will have plenty of opportunity to catch a rerun." *Besides*, she thought, *there's a far more courageous performance waiting in the wings for him.*

Uncertain of Logan's reaction and fearing the worst, Emma dreaded the unavoidable confrontation. *Coward!* Why was she so scared to face him? He loved her. He'd proven that countless times throughout her ordeal. A lesser man would have deserted her the moment she was arrested, but Logan had raced to her side. He'd protected and defended her at great risk to himself and his business dealings.

Unlike her own sons, the child she carried in her womb was a miracle of love. Phillip had gotten her pregnant with James as a means to an end. Kevin was his insurance policy. An heir and a spare. Why was she so fearful that Logan would think she'd committed a similar act?

You're being totally irrational, she silently screamed at herself. They had used protection each time, and if that protection had failed, it wasn't her fault any more than his. But still she worried. Her only previous relationship had been with a man who distorted the truth, shaping it to conform to his own twisted version of reality.

"Emma? Are you all right?"

Ned was holding the elevator door open for her. Nodding, she smiled slightly and stepped out. "Fine. Just tired," she assured him.

Chapter 46

As the jet taxied down the runway to the gate at Philadelphia International Airport, Logan reset his watch to Eastern time. Six A.M. Too early to go directly to the hospital. Too early to contact Ned Ralston. He'd hail a cab to the Four Seasons, take a quick shower, then head over to see Emma.

Although Ned had assured him that she was safe, Logan wouldn't be convinced until he saw her for himself. Ralston hadn't explained why she wasn't in her room when he called, and that worried him more than anything. Lack of sleep caused his mind to conjure up all sorts of horrid scenarios. It had taken massive willpower to force the lurid images from his thoughts and concentrate on giving his deposition. At least that damn nuisance was behind him.

Logan stifled a yawn. Rubbing his stubble-covered chin, he tried to remember the last time he'd slept, but he wasn't even certain what day it was. With mounting impatience, he watched as the flight attendants prepared the plane for disembarkation. As soon as the hatch opened, he bolted from his seat and raced down the Jetway into the terminal.

A horde of aggressive reporters, all vying for his attention, stopped him short.

"Mr. Crawford! Your thoughts on the new developments in the Wadsworth case."

New developments? "No comment," he muttered, shouldering his way through the crowd.

"Did you play any role in getting the charges against Mrs. Wadsworth dropped?"

Charges dropped?

A microphone was thrust in front of his face. "How do you feel about Leslee Howell's arrest?"

"And D.A. Harper's sudden resignation?"

Logan shoved the microphones out of his face and bolted down the corridor. What the hell was going on?

At the first newsstand he came to, he fished two quarters from his pocket and grabbed a copy of that morning's *Philadelphia Inquirer*.

PRINCESS CLEARED. The two-inch-high headline screamed at him. The sidebar proved equally fascinating: *Secret diaries implicate city official as Korat's accomplice. Leslee Howell charged with attempted murder of tabloid photographer*. With the paper clutched tightly under his arm, he headed for the taxi stand.

Half an hour later, Logan let himself into the hotel suite. Taking care not to awaken anyone, he tiptoed across the living room and quietly opened the bedroom door. He found Emma curled up on one side of the king-sized bed. He smiled down at her. If only he could make her understand how much she meant to him, how she'd changed his life. How the secret she harbored filled him with joy.

He slipped out of his clothes and joined her in bed. In the early light of morning he folded her into his arms and caressed her body.

Emma stirred, snuggling closer against his. Her eyes fluttered open. Her lips curled up into a smile. "Are you really here, or am I dreaming?"

"I'm really here."

"I'm free. Cleared of all charges."

"So I understand. Thanks to Anita, I missed all the excitement."

Emma reached for the remote and clicked on the television. "They'll milk this story for months," she said, rubbing the sleep from her eyes. She burrowed back down under the quilt and nestled against him while he watched the early morning news account of last night's events.

After viewing Emma's confrontation with Harper, Logan clicked off the television. He rested his hand on her abdomen. "You found your courage."

Emma stared at his hand, her mouth open. *He couldn't possibly know, could he?* Her guilty secret was making her paranoid. She had to tell him. "I . . ."

Logan silenced her with a kiss. "Not now, love. We'll talk later." He rolled over and entered her.

Emma noted he took no precautions but said nothing. Did he know? Was this Logan's way of telling her she had nothing to fear?

Several hours later, after some much-needed sleep, Logan ordered James and Kevin back to school. "Holiday's over," he said. "Time to hit the books again."

After Beryl left to escort the boys back up to New England, he hustled Emma out of the hotel.

"Where are we going?" she asked as they settled into the rental car.

He started the engine, then turned to face her. "Do you trust me?"

"With my life."

He glanced down at the hands she clasped protectively against her belly and smiled. Poor Emma. He wanted to put her out of her misery and tell her he knew about the baby, reassure her she had nothing to worry about. But she had to overcome her past on her own. He could support her. Encourage her. But she would never be totally free of Phillip's controlling grasp unless she took that last leap of faith by herself. With his free hand he patted both of hers. *No, my love. You still don't trust me fully. But soon.*

An hour later, Emma gazed out the window and studied the passing landscape. "We're going to Cape May!" Her face lit up. "The Christmas Inn?"

"The Angel Suite for my angel. A full week of non-stop peaceful solitude and pampering."

She nestled her head against his shoulder. Her throat constricted with emotion. His thoughtfulness overwhelmed her. With a multitude of business problems and a lawsuit threatening to create havoc with his life, his only thoughts were for her. In everything Logan did, he made clear how important she was to him.

So why did she still hesitate to tell him about the baby? *Tell him, you coward!* But the words remained trapped in her throat. A shudder coursed through her body.

"Cold?" He reached over and switched the heater up a notch.

But Emma wasn't cold. She was consumed with irrational terror. She pulled away and huddled against the passenger door, staring out at the bleak wintry landscape. *This makes no sense! He's not Phillip.*

He's Logan. And he loves me. But the words refused to come. As much as she fought to break free, the past still held her captive. Once upon a time, she erroneously thought Phillip loved her, and look how that had turned out.

Forty-five minutes later, they stepped over the threshold of The Christmas Inn. A roaring fire filled the hearth in the parlor, and lights twinkled in each window, but the inn appeared deserted. Logan took Emma's hand and led her toward the staircase.

"Shouldn't we wait for Nick?" she asked. "We haven't registered."

"It's all taken care of."

They climbed the steps to The Angel Suite. Once inside, Logan closed the door behind them. He helped her out of her coat, then removed his own.

Emma walked over to the four-poster bed and lifted the baby angel doll reclining against the pillow shams. "Logan?"

"Hmm?" He crossed the room toward her, but she backed away until she'd put half a room's distance between them.

Emma leaned against the back of the love seat, clutching the doll to her chest, her eyes averted. "Hypothetically, suppose a situation arose between two people." She stole a glance at him. "Something unexpected and neither person's fault."

"Yes?" Smiling to himself, Logan crossed his arms over his chest. Inwardly, he cheered her on, grateful she'd finally found the courage to tell him. Outwardly, he gave no sign he knew where the conversation was leading.

"And the first person was afraid the second person might want to remedy the situation."

"Remedy the situation? As in solve a problem?"

"Not exactly. More like get rid of it. Pretend it never happened."

"But the first person couldn't do that?"

Alarm spread across her face. "No! I . . . she couldn't, but she, the first person, was afraid the second person would think she'd tricked him in some way."

"But she hadn't."

"No, of course not!"

"And what makes you . . . I mean, the first person believe the second person is upset by this hypothetical situation? Don't you think that's a bit presumptuous on her part? Maybe he's actually thrilled by this unexpected occurrence."

Confusion spread across Emma's face. The doll slipped from her hands. She bent to retrieve it and sank to the floor. "Thrilled?"

"Did that reaction not occur to the first person?"

"Yes. Maybe, but . . ."

Logan crossed the room and raised her to her feet. He cupped her face with his hands, lifting her chin until their eyes met, and smiled down at her. As much as he wanted her to come out and say the words, he couldn't stand seeing her suffer further. It was time to end her pain once and for all. "Don't you think it's about time the first person told the second person he's going to be a daddy?"

"You know?"

He nodded.

"And you're not angry?"

"Angry? I'm furious with you!"

Blood drained from her face. A frightened animal sound sprang from inside her throat. She struggled to free herself from his grasp, but he refused to release her. "You foolish woman. I'm furious you didn't tell me sooner! How could you keep something like that bottled up inside you with everything else that was happening?"

"You're thrilled?" she repeated.

"Ecstatic."

Emma went limp in his arms, her body wracked with a combination of hysterical laughter and choking sobs. Logan scooped her up and carried her to the bed. He held her while she cried.

He reveled in her tears. Where once he'd berated himself for constantly making her cry, he now realized her tears were a gift. He was the only man Emma couldn't hide her emotions from. And this was the ultimate trust. When two people shared emotional honesty, everything else fell into place. Perhaps that was why he'd known from the very beginning, from the first tears he'd caused her to shed, that they were destined to spend their lives together.

He stroked her belly. "A baby. Growing right here?"

She nodded.

He grinned and spoke to the child. "Well, sweetheart, I suppose I have to apologize for saddling you with such a foolish mommy. But what can I do? I love the silly girl, and she damn well better agree to marry me because I can't imagine life without her."

"Oh, Logan! I knew I was being irrational, but I was so frightened you'd think I'd tricked you in some way." She paused and studied his face. "Forgive me?"

"Hmm . . ." He cocked his head and scrutinized her for a moment. Then, resting his head on her abdomen, he once again spoke to the baby as though she were already in his arms. "Well, what do you say, little one? Think she deserves a second chance?"

"I'm sorry for not telling you sooner."

"No. It's my fault. I caused you needless worry. I should have said something when I first realized."

"And when was that?"

He raised himself up on one elbow and brushed away the remaining moisture from her cheeks. "Sooner than you, I think. I never bought that crap about bad shrimp. Especially since six of us ate the same meal that night and you were the only one stricken."

"And from that, Dr. Crawford concluded the patient was with child?"

"That and having four married sisters. With nine children among them, we haven't had a Christmas dinner in years without one of them going on about morning sickness and assorted other discomforts. Makes it difficult to enjoy the turkey and dressing."

"Ah! So that makes you an expert on obstetrics?"

"Among other things. I've also changed a diaper or two in my day and burped a few babies, so don't think you're getting stuck with a chauvinist here. Contrary to what the press would have you believe, I'm a rather sensitive, New Age sort of guy."

"And a pediatrics expert, to boot." Emma chuckled. "Interesting talents for an old bachelor."

Logan rolled on top of her, trapping her beneath him. "Old?" He tugged at her sweater and drew it over her head.

"Nearly forty. I'd say that's ancient." She unbuttoned his shirt and stripped it from his chest.

"Fighting words if ever I heard them. You'll find I still have a few tricks up my sleeve."

Emma contemplated his bare chest. "You have no sleeves."

"Then down my pants."

She reached for his belt buckle. "Prove it, old man."

"With pleasure."

Chapter 47

Emma sat in the car and stared at the house. Remnants of yellow crime tape still clung to several low evergreen boughs. Conflicting emotions tore at her. This was her home. But it had also served as her prison. Could she walk its rooms without conjuring up visions of years of unhappiness? She turned from the window to Logan. "Why are we here?"

"This is your home, isn't it?"

A long time ago, she thought. Once upon a time, laughter sang within the walls of the old estate. Now it was just a shell housing a myriad of ghosts and far more disturbing memories than pleasant ones. "I suppose I expected us to go back to the hotel."

Logan shrugged. "If you wish. But since we're here, why not go inside and pack up some extra clothes and anything else you might want."

Emma hesitated. She hadn't been inside the house since the day the police led her away in handcuffs. So much had changed in such a short period of time.

She took a deep breath and smiled at Logan. *I can do this!*

Logan stepped from the car. A moment later he held her door open for her. Emma stepped from the car without hesitation. A newfound confidence infused her. He reached for the key she fished from her handbag, but she shook her head. *I can do this!* With a steady hand she inserted the key in the lock and pushed open the door.

It took a few seconds for her eyes to adjust to the interior light. She blinked, unable to believe the sight before her. Was she hallucinating? "No," she whispered. "This . . . this is impossible."

Logan grasped her elbow and led her into the living room. Her heels clicked against the wide planking of the newly waxed hardwood floor, no longer hidden by thick carpeting. "Anything is possible given enough time."

Emma stared across the room. Gone were Phillip's antique swords and pistols. Hanging above the mantel was her father's prized Gilbert Stuart portrait of his ancestor, John Oliver Brockton. The antique Paul Revere candlesticks sat at each end of the mantel in place of the hideous pornographic French urns. The walls, once covered with gaudy velvet-flocked wallpaper and heavy drapes, wore a fresh coat of warm ecru paint. Delicate lace curtains filtered the late afternoon sun into the room.

Her head spinning, Emma raced from one piece of furniture to the next. Her mother's furniture—the graceful, antique Chippendale pieces she believed were long gone, replaced years before when Phillip had transformed her home into something out of a bordello.

And there in the corner, in all its regal magnificence, stood the hand-carved, claw-foot grand piano. Emma sat down at the bench and tentatively stroked a few keys. "It's in tune!" She cast a perplexed look at Logan. "How in the world did you do this?"

Instead of answering, he drew her off the bench. "Come with me." He led her on a tour of the lower level of the house. Each room had gone through a miraculous transformation, restored to its past splendor and elegance. It was as if a magician had waved a wand and erased the past sixteen years from the life of the house.

When they came to the foot of the staircase, Emma hesitated, eyeing the upstairs with trepidation. She shook her head. "I don't go up there anymore."

Logan stroked her cheek. "Trust me?"

She gazed into his eyes. How could she not trust him after all he'd done for her? She sucked in her breath, bit down on her lower lip, and began the long, painful trip up the staircase.

The door to the master bedroom stood closed. Emma hesitated. "I don't think I can do this."

"He's not here anymore. Even his ghost is gone. Open the door, Emma. Not for me. For yourself."

Placing her fingers over the brass knob, she glanced up at him for reassurance. When he gave her a smile of encouragement, she turned the knob and push the door open.

The room, like the others, contained no evidence of Phillip Wadsworth. Instead, she felt the presence of her parents. In her head, she heard their voices, their laughter.

She stepped across the threshold but stopped short. Her eyes focused on the seventeenth-century rope bed that had seen the birth of generations of Brocktons. She couldn't believe what she saw spread across the chenille spread. Photo albums! Her baby pictures! Her parents' and grandparents' wedding albums!

Emma sank onto the bed and opened one of the volumes. For the first time in years she beheld the images of her parents. Tears cascaded down her cheeks, blurring the smiling faces. Logan sat down beside her and held her close.

"I don't know how you did this," she said between gulping sobs of joy, "but thank you. Thank you so much."

"You can thank Beryl."

Emma looked up from the photographs. "I don't understand."

"Molly told me about Autumn Summers, the exotic dancer who redecorated the house while you gave birth to James. When I related the tale to Beryl, she remembered seeing the name somewhere during her travels around the city. Autumn Summers operates a massage parlor on South Street."

Emma sniffed back some tears and smirked. "Really? And here I thought she'd gone on to have a highly successful career decorating whorehouses."

Logan chuckled. "No, but apparently she did suspect your parents' possessions had value. Although I seriously doubt she had a clue of their actual worth. Instead of trashing them as Phillip had instructed, she stored them in an uncle's warehouse, hoping one day to auction the items off. She considered it her retirement nest egg."

"And you bought them from her?"

A sheepish grin spread across Logan's face. "Let's just say Beryl made her an offer she couldn't refuse."

Emma smiled. "Thank you for giving me back my life."

"No. Thank you." He caressed her abdomen. "For everything."

Another shower of tears spilled over her eyelids and down her cheeks.

"I'm always making you cry," he said.

Emma shook her head. "I never cry."

Talk Gertie To Me

LOIS WINSTON

Nori Stedworth is living the good life. That is, until the dot-com company she works for goes bust, she finds her fiancé cavorting in the Jacuzzi with her best friend, and her mom flies in for a surprise visit....

Now suddenly, from out of nowhere, Nori's alter ego from adolescence, Gertie, is throwing her two cents in about everything in Nori's life. Like, Nori's new job at a radio station might finally be her niche. Like, Nori's droolworthy boss, Mac, just might be the man of her dreams. Like, it's time Nori stopped hiding in the shadows. Move over, Gertie—Nori's stepping up to the mic.

KILLER *in* HIGH HEELS

Gemma Halliday

L.A. shoe designer Maddie Springer hasn't seen her father since he reportedly ran off to Las Vegas with a showgirl named Lola. So she's shocked when he leaves a desperate plea for help on her answering machine—ending in a loud bang. Never one to leave her curiosity unsatisfied, Maddie straps on her stilettos and heads for Sin City.

There she finds not only her dad, but also a handful of aging drag queens, an organized crime ring smuggling fake Prada pumps, and one relentless killer. Plus, it seems the LAPD's sexiest cop is doing a little Vegas moonlighting of his own.

KATHLEEN BACUS

CALAMITY JAYNE GOES TO COLLEGE

Ace cub reporter Tressa Jayne Turner is carrying a full load—and we're not talking post-holiday pounds. Back in college for the fourth time (but who's counting?), she's also looking to nab a raise from her stingy boss at the *Gazette*. So, what's to stop her from making the grade? Could it be the botched betrothal that's more than just schoolyard gossip? Or maybe it's the two men in hot pursuit of her heart. And let's not forget the campus criminal that's out to teach the student body a lesson— one crime at a time. It's a case of murder and mayhem by the books…and failure is *so* not an option.

REMEMBER THE ALIMONY
BETHANY TRUE

Tips from Delaney Davis-Daniels, former Miss Texas:

Avoid sleeping with the enemy. Even if your ex's attorney is the most luscious man ever and you had no idea who he was when he gave you the most incredible night of your life.

Never let 'em catch you crying. When your slimeball former husband turns up dead and you're suspect #1, stay strong. After all, you have a gorgeous lawyer willing to do anything to help you prove your innocence—as long as he doesn't get disbarred first.

And remember: *Love never follows the rules.*
